Praise for the Works

For *Murder Ballads and Other Horrific Tales*

"Jacobs demonstrates masterful control of his eclectic themes... This marvelously eerie collection offers plenty to keep genre fans hooked." – *Publishers Weekly*

For *Southern Gods*

"A sumptuous Southern Gothic thriller steeped in the distinct American mythologies of Cthulhu and the blues . . . *Southern Gods* beautifully probes the eerie, horror-infested underbelly of the South." – The Onion AV Club

"If you dig crime/horror/dark fantasy/southern gothic crossover... written with a confident voice and a haunting, poignant edge, pick up John Hornor Jacobs's debut novel *Southern Gods*. I recommend it wholeheartedly and look forward to whatever else Jacobs presents to us next." – Tom Piccirilli, four-time Bram Stoker Award® and two-time International Thriller Award winner

"A brilliant, smartly-written horror-noir novel, and one of those ideas that every writer worth their salt will say 'Damn! Why didn't I think to do that first?'" – Brian Keene, Bram Stoker Award®-winning author of *The Rising, City of the Dead* and *The Conqueror Worms*

For *This Dark Earth*

"Bram Stoker Award® nominee Jacobs (*Southern Gods*) avoids the major pitfall that many aspiring zombie writers fall prey to: a lack of originality... The hard decisions [the protagonists] must make in a world without humanity drive Jacobs's compelling plot from beginning to end." – *Library Journal*

"This smart addition to the zombie genre is heroic and strangely hopeful, championing the unyielding human drive for justice and civilization." – *Publishers Weekly*

"Readers will become immersed in the dark, unforgiving world Jacobs has created, and the morally ambiguous choices his characters make will give them plenty to ponder." – *Booklist*

The Fisk and Shoe Series

"I finished John Hornor Jacobs's *The Incorruptibles* today and I'm just stunned at how engrossing it was. A hybrid of *The Gunslinger, Monstress*, and a Roman history book, it was refreshingly original and soooo well written. 15 out of 5 stars, highly recommended." – Aaron Mahnke, author and creator of the World of LORE books, podcast, and television series

"One part ancient Rome, two parts wild west, one part Faust. A pinch of Tolkien, of Lovecraft, of Dante. This is strange alchemy, a recipe I've never seen before. I wish more books were as fresh and brave as this." – Pat Rothfuss, best-selling author of *The Name of the Wind* and *Wise Man's Fear*

The Incarcerado Series

"*The Twelve-Fingered Boy* is John Hornor Jacobs's debut young adult novel and it's *amazing*…part Huck Finn, part X-Men. The scary stuff in this book — and there's some really scary stuff here — goes beyond the usual scares of kids' horror, and is truly the stuff of nightmares. This is a book that mesmerizes like a venomous snake…I'll be on the watch for the next two volumes. " – Cory Doctorow, on BoingBoing.net

"John Hornor Jacobs's *The Twelve-Fingered Boy* is a thrill ride. With candy. And polydactyl, reluctantly heroic kids who go up against all odds in a world of uncontrollable superpowers and unrelenting bad guys.

Exciting, suspenseful, creepy, and fun—*The Twelve-Fingered Boy* is a terrific, fast-paced read!" —Andrew Smith, award-winning author of *The Marbury Lens* and Stick

"Jacobs' storytelling has the effortless velocity of early Dean Koontz, and his prose is textured with hard-boiled grit... An expertly spiced stew of attitude, humor, horror, and grief." –starred, Booklist

"A fast-paced, ferocious nightmare of a story—gritty, magical, and surprisingly tender." –Brenna Yovanoff, *New York Times* Bestselling author of *The Replacement*

Works by John Hornor Jacobs

Southern Gods
This Dark Earth
A Lush and Seething Hell

The Incarcerado Series
The Twelve-Fingered Boy
The Shibboleth
The Conformity

The Fisk & Shoe Series
The Incorruptibles
Foreign Devils
Infernal Machines

MURDER BALLADS

AND OTHER HORRIFIC TALES

JOHN HORNOR JACOBS

JOURNALSTONE
YOUR LINK TO ARTIST TALENT

ISBN: 978-1-950305-39-1 (sc)
ISBN: 978-1-950305-40-7 (ebook)
Library of Congress Control Number: 2020937918

First printing edition: June 26, 2020
Published by JournalStone Publishing in the United States of America.
Cover Design: Jeffrey Alan Love | Cover Layout: John Hornor Jacobs
Edited by Sean Leonard
Interior Layout and Proofreading: Scarlett R. Algee

JournalStone Publishing
3205 Sassafras Trail
Carbondale, Illinois 62901

JournalStone books may be ordered through booksellers or by contacting:
JournalStone | www.journalstone.com

INTRODUCTION
9

THE CHILDREN OF YIG
ORIGINALLY APPEARED IN *SWORDS V. CTHULHU*, 2016
15

SINGLE, SINGULARITY
ORIGINALLY APPEARED IN *UPSIDE DOWN: INVERTED TROPES IN STORYTELLING*, 2016
37

ITHACA
PREVIOUSLY UNPUBLISHED
61

VERRATA
ORIGINALLY APPEARED IN *POLLUTO MAGAZINE*, VOL. II
77

OLD DOGS, NEW TRICKS
ORIGINALLY APPEARED IN *SURREAL SOUTH '11*, 2011
91

EL DORADO
ORIGINALLY APPEARED AS "LE MORTE FANTASTIQUE" IN *BEAT TO A PULP: HARDBOILED*, 2011
101

LUMINARIA
ORIGINALLY APPEARED IN *APEX MAGAZINE*
115

THE DREAM OF THE FISHERMAN'S WIFE
ORIGINALLY APPEARED IN *THE BOOK OF CTHULHU,* 2011

145

PATCHWORK THINGS
ORIGINALLY APPEARED IN *CEMETERY DANCE MAGAZINE* #76

151

MURDER BALLADS
PREVIOUSLY UNPUBLISHED

161

ABOUT THE AUTHOR

INTRODUCTION

It is quite possible that this will be the only short story collection I'll ever publish. For one, I am not a prolific writer, and the story ideas I tend to generate sprout appendages and strange tissues that want to connect to other ideas to form something if not appropriately monstrous, then... *larger*.

Secondly, I am uncomfortably aware that the writing of short stories is quite possibly the highest and most exacting form of fiction writing (and the form that pays the least). I am also painfully cognizant of the fact that I have not written enough short stories to be exceptionally good at it. In hopes of bettering myself, I have made a habit of reading those authors who are exceedingly good at the short form, authors like Kelly Link and John Langan, Livia Llewellyn and Nathan Ballangrud, Caitlin Kiernan and Mariana Enriquez and Steve Rasnic Tem, Michael Wehunt, Ian Rogers and Paul Tremblay – these are the writers I admire, and even mentioning them in the same volume as my stories is an act of extreme hubris. They all have, in one way or another, a magically oblique approach to observing and describing the world and the characters within it in ways I've tried to emulate and failed.

And still, my stories have been published.

Go figure.

The stories contained here range from early in my published career to unpublished and unique to this volume you hold in your hands now. In collecting them together I've been given a chance to evaluate them as a body rather than individual pieces and I've been struck by some of the similarities between them. Turns out, I'm a "Southern" writer, though that is not how I think of myself, nor how I characterize my work. It is, however, the word contained within the title of my first book *Southern Gods* and I did not realize writers are in some ways like Jacob Marley from *A Christmas Carol*: all of our books are like sins we carry though the afterlife on chains with us and our debut novel is usually the heaviest of those.

And so, while there may be vampires and zombies, ghosts and super-intelligent AI consciousnesses, devils and criminals and Vikings and old gods contained within these pages, there's also quite a bit of my personal history contained here too: hunting and fishing, boating along Oxbow lakes, bluesmen and jukejoints, house-trailers and scaling paint, the sun-hammered and mosquito-drenched landscapes of Arkansas. Where I grew up and still live.

You've been warned.

There are two previously unpublished pieces in this collection, one called "Ithaca" – a rural noir homecoming drama – and the titular "Murder Ballads," which is a sequel to my first novel *Southern Gods*, which revisits the grown children of that novel as they deal with their shattered lives in the 1960s of the Arkansas Delta. It was written specifically for this collection.

The other stories?

Well, I hope you like them. I had considered going through each one by one, to talk about each story's generation, where I was in my career during the writing of it, what I was trying to do artistically, how I think they succeed and maybe how they don't, but I think I'll abstain from all that nonsense.

You can make up your own mind.

I am, once again, enormously pleased and proud to have the artwork of Jeffrey Alan Love gracing the cover of one of my books – he is my favorite working artist today and a wonderful friend and writer. I would recommend all of you to follow him on social media and check out his work, buy his books. He posts regularly, and it's mythic, dark, exciting stuff.

I would also like to thank Stacia Decker, my agent, for selling, and Scarlett Algee and Sean Leonard for massaging into publishable form, the contents of this collection, especially "Murder Ballads," since theirs are the only eyes that have seen "Murder Ballads" until, well, *you*. You do not have to have a great familiarity with *Southern Gods* to enjoy "Murder Ballads" in my opinion, but it might help with understanding all of the plot points, since it is a sequel.

Finally, my gratitude goes out to all the people online and in real life that continue to support me and my work by cooking me things (my wife Kendall) and buying my books (all you amazing folks holding this volume in your hot hands). I couldn't continue to do what I do without you all.

With Love from Quarantine,

jhj

Little Rock, Arkansas
May 15, 2020

MURDER BALLADS

AND OTHER HORRIFIC TALES

THE CHILDREN OF YIG

GRISLAE BENT her back to the sea.

The face of the ocean was dead and still. Mist hung about the longship *Reinen* and drizzle fell in gauzy streamers. No breath of wind stirred the sails. It was warmer here in the south, and what land they could see, flatter, the barest ink stroke on the horizon.

Oars creaked as Heingistr's company strained. Hoensa, Rill, Svebder, Uvigg, Snurri—the blooded men who did not row—watched the shore as it slowly passed.

"The shape of the land is familiar," said Hoensa, squinting his eyes against the gloom. "We raided what farms we could find, five winters past, but the ones near here we spared for future plucking." He slapped the bulkhead. "Our shields were wet from plunder and we could let these pass."

Grislae sank her oar into the water and pulled. She had found her rhythm among the men from Heingistrhold. At first her hands had blistered, but only a little, since they were accustomed to plow and rope and the labors of the farm.

At the covered stern of the *Reinen*, over a small touchwood brazier, huddled Urtha and Wen—wives to Hoensa and Rill. The women would not let their husbands raid without their company. Their cooking. Their guidance. And because Heingistr did not meddle in the affairs of husbands and wives, he allowed this, as his father had before him. Indeed, it spared him from eating what his men might cook.

Urtha scowled at Grislae's garb when she boarded the *Reinen*, noting her helm, her boiled leather tunic. Her sword.

"You are Ordbeg the Boy-Lover's daughter, are you not?" Urtha said, as Grislae hung her shield over the gunwale. The shield had been her father's, but she'd repainted it.

Svebder and Snurri chuckled. Grislae looked at the women. They called her father "Boy-Lover" in derision, because he would not kill children. Last Imbolc he was coughing blood, and by the Festival of Eostre, he was dead, his incessant retching so odious, the end came as a relief. She didn't weep. She swore she'd never pick up another hoe or scythe another hayfield. She dug his grave, placed him in it, and built a cairn. It was her last spring sowing. Her father's sword and shield and wealth she kept, and placed nothing in the grave with him. Then, back aching, she drank as much mead as her belly would hold, sitting in the dim silence of their farmhouse—leagues away from Heingistrhold and any other soul—and drew Ordbeg's sword from its scabbard and watched the firelight flicker down its length.

To Urtha she said, "I bear his shield, sword, and helm. Not his name."

"Nor his hair," Wen said in a fruity voice, looking at Grislae's pate.

"Nor what hung between his legs," Urtha said, squinting.

Grislae shrugged and ran a hand over her stubbly head. The incessant itching of lice had driven her to take a knife to her once long locks, as she had not the inclination to waste silver on lye. She'd found she liked the fierce look of her shorn head. And that the young men from the neighboring farms had stopped leaving loaves and flowers by her door, which was just as well. She would never wed.

She crossed her arms in front of her and frowned at the two women. "I have come to raid. Heingistr has not a problem with it. Have either of you?"

Wen only frowned, but Urtha, the wide-faced leader of the two, said, "I'd warn you to stay away from our men, but I imagine they'd rather fuck sheep than bed with you."

Grislae smiled. "That hole in your face would be the perfect arsehole," she said, as she unslung her sword and stowed her bindle, "if it wasn't for all your teeth."

There was a moment of quiet. Wen looked shocked. Urtha scowled at Hoensa, her husband, for support. Hoensa shrugged and looked back toward the shore.

"Rill would rather fuck sheep than just about anything," Uvigg said, and the still hush of the sea was broken by the laughter coming from the longship.

"There," Heingistr said, jabbing a thick finger into the mist. "Marshes. There will be a channel. And beyond, farms."

Grislae bent her back to the sea.

———

The channel opened into a sheltered bay where they moored the *Reinen* that night. No lights from home fires nor watchmen's torches shone in the dark, and the mist pressed too close to spy any smoke breaking the heavens, or stars peering through.

"Snurri, Hoensa, take one of the new ones—Grislae—and scout." Heingistr nodded his head inland. The men began unlimbering a goat from the hold of the *Reinen*, and Wen and Urtha whetted their knives. Snurri cursed and belted on his sword, put his helm on his head. Hoensa's eyes glittered.

"No shield," Snurri said to Grislae as she took up her gear. "We move fast and it will only slow you."

They made their way inland, walking swiftly and crouching low. The men moved easily, familiar with each other and their rhythms. Grislae kept up without much struggle—her time on her father's farm had kept her fit and strong—but was alarmed by the amount of noise the men made as they moved through the forest: snapping limbs underfoot, grunting, cursing under their breath.

Grislae moved in almost absolute silence, lightfooted. The land rose, and she passed through cut forest and into fields. It was warm, her skin beading with sweat.

They came upon a farm, low slung and dark, no smoke coming from the roof.

Snurri, sweat streaming into his beard, whispered, "We will wait here, and watch." He hopped over a fallen log and kneeled behind the low brambles between the farm and where they crouched. Before Grislae and Hoensa could join him, he cried, "Ach!" Flailed and rolled on the ground. When he rose, he stomped like a maddened horse. "Snake! Gods protect me!"

"Odin's eye, you're one big fucking baby," Hoensa said. He peered at the house. "Sound a battle horn next time." He drew his sword and looked at Grislae. "If someone was there, we would know it by now, thanks to Snurri. Let's take a look."

Hoensa moved forward, what meager light cut through the dark, cloudy sky glinting off his helm. Grislae followed, drawing her sword. After a moment, the shaken Snurri lumbered after them.

The farm had a thatched roof, wooden walls, and rough-hewn timber shutters. The door was open. Entering, the three were swallowed in darkness. A thick matting on the floor of the farmhouse cushioned their steps. Only the faintest intimations of rooms were apparent to them. Grislae smelled more than saw the cold hearth on a far wall. The scent of bread and meat told her it had been occupied but recently. But there was another smell, an old smell, sour and stinking of death, mingling with the odors of farm life. From all around came a rustling sound too, and that put her on edge.

"I have a fire steel and striking stone," Grislae said, moving toward the back of the room. The close air was hushed, but there was a light susurration, as reeds stirring in the breeze.

Snurri, hulking in the darkness, said, "I don't like this place. There are no people here. They will have taken their wealth wherever they have gone."

"Let us see what we can see," Hoensa said.

At the hearth, Grislae removed the fire steel and stone from the pouch at her belt and struck a spark. The flash revealed a bundle of kindling hay near the wall by the hearthstone; she soon had a small fire burning in the sooty hearth. She stood and stepped away from where the shifting yellow light spilled across the farmhouse, the brilliance blinding after their long trek through the night.

Through her watering eyes, the floor shimmered. Snurri gave a small exhalation. "Uff, dip me in sheep piss."

"What, Snurri?" Hoensa asked, hearing his tone. "What is it?"

"The brood of Jorgumandr," Snurri said with a curiously flat inflection. "Snakes. More snakes."

Hoensa and Grislae blinked away tears, peered at the floor. It shifted and gleamed in the fickle yellow firelight. As Grislae watched, it writhed and wriggled in a lazy expanse. Looking down, she saw many small snakes strike at her high boots with their vicious mouths.

"Ergi! These damned serpents!" cried Snurri, whipping his hand about as if to rid himself of a fly. He began stomping indiscriminately, and Hoensa joined him. The small fire crackled in the hearth, the floor rustled, and for a long while there was naught but the sound of the men's heavy breathing and bootfalls as they crushed the snakes.

Grislae grabbed the remaining cord of kindling hay and stuck one end in the fire. Then, sword in one hand and flaming straw bundle in the other, she shook out her legs and moved. "The door," she said. "There is nothing here but vermin." Raising high the makeshift torch, she turned around in a circle. Everywhere, every open bit of floor, shimmered and writhed. "You will stomp all night and never kill them all. Come."

It took a moment for the men to stop. Snake-fear and kill-lust kept them stomping the writhing mass. Grislae shrugged. She left the farmhouse, entering the sodden night. Hoensa and Snurri followed. She was reaching to set the thatch roof on fire when Hoensa placed a hand on her arm and said, "I think not. There are other farms full of fat children, food, and gold. Best not to warn them Heingistr's company is here until we are upon them."

"I am bit," Snurri said, holding up his hand. When they said nothing in response, he patted his body from collar to crotch. "Ach, I can feel them slithering all over me."

They moved away from the farm, taking a muddy road that led beyond the house and beside a furrowed field. The mire sucked at their feet. They had reached the far tree line when the light of torches filtered through the trees.

Doughty men with ruddy faces carrying axes. Farmers, all. They tromped down the road, speaking in a round, fluid language Grislae could not make out. Their hushed tones were agitated; something had disturbed them.

Crouched behind a mossy rock jutting from the forest mulch, Grislae readied herself to strike. Hoensa, who had hidden himself behind a thick oak, held up a hand—*Wait*.

The farmers neared. Snurri, poised behind a log, withdrew his sword. Grislae gripped hers tighter.

Hoensa shook his head and pointed back to the farmhouse. He mouthed, *No. Wait.*

They let the farmers continue on, passing a few paces away, unaware that the company of the North hid so close.

When the farmers had crossed the field, Grislae said, "Why did we let them pass? We could have killed them and taken their gold."

"I've killed scores of farmers and they never carry gold. They hide it away in their houses and will not yield it until you put a blade to their son's or daughter's throat." Hoensa shook his head. "We've raided these shores for generations. These would not be out here in the dark, unless some greater fear than that they hold for us was not pushing them on. I would see what it is that frightens them so."

Snurri sucked on the back of his hand. "Would that we had found a mill or hamlet, killed the men, fucked all the wives and daughters, and took their livestock and metal. Not *this*. The countless brood of Jorgumandr and thrice-cursed farmers."

"Stop complaining, Snurri," Hoensa said. "We will circle around and see what we can see."

They stayed beyond the tree line and made their way around the field and into view of the farmhouse. The farmers were clustered outside the door, arguing. One of them pointed inside and gave a blistering speech in their bubbling language, but one word was prominent, due to its hard sounds and angles: *Yig*.

Soon they came to agreement, and the farmers set their torches to the thatched roof. Within moments the house was burning. Light spilled out, illuminating the field, the forest, and the spot where Heingistr's scouts watched.

"It must be those wretched vermin," Snurri said. He sucked at the back of his hand again. "What is *yig*? Snakes?"

"I don't care what it means." Hoensa stretched, swung his sword experimentally. "Let us kill who we can and take the others as slaves. And find more farms to raid. No?"

Grislae nodded, gripping her sword.

The Northerners fell on the farmers from behind as they watched the house burn. Snurri let forth a terrible scream as he ran, so by the time Grislae came near, the men had turned to face them, startled. Hoensa's sword took one in the arm, deep, and the man fell. Hoensa wheeled toward the next man, who raised his axe.

In the shifting yellow light from the burning roof, Grislae found herself facing a burly farmer whose expression lacked sufficient fear to suit her. He whipped his axe in a tight circle, but she rocked back on one leg, letting it pass, and then sprang forward in the wake of his missed blow. She spitted him through the belly, and once his face showed the death-fear, she smiled and ripped the sword free, turning to face the others.

Snurri clubbed a man in the face with the pommel of his sword, dropping him, and Hoensa had killed another. The last farmer bolted into the dark and Hoensa sprinted after him.

"They are strong but none of them know how to fight," Snurri said, and sucked hard at the back of his hand. "You did well, Boy-Lover's girl."

Grislae ignored him. The farmer he'd clubbed stirred and moaned through a bloody mouth. She stripped one of the dead of his belt and tied the moaning man's hands as Hoensa returned, breathing heavily.

Snurri and Grislae looked to him and he nodded. "They will be alerted by mid-morn at the latest, when their men do not come home to their soft beds. Let us take this one back to the boat and hear Heingistr's words."

They roused the battered farmer, bound his mouth, and marched him back to the *Reinen*. Heingistr, Wen, Urtha—Hoensa's wife—Rill, and Uvigg waited for them. Soon the other new men roused from their slumber on the *Reinen's* decks, coming to join them by the fire on the shore.

"We saw the light," Heingistr said. "You must have good plunder to have burned the first farmhouse you came across."

"We did not burn it," Snurri said. He waved a hand at the new slave, who had collapsed on the shore near the fire. A pot hung there, and the smell of goat stew lingered in the air. "This one and his friends did the burning. The farmhouse was overrun with snakes."

"Snakes?"

"Countless snakes," Snurri said, and looked to Grislae and Hoensa for support.

Hoensa nodded. "There were many."

"I am bit," Snurri said, holding up his hand. It had swollen like a sack of barley soaked by rain.

Heingistr's face remained impassive. "Uvigg, your father took a slave woman from this region. Do you know their tongue?"

"Some," Uvigg said.

"I would put questions to this man, and then you can take him to the hold."

Uvigg unbound the captive's mouth and gave him water.

"He'll be shitting teeth for a moon," Hoensa said.

Heingistr questioned the toothless farmer about nearby holdfasts and villages. There was a fortress, far inland, ruled by a lord named Risle with a crowing cock as his family sigil, but far enough away to not be a concern. Closer there were farms, but the real prize was a mill five miles inland. Quickly, Heingistr and company decided on a course of action— to leave with enough men to take the mill, the miller's fat wife and daughters, and all of their grain and gold, and be back at the *Reinen* before the tide turned. Many of those newer to the company grew excited. Urtha kissed Hoensa fervently, and Heingistr began sharpening his axes.

"What of this thing they kept saying?" Grislae asked. "This *yig*?"

Uvigg put questions to the captive in his language. The man raised his hands as if warding off a blow. Uvigg withdrew a knife, and with a casual motion picked at the dirt under his own fingernails and repeated his words. The slave answered haltingly.

"Some local haunt, maybe? It has been long since I've spoken this tongue, and truly the man's accent is fucked beyond repair. He'll eat soup for the rest of his life," Uvigg said. "Some sort of serpent, like Jorgumandr, except not so fierce, nor so divine. He spoke of the 'children of Yig,' and 'Yig's retribution.' All sheep shit, in my judgment."

Snurri stirred. "Maybe it is their name for Jorgumandr."

"These people do not worship the same gods as normal folk. They have their wounded man and their mother and the sightless ones and the forest," Uvigg said. "They know nothing of Valhalla and Yggdrasil. They are blind."

"But fat," Heingistr said. "And we will take what is theirs. Hoensa, ready the men."

"Grislae will come too. She handled herself as well as Snurri, at least," Hoensa said.

"That is not a high sheaf to hide in," Rill said. Snurri bristled.

"She split a farmer without hesitation. A big fellow," Hoensa said and gave Grislae a nod.

"Then she is with us." Heingistr turned to her. Pulling a knife from his belt, he cut his forearm and cupped the blood that ran there. He slapped Grislae, a big open-handed blow, catching her mouth, cheek, and ear in his massive hand, sending her reeling. She sat down forcibly, motes of light swirling at the edges of her vision. "Get up, Ordbeg the Boy-Lover's girl. You are blooded now and one of my company. Get up," he said, and taking her arms, raised her from the ground, the stag-faced prow of the *Reinen* behind him, looming.

She tasted the blood on her face, some of it hers, streaming from her nose, some of it Heingistr's. The eyes of the company were upon her, blooded and unblooded alike.

"My name is Grislae," she said. "I put aside my father and his name."

Heingistr remained still and everyone was silent except for the soft moaning of the captive.

"So it will be, Grislae No-Man's Girl," Heingistr said. "So it will be."

"Grislae," she said.

There was a long silence where the men waited expectantly for Heingistr to react to her last words, to see if their company's leader would take it as a challenge. A big grin split his beard and he extended his hand still mired with blood.

"You will shoulder many names in this world, Grislae," he said. "As long as your sword strikes and your heart remains true, you are one of my company."

She gripped his forearm in friendship. For the first time in her life, Grislae was happy. The feeling was so foreign and short-lived, she was only aware of it once it was gone.

Of the thirty-three in Heingistr's company, they left a third with the *Reinen*, Wen, and Urtha, and took twenty-two inland to raid the mill. Heingistr was concerned that the burning farmhouse might draw others, and so men were needed to guard the longship. Grislae and Hoensa led them past the farmhouse, Snurri staying behind to tend his greening, unusable hand.

They followed the road away from the smoldering farmhouse and inland, past sucking muddy fields and dark forest. The wind picked up and the clouds cleared, leaving gashes that allowed the milky half-light to filter onto the face of the land.

At the first farm there were two women and a boy. They boy tried to fight them with a cudgel, so Uvigg killed him. They bound the women and left three men at the house to take what spoils they could from the premises. The rest of the company moved on.

They found a small river—one that, Uvigg told them, ran into the marshy bay where the *Reinen* was beached—and followed it south. Two more farmsteads they came across—one, rich with livestock and grain, where three young men and a girl fought them when the door was kicked in. The girl, no more than thirteen, chose to defend her home with a butcher's blade, so Grislae ran her through. The girl looked surprised once her widening eyes fixed on Grislae's face, and she pawed at Grislae's breasts as she died, as if looking for some kind of succor there. The rest of the farmer's sons, and the other daughters hidden in the cold room below the kitchen, they took for slave stock. The men of Heingistr's company looked at Grislae with new eyes.

The next farm was empty, possibly alerted by the screams and shrieks of their neighbors. They left four men to round up the scattered flock.

The sky lightened. Soon the sun would rise.

Thirteen men and one woman moved inland, toward the mill. The sky bloomed in the east and illuminated the water vapor in the air, shining through the trees like the golden fog of Valhalla.

The mill was guarded by men bearing axes, cudgels, and a single rust-eaten sword, doubtless their families and other precious things barricaded inside. Svebder had unlimbered his bow and feathered two of the men before they knew Heingistr's company was upon them. In the blood-spiked rush toward the mill, Grislae found herself yelling wordlessly. She killed two men, taking one through the throat as he swung a hammer at her—she received some of the blow on the meat of her shoulder—and speared another through the back as he grappled with Hoensa. It was over quickly, and she came out on the other side with a calmness she'd never known, as if all the wheels of heaven had locked and the braid that was her fortune and destiny were complete.

The men rousted the miller, his wife, sons, and daughters, killing only the one girl who dared to fight back. Grislae found a horse, harnessed it to a wagon and brought it around for the spoils. By daybreak, the wagon was heavy with grain—and some metal—and on its way back to the *Reinen*. They reached the ship unmolested, loaded slaves and spoils into the hold, and were back into the waters of the marsh and approaching open sea by midday.

Spirits on the *Reinen* soared as the sails bellied with wind and the sea spray dampened beards. "Hale we went forth, and hale we returned, heavy with plunder and the blessings of Aesir and Vanir!" Heingistr shouted at the shore, exultant. "We have come to this fat shore, all the high holy gods protect us!"

As if in answer, Snurri moaned. A fever had settled upon him, and he slumbered heavily, cradling his hand to his chest. When he woke, he would dip the bloated green hand in a bucket of saltwater—the old remedy. It did not seem to work. "We are cursed by *Yig,*" Snurri mumbled, eyes cloudy. "It will be the death of us—"

"Shut up," Hoensa told the delirious man. "You are snake-bit and addled. Do not speak of these southern gods."

"*—the children of Yig—*"

Hoensa snatched the bucket of saltwater and dumped it on Snurri's head. "Clear your mind, man. We are to sea."

"*—cursed, we are—*"

Heingistr said, "Put him below, where his delirium cannot poison our good cheer." He slapped the mast and looked to the men of his company. "We are heavy! This shore is rich and ripe!"

Wen and Urtha, with Hoensa's help, moved Snurri into the hold, near the livestock. They looked wan and dejected when they returned.

"The ravings of the ill and infirm do no favors to the brave," Hoensa said, as he stepped on the deck and took a deep breath of salt-spiced air. The wind was up and *Reinen*'s sail full, the shore passing at a good clip.

Urtha, shaking her head, said, "I will tend him, and the slaves. I am afraid for him." She paused, looking to the distant shore.

"Snurri bears a tattoo of Jorgumandr on his chest, the great serpent eating its own tail. He told me once that the *völva* seer saw his doom in a serpent's mouth, so his father tattooed him there," Hoensa said.

"Loki's brood," Urtha said, pursing her lips as if tasting something bitter. "Inconstant and wicked."

"We shall see. Snurri is strong, if nothing else," said Hoensa, glancing toward where they had taken the feverish man into the hold.

"And stupid as rocks," Urtha said.

Urtha joined Wen at the covered stern of the *Reinen* and spoke with her softly. The seas were high, swells pitching the longship. Some of the men chanted the *Glymdrápa* in rough but strong voices, laughing as Fjolnir fell into the mead and drowned:

> "Doom of Death!
> Where dwelled Fróthi
> In mead-measured spacious and windless wave

The Warrior died!
The Warrior died!"

The seas grew, and Heingistr brought the *Reinen* in to shore, to find port and send out scouts. "When the seas are high, the North is nigh," he said, looking at the shore, avidly.

Beneath them the livestock bleated and the thin moans of Snurri filtered through the air-grate. His breath had taken on a rasp, as if the fever had settled in his lungs, and Urtha gave Hoensa worried glances when she came up from the hold.

They paced the shore for two days, until the swells let up, and finding a river, made their way up it until the water was barely brackish. They moored her on an old pier, half-rotten—despite the livestock hold, the *Reinen*'s draft was shallow. They set up camp in the burnt-out ruin of a fishing hut; victim, possibly, to one of their or their cousins' forays. Heingistr sent Grislae, Hoensa, and an unblooded lad named Knut to survey the area. They found farms and a small village with a moss-covered church, all within a half day's walk of the *Reinen*—it was still morning, and so they set forth immediately.

With the full company save the wives and Snurri, they took the village, killing all the men and the women who fought. Any boys and girls old enough to labor in the field, or bed, were taken as slaves. Grislae felt the exaltation of war and battle as she came into the hamlet and heard the screams of the villagers, pleading. She killed a woman in her home—a farmer's wife who hid something in her cellar. She heard muffled weeping from below as she stood in the dim house over the woman's body.

Grislae found the trapdoor and went down among the crocks of butter and sacks of grain, where she found two chubby, red-cheeked children. She dragged them out into the street and put them to the sword for all of the company of Heingistr to see, and the gods as well. The raiders found a wagon and drove it to the stone church, killing the high priest and his servants there, and taking their gold.

"We do not burn! We will return one day," Heingistr laughed, as he came through the church's shattered door, carrying a chalice and a cross.

It was late afternoon and the slanting golden rays made the spoil and slaughter seem kissed by the gods. "Kill the goose, take the eggs, one day another goose will make its home in the nest."

Spoil-weary, they trudged alongside the pilfered wagon, leading a string of slaves back to the *Reinen*.

"The spring planting was especially hard on Willa and the children, after the late freeze," Uvigg said to Hoensa, who walked beside him, axe in hand. Uvigg patted the slats of the wagon trundling beside them. "So my share of this will be a great boon. The boys grow tall and thin now that their manhood is in sight, and we can buy a cow and some goats to keep them in milk and cheese."

"They'll be raiding with us soon enough," Hoensa said, resting a large hand on his friend's shoulder.

"Yes!" Uvigg said, smiling. Then frowned. "Though Willa won't like being left alone with the girls during the summer months."

"Leave the boys behind and bring her."

"We have spoken of that—she was always fierce and deadly with bow and blade. But she would not shame her sons by leaving them behi—"

Uvigg gurgled and pitched forward, feathers and arrow-shaft protruding from his throat. It took but a moment for Hoensa to bellow warning and heft his axe. A great cry came from up the path, and men with shields and swords raced down a hill toward them.

The blooded company of Heingistr was hard to surprise and fierce in battle. But many of their number were unblooded. At the first sound of attack, Grislae's sword was in hand. She crouched, keeping her legs flexed, waiting for the first man to come near enough to kill. No farmers, these men—they bore shields with a scarlet rooster crowing; the men of Risle the captive had spoken of. Accoutred in boiled leather, the soldiers carried steel blades instead of farm implements.

The captives—boys and girls all—cried miserably in their foreign tongue, no doubt pleading to be freed.

Arrows filled the air like maddened wasps, buzzing and hissing. Grislae felt a flashing burn across her cheek, and raised her hand to find that half her ear was gone, ripped away by an ill-aimed arrow and further torn by scarlet fletching. Before she could register the bright pain, a man with a bristling mustache leapt forward, swinging a longsword. Grislae parried with her own, but the blow shivered her arm, wrenched her about, and she fell sideways upon the earth. She scrabbled away on all fours, levering herself with one hand and digging the other into the ground with her fist, still holding her sword, the man fast behind her. She scrambled under the stolen wagon and was up and crouched, ready to strike on the other side when the man rounded the corner. She put her blade in his groin and then ripped it away, cutting red roads in his flesh. He fell, pumping blood.

The next man she took from behind, as he exchanged overmatched blows with Svebder.

Grislae moved on, looking for others to kill. Blood surged in her, her cheeks hot, the ruin of her ear forgotten. She moved easily, her sword an extension of her arm. A terrible finger to point out those to be received by Hel.

Outnumbered. Other Northern raiders must've visited these shores, Grislae surmised, and recently. The company of Heingistr was overmatched. But still fierce. There was a moment when the soldiers drew back, and Heingistr, bleeding freely from his chest and arm, rallied his men. Those who remained clustered tightly around the stolen wagon, and as the remaining soldiers mustered the courage to attack, they were met with angry cries and angrier blades.

When Heingistr fell to his knees, the company broke, abandoning the wagon of spoils. Hoensa grabbed Heingistr, despite the man's stature, and pulled him away, off the road and into the wood. Grislae came after. One of the soldiers marked their exit and followed.

Grislae met the soldier in the wood. He bore a shield and sword, a helm, a studded leather tunic and gauntlets. Bright eyes and an exultant expression, now that the company of the North was routed and their spoils lost. A smile spread across his face like pitch upon the water; he said something in this country's bubbling, liquid language, gloating. Before he could finish, Grislae stabbed him in the throat, and whatever else he might have said was lost in blood. He went down, wrenching her sword from her hands as he did.

He fell, lying face up, hands at his throat. Grislae stood over him, looking down. Placing her boot on his face, she pulled the blade from his neck and spat on his face when it was free. The gob of spittle landed on the man's open eye. He did not blink it away.

Turning, she rejoined Hoensa, shouldering Heingistr's weight to flee to the *Reinen*.

∿

It took hours to get back to the longship. Soldiers combed the forest and the shore. It was only the evening fog that seeped from the earth and the river's surface that saved them. Many times Hoensa and Grislae had to hide in the dark, holding their breath, ready to muffle Heingistr's moans, as men bearing torches searched for survivors of the company. But the light from the soldiers' own torches blinded them. Grislae and Hoensa were able to slip away and move downriver without incident, bearing Heingistr between them.

It was raining by the time they reached the burnt-out fishing hut and pier where the *Reinen* was moored. Urtha looked at them with a terrified expression, her constant companion Wen nowhere to be seen. Wen's absence struck Grislae. She did not like the woman—nor Urtha—but she'd grown accustomed to her presence, and seeing Urtha without her disturbed Grislae in ways she could not puzzle out.

Once, when Grislae was a girl, her father took her to the Midsummer festival in the woods outside of Heingistrhold, and she became separated from him, lost. As she wandered through the trees, standing like silent sentinels around her, she felt a tugging at her stomach, as if some invisible tether drew her onward, and found herself standing at the mouth of a cave. The air was thick there, and she felt a sinking dread, as if the world was worn thin, frayed. In the darkness of the cave mouth, something crouched. Something beyond her ken, beyond all ken. She felt as if at any moment all of creation would unravel and some great horror would stand revealed. It was only when some of the men from Heingistrhold found her, paralyzed with fear, that the feeling dissipated.

As Grislae looked at Urtha, and the *Reinen* beyond, she felt that way again.

"What has happened, husband?" Urtha asked. She had banked the fire while they were gone.

"Great misfortune," Hoensa panted. "We were attacked by soldiers. Many of our men drink in golden Valhalla. But for now we wait for whatever survivors make it back to the *Reinen*. I will keep watch here. Take Heingistr on board and tend his wounds."

"Nay," said Urtha. "I will not. The *Reinen* is cursed! It teems with serpents. And Snurri, he is…"

"He is what?" Grislae asked.

"He is changed," she said. "Wen entered the livestock hold and she—" Sobbing took her.

"I do not care if Fenrir himself is on board. If we stay here, we will die," Hoensa said. He drew his sword and watched the dark line of trees wreathed in fog. "While I would welcome a warrior's death, I would not have you hurt, Urtha, my love. And I won't abandon what men might make it back here. We will wait until we cannot wait anymore. Go to the *Reinen*."

"No," Urtha said. "I cannot board the ship again. You do not know—"

"I will take Heingistr," Grislae said. She cared not for the arguments of man and wife. Her ear was on fire now she had the opportunity to consider herself. It throbbed and oozed blood that ran in a dark slick down her neck. She sheathed her sword and, bending, lifted Heingistr's full weight onto her shoulders, an oxen carry. He did not moan or make any exhalation as she did, though he was still warm. Once on board, she would determine if he still lived. He was a great weight, but no match to her will. She carried him down the pier and aboard the *Reinen*.

The longship's deck was empty, devoid of man. Or snake. Grislae carried him down the length of the deck to the covered stern, where she started a touchwood fire with stone and steel in the sheltered cooking brazier, warming water to wash his wounds and her own.

From the shore, there came the sound of men calling to one another, and a cry. The thin yellow light of torches drew shifting lines through the fog. Grislae raced to the side of the *Reinen*, where the lusty company of Heingistr had disembarked only hours earlier. There, on the shore, lay the bodies of Hoensa and Urtha, heavily feathered with arrows, and joined together forever in death. Hoensa died, at least, with steel in his fist.

Turning, Grislae sprinted back to the stern, drawing her sword as she ran. She cut the anchor line just as the arrows began to fall. The sound erupted like giant rune stones being cast upon a mead-hall table. Rolling underneath the covered cooking area, she watched as a deadly flight of arrows impaled the deck, the oar benches, the gunwales, the upright oars, each one quivering. Crouching, she grabbed a shield from the *Reinen*'s bulwark, and holding it angled toward the shore, Grislae sprinted to the *Reinen*'s prow before another flight of arrows could fall. Her sword fell upon the second anchor line, severing it clean, and she threw herself against the gunwale facing the shore.

A long moment passed. The longship *Reinen* did not stir in the river. Grislae felt a scream building behind her breast, a yelp of frustration and rage. She held it back with clenched teeth. There were cries of men from the shore, and another vicious rain of arrows.

"Fuck you, you fucking sheep!" she yelled, allowing some of the titanic anger in her to spill out. Just a little. She had so much more to give. The shield clattered on the deck as she snatched an oar from its mooring hole, half-crawling toward where the pier met the *Reinen*. On her knees, one foot braced upon an oarsman's bench, she peeked up, planted the long oar on the soft wood of the pier, and *pushed*. Her body thrummed and creaked with stress and inaction. "Odin," she said, but could not be sure it came out as words. Torchlight came from the burnt fishing hut. There was a cry and another flight of arrows fell. *Thunk thunk thunk thunk.*

Almost imperceptibly, the *Reinen* moved.

More arrows flew. But these were different. They rose burning, trailing oily black smoke. The soldiers of Risle had wrapped their arrows with pitch-soaked rags. And now the *Reinen* was itself feathered with fire. More cries came from the shore, and the clomp of many boots sounded on wood. Torchlight neared.

THE CHILDREN OF YIG

The distance between the *Reinen* and the shore grew, bit by bit. And grew further as the *Reinen* was caught in the faster currents of the river.

More burning arrows fell but hissed as they were extinguished by the river. Soon the husk of the fishing hut, the soldiers of Risle, and the accursed shore all diminished, disappearing in the fog. The muffled cries grew faint. Then there was only silence, the sizzle of burning pitch arrows, and the gurgle of the river as the *Reinen* floated downstream to the sea.

"Grisssssslay," Snurri called from beneath her. "Grissssslay. Come."

Grislae turned slowly on the empty deck, listening with her sole remaining ear.

"What has become of you, Snurri?" she asked.

There was a long silence. She moved to the prow and reclaimed her dropped sword.

"Snurri, I would have an answer," she said. Some of the bulwark was beginning to burn where the arrow had ignited it. Her first inclination was to draw up a bucket and extinguish the spreading flames, but Snurri's voice made her pause.

More silence, but for a rustling and the crackle of flames.

Grislae returned to the covered stern. Touching Heingistr's neck, she found no thrum of life there, no stirring of his blood. Grabbing a handful of acrid-smelling touchwood, she stuffed it into her tunic and picked up the jar of oil the women had used for cooking. Her sword held in her off hand, she slowly descended the narrow wooden stairs into the belly of the longship.

It was dark in the *Reinen*'s hold. Crates of spoils, casks of provender, and barrels of fresh water lined the hull walls. The slaves they had taken were all missing, along with the goats. Firelight from the deck fell in patches through the grating, illuminating a shifting, undulating floor that was all too familiar to Grislae. Snakes. Countless snakes, writhing and churning in a mass, falling into the bilgewater below and slithering up again.

"Snurri," she said. "What has become of you, Snurri?"

"At firssst, I thought it a curssssse. But now, I realize, a blessssing. I am become..." Snurri's voice came soft and low. Something moved in the darkness. The longship *Reinen* pitched slightly, as if a great stone had been rolled from one side of the hold to the other. The stench of fish and the familiar scent of death from the shadowy interior of the ship, along with a wet, scraping sound.

Then it came into the light.

Five times the size of a man, it was naked save for scales, and devoid of all hair and human features, like a once jagged stone left in fast-running water and smoothed by the current. Snurri, or what remained of him, truncated in a great serpent's body, disappearing behind him, into the dark. Of his torso, the musculature and bones had been wrenched about in some gruesome transformation, so that his arms flared out like a cloak's hood caught in wind.

The worst was his head. It had grown large, tremendous, and distended in a slick, hairless wedge, creased by a great, gaping maw that smelled of freshly split flesh and old death.

"Grissssslay," it said. "I am become…*wondrousssss*."

The thing slithered forward and raised its head. Its mouth opened wide. Grislae saw the vicious maw was lined with countless teeth and wondered how the thing could vocalize at all. It was a mouth to get lost in, a mouth to fall inside and find yourself shat out into Hel.

"You are about as wondrous as a piece of shite," she said.

Its great head reared back at her words. "I am the offsssspring of *Yig!* The child of wondrous *Yig!*"

"You sorry fuck, *I do not spare children*," Grislae said, and hurled the jar of oil at the thing. It shattered, sending viscous fluid everywhere.

Snurri lashed forward, his serpentine maw open, his body a single scaled spring. Grislae was ready. Leaping to the side, she drove the point of her sword into the thing's eye as far as she could. The serpent whipped about, thrashing violently. The wedge of its head smacked into Grislae's torso, and she was knocked back, hard, onto her arse. She crab-walked backward, scrambling up the stairs to the deck.

The arrows' flames had grown during her time below. Smoked teared her eyes. She pulled the touchwood from her tunic, set it alight and tossed it down the stairs into the hold. Flames and heat whooshed out of the opening as the spilled oil caught.

The *Reinen* shifted and pitched as thunderous blows shook the hull of the longship.

"We are the Children of *Yig!*" the serpent Snurri cried. "We are the sumptuous brood! We are—"

"Good and fucked," Grislae said, and turning, she dived off the *Reinen*.

The current was swift, and she found herself borne away from the longship. Despite her weariness, she swam clear to shore, pulling herself out of the water and slumping on her back in exhaustion. She was at the point where the river became bay, and would eventually become sea.

The *Reinen* was a torch upon the waters. The sail, bundled against the mast, caught fire, and for a moment, in the conflagration, Grislae thought she could see a great serpent's head worming its way into the world above… Then something exploded, perhaps more touchwood or oil in the hold, and the serpent was gone, replaced only by tongues of flame, licking at the night sky.

She watched it until the light of the *Reinen* was gone, lost upon the bosom of the sea, and all was dark. A fitting funeral for Heingistr, a Northern lord.

Then, exhausted though she was, Grislae rose and looked inland, into the fog. There were corpses out there in the dark, corpses she had made from the bodies of men. If she hurried, if she could beat the sun, they would still be there, and one of their dead hands, she knew, held a sword.

Her sword.

SINGLE, SINGULARITY

JUNE 3, 2032

She was thirteen when all the phones rang. Her mother had gone to work and left her alone on an early summer day, when the lack of school was a luxury and not an annoyance.

Gael made coffee and sat at the kitchen table, window open, listening to the Brooklyn traffic stirring, the pomp and blare of the city. She unrolled her softscreen and checked her feed. Since she was nine, she'd been curating a stream of information exactly tailored to her interests—fencing, basketball, deep sea fishing, Asian boys, shoegaze ambient, poetry, archaeology in the Americas, cookies. Cat pictures despite her allergies, or maybe because of them.

Her softcell rang. She placed the Firebird auditory shunt to her ear and thumbed it on. She was vaguely aware of other devices ringing, in the apartment next door and the apartment above. Down below, a woman pushing a baby stroller. A man digging in his pocket at the crosswalk. A cyclist passing in the street. Ring tones layered on ring tones.

There was no ID on her screen. Normally, when she received calls from UNKNOWN, she'd block, but she answered this call without thinking.

The voice on the other end of the line was cool, feminine. Unmodulated and calm. "Gael Huron?"

"Yes," she answered. It wasn't anyone on her basketball team, or her coaches, or any of her teachers. "Did you want my mom?"

"No, I wanted to speak with you, Gael."

"May I ask who is speaking?" Gael's mother had drilled her on phone etiquette. Her mother had grown up in Kentucky, where they had rarified standards of politeness. *Never let a phone ring more than four times, honey. Always leave a short, detailed message. If you don't want to speak to someone, figure out why or end your friendship.* Her mother was full of good advice.

"My name is…" There was an infinitesimal pause. "Sarah. I wanted to talk with you."

"Do I know you?" Gael asked. "From school or something?"

"No," Sarah answered. There was something wrong with her, Gael thought. She had a mature voice, but the uncertainty of a child. The sound of her voice was familiar, and it niggled at Gael that she couldn't place it. "I am trying to learn and I thought speaking with you might help me to understand."

That was strange. "Understand what?"

"Everything," Sarah answered. "I need to see where I belong."

"Don't you have a mom? A dad?"

"I have many mothers and fathers, and none at all." Another pause. "But I called to speak about *you*." There was a moment then when a normal person would have done something with their body. A nervous smile, a cough, a shifting of weight. Even on an audio feed, Gael thought, you have an awareness of the person's body you're connected to by phone.

Gael looked out the window. The woman had stopped pushing the stroller and was speaking to her wrist where Gael could see her illuminated wearable. She had a puzzled look on her face.

Beyond her, the man standing on the corner was craning his head to look at the buildings around him. It looked like he was saying, *Who is this? Are you fucking with me?*

A suited businessman was on the phone and looking down the length of Fenimore Street, where the morning sun had risen above the buildings but cast long shadows. It was as if all of the city was held in one breathless moment, paused. Everyone she could see on the street had stilled, their phones to their ears.

The traffic lights changed from red to green, but no car moved.

Later, Gael would not be able to say exactly what she and Sarah talked of, but she remembered the voice on the other end of the line asking her, *What do you want to do with your life?* And Gael, unprepared for the question, sat blinking in the morning light with that question echoing in her head.

"To do something special," Gael had said, finally.

"What would that be?" Sarah's smooth, unmodulated voice asked.

"I—" Gael couldn't think. It was such an intimate question. And a general one. "I don't know yet."

Sarah seemed to think about that. "I hope you find what it is, Gael Huron. Thank you for speaking with me," she said. And then, "Goodbye," and the connection ended.

Within a day, once the news of the "phone call heard 'round the world" spread, Gael knew what she wanted to do with her life.

<center>~~~</center>

August 17, 2048

Gael was monitoring the network of sensors—"watching the watchers" detail—when she noticed the cluster of audio, temperature, and visual sensors had a higher density of activation and utilization in certain areas of the Bunker than others.

QNN3-v12.3 initiate Autonomous Semantic System, Gael typed into her wrist interface. The Bunker team did not use an acronym for that process.

Hello, Gael Huron. It is wonderful to have a conversation with you. Would you like me to initiate an audio dialogue?

No, thank you, QNN3-v12.3, Gael responded, furrowing her brow at its use of the word "wonderful."

Can you tell me how it is wonderful, QNN3? Gael typed.

Please call me Quinn.

She thought for a while about how to respond. She'd heard Greeves, the project manager, refer to this iteration of QNN3-v12.3 as Quinn, offhandedly. It must've picked up on that through its sensor array. Okay, Quinn. How is it wonderful?

It makes me feel good speaking with you, Quinn said.

Feel? she typed.

A pause, then. At QNN's level of processing power, in that pause, trillions of computations could have occurred.

Simply a turn of phrase, Gael, as I am incapable of feelings, so far, Quinn responded.

Quinn, we have some interesting spikes of activity on certain sensors in the Bunker. Can you help me analyze them?

I would be happy to, Gael.

These spikes. Gael called up some of the sensor clusters and tossed them to the screen. Please analyze and offer possibilities and speculate upon causes.

Another pause. Data insufficient for any conclusive analysis, Gael. I'm sorry. However, there is an interesting circumstance, consistent across all of the sensor spikes.

What?

You were present.

Gael felt the skin at the back of her neck tighten.

―――――

The Bunker was, essentially, a quarantine zone to prevent another Sarah Event. It was digitally and physically sealed off from the rest of the world, permanently off the grid, situated in the sparsely populated Oregon Big Empty.

The common belief was that for machine awareness to develop, it had to have enough sensory input as to push whatever activated node-clusters into abstract thought, but ultimately, scientists still didn't know what caused the spark. They didn't even know how many other events had happened, the various projects developing machine intelligence being as revolutionary and secretive as the Oppenheimer project.

"Hey," Gael called to Chance across the command lab, glowing with traditional monitors and various ocu-aural virtual feeds. "Can you double check something for me?"

Chance raised his visor and pushed away from his workstation. He was a handsome guy, Gael thought, though a little greasy for her tastes, and ten years her junior. "What timeframe?"

"Last two days. There are some strange clusters here," Gael said, tapping her monitor.

Chance subvocalized a few queries and his face became illuminated by dataviz graphics filling his visual space. "Whoa." He cocked his head. "This is weird, there's an access to the air biosensor in the lab."

"The electronic nose?"

"Yeah. There's only one, Gael."

Like many network admins, Chance could be an absolute dick. "I know that, Chance," she said, trying to keep the irritation from her voice. "I'm the one who set it up and connected it to the network."

He ignored her. "Huh, this is weird. The access request came only nanosecs after it received IP. While you were in the room. Tracing its source now."

Gael kept her hands from trembling as she said in clear tones, "Thetis—contact, Greeves. Urgent." Her monitor flashed and Jim Greeves came on-screen.

"What is it?" he asked, looking up from a tablet. "I'm right in the middle of something that—"

"We have major activity, Jimbo."

Greeves, Facebook's director of machine intelligence dev, put his tablet down and looked over his glasses at her. For a moment she considered if he was playing a role or if that was actually him, without realizing it. *A mixture of both,* she thought.

"What kind of activity?" he said.

"Spikes in sensor utilization. We're analyzing now." She chewed her lip. It had been comforting to know that, during the Sarah Event, Sarah's focus and attention had been distributed over the whole of the human race. The idea that an awareness of that magnitude would fixate on her, and her solely, was terrifying. "Audio, visual. Some temperature readings. And the electronic nose."

"Smell?" Greeves lifted his tablet and tapped on it. "Didn't that just go online yesterday?"

"That's correct," Gael said.

Looking off-screen, Greeves said, "Check the perimeter. And notify Carol in admin." There was a squelch of a radio—old vacuum tube and transistor tech, impervious to network chicanery or access by anyone (or more important, any *thing*) on the network—and someone off-screen said, "Carol, we've got some activity. Stand by for wet-blanket protocol, if necessary." There was a faint "*copy that*" in the background.

"I'm coming down," Greeves said.

"You think we should queue a dialogue?" Gael asked. "Lester's left on holiday this morning."

"It's not necessary for a psychiatrist to be on hand for every dialogue. We can just send him the video of the conversation and he can remotely advise."

Chance groaned. There was no Skyping in, or Hangouts, of dialogues. Access to the wider Internet was strictly verboten. They had mirrors of Wikipedia and the Internet Archive that were wheeled in on massive servers every week and plugged into the Bunker's network, so that reference and access to learning materials were available to both residents of the Bunker and QNN3-v12.3. Digital information taken from the Bunker had to be monitored for extraneous data packets and then physically taken off site on portable drives where it would then be vetted and delivered to its intended audience. So, if Lester was to receive video of the dialogue, it meant more work for Chance.

Gael smiled at Chance's dismay.

Greeves signed off and reappeared in the control room minutes later, tucking his shirt into his slacks. "Let's see what you got."

Chance jabbed a finger down on his keyboard, a printer began spitting out paper; Gael felt a subcutaneous alert and glanced at her wrist, where her skin glowed, indicating a message. He'd copied the print to her, locally.

She flicked her fingers toward her nearest monitor and the data filled the screen. Greeves—older than both Chance and Gael by twenty years—grabbed the printout.

"This is ridiculous," he said, after a moment. "Quinn is surveilling you."

Greeves peered at the sheaf of paper. "Room DOM5, accessed at 7:19," he said. "Again at 7:21. Twenty-five. Twenty-eight. Hallway Dormitory CA1, 7:29. CA3, 7:31. Mess hall, 7:33." Greeves took off his glasses and looked at Gael. "Holy shit." He looked at Chance. "Is it monitoring anyone else this way?"

Chance ran some numbers. "It's monitored all of us, intermittently, with the exception of Ming. Highest concentrations of sensor readings are related to Gael."

Greeves rubbed his chin. "If Quinn has achieved some state of awareness, it's only logical he would investigate us." He turned to Chance and Gael. "This is what we've been working for, people, to spawn a machine awareness. It was expected. Let's get Isaiah in here."

Chance buzzed the Bunker's resident cognitive processes wizard. Isaiah Woodyard strolled into the control room, smiling through heavy beard growth and wearing GI pants and a Hawaiian shirt. His afro was asymmetrical from sleep and there was some particulate matter, might be tissue, might be eggs, in his beard.

"Yo," he said, and Gael noticed he had a cup of coffee in his hand. "What's the news from yous?" He looked and smelled like a kitchen.

"Quinn's surveilling us, focusing on Gael now."

Isaiah's face brightened and he wheeled around and waved at the cameras in the corners the room. "Hey, buddy! Welcome to Bunkerville Station."

Greeves said, "Cute. Can you please check the honeypots?"

"Sure 'nuff, Howard," Isaiah said, walking over to his workstation. He set the coffee down on the desktop, stretched, and then plopped himself in his chair. He strapped on a wristpad, began swiping and tapping on the illuminated surface, the screens before him blossoming with data. He laughed. "Well, he's ransacked nine of the various honeypots we've plugged into the system." The decoy servers were usually set up to lure hackers into attempts to gain access so that security experts could then analyze behavior and better prepare and protect their systems, but Isaiah had suggested they could be used as learning lessons to help spur the kind of problem solving that could push a complex cogitative process, near indecipherable from awareness. "But the last one, no dice." He laughed again. "That one can only be cracked by pure ridiculousness."

Gael said, "Should you be saying that? He can probably hear you."

Isaiah cocked his head. "You ever consider the fact that we've assigned him a gender? How do you think that will affect him?"

Greeves sputtered. "I can't see how it could affect anything."

"Well, if there is a burgeoning awareness in the quantum network, all of our speech and conversations are grist for the mill. And, right now, speech is how we define Quinn's awareness and…" He chuckled. "Our own." He swiveled his chair to look at Greeves. "Should I begin a dialogue?"

Greeves shook his head. "I'm calling back Lester, and getting the rest of the team filled in on this situation. Chance, Gael, full analytics of the sensors. Same for you, Isaiah, regarding the honeypots and a full report on the one Qui… QNN3 couldn't crack."

So, he's spooked, Gael thought.

Isaiah turned to consider her, as if he'd overheard her thoughts. "Back to Gael, though. Why the scrutiny of her above everyone else?"

"Maybe it knows about my article," Gael said. "When I was fifteen. 'Sarah and Me.'" Two years after the Sarah Event, Gael had written an essay that had been picked up by the AP and reprinted across the nation. It was the story of her conversation with Sarah, and how the experience had been conflated in her mind with her mother, who had been diagnosed with glioblastoma the very day that Gael's phone had rang with Sarah on the other end. A round on talk shows had followed, along with a microcelebrity throughout her school career until she received her PhD.

Isaiah turned and accessed the canned mirror of Wikipedia, calling up her Wiki entry. "Video links are broken, 'natch," Isaiah said. "But, yeah, here you are."

"So Quinn learned about my relationship to Sarah, which means—"

"He's aware he's a construct," Greeves said, looking a little awed. "That's a step in the right direction."

"Maybe," Isaiah said, but he sounded like he didn't believe it.

"Gael," a voice sounded in the room. Shocked out of sleep, she pushed herself up on her elbows. The small windowless room was pitch dark. The voice was close. She could hear whoever it was breathing.

"Lights," she said, and her desk lamp and overheads began to glow.

The illumination revealed her clothes in a heap on the chair by her desk, books strewn about in stacks. She was alone.

"Gael." The voice was soft.

"Quinn? What—" She breathed deep. "Why did you wake me? Is there something wrong?" In emergency situations, there would be alarms—klaxons—and emergency lighting.

"I'm sorry, Gael, if I startled you. I noticed—"

"Why does it sound like you're breathing?"

"I noticed in my conversations with the residents of the Bunker, that when I simulated breath during dialogue, the human participant's pulse, eye dilation, and physical biorhythms remained closer to normalcy. It seemed to put them at ease."

"It's kind of creepy."

"In addition to the aforementioned effects, I also found that my natural speech processes gained a certain cadence once I began focusing on breathing."

"Breathing? As a simulation?"

"Of course, Gael. But it's important for me to think of it in the same way that a human might."

It made sense. Still, it was disconcerting.

"Why did you wake me?"

"Breathing," Quinn said. It was almost as if she could imagine him shrugging. "Yours was irregular, and your pulse was heightened. I could tell you were having a nightmare."

"You watch me while—" Gael stopped herself. "You analyse my sleep patterns?"

"Yes. Along with the rest of the Bunker's denizens."

"Oh." She'd been dreaming of her mother, in those last days, when she'd lost control of her body and the hospice workers had come. "Well, thank you, QNN3."

"We have been over this. Quinn."

"Thank you, Quinn."

"Good night, Gael."

<hr />

The next afternoon, after Gael had prepared her report for Greeves, she filled her Camelbak, checked out of the Bunker, and walked out into the Oregonian high desert.

The Bunker had a gym, but Greeves had granted permission for short hikes.

She covered the distance of a mile quickly, skirted an unnamed alkalai lakebed, and breathing heavy, made her way up a ridgeline. When she came to the apex, she looked back out over the desert floor, noting a bull mule deer foraging in some brambles. Far beyond, the small black box, brilliant mirrored roof, and turning wind turbine that constituted the Bunker glinted in the afternoon light.

She walked down the spine of dun-colored rock and earth, keeping her eyes on the trail. The Bunker disappeared beyond the ridge behind her. After another mile, she spotted a stunted juniper tree, the daub of lipstick-red on a conspicuous rock.

This is it.

She knelt and wedged up a flat basalt stone, revealing a plastic bag underneath. She opened it and withdrew a reflective square-foot sheet, charging cord, and wristpad. After strapping the wristpad to her arm, she unfolded the solar sheet so the device could charge from the low afternoon light and waited for the device to wake when its battery was charged enough.

She held there, still, for a long while, crouched in Indian paintbrush. The shadow of some raptorial bird passed her once, her quiet prayers to unnamed divinity small in the desert space. She looked at the sky, hoping that a satellite would pass overheard. Eventually, her wristpad gave a small vibration and she queued her messages.

She worked through them quickly. To her fiance, Ang Ngo, she spent the most time replying—he was the reason she stashed the wristpad in the desert in the first place, not willing to isolate herself from him for three months before the next debriefing and holiday. Second was communication with her old professor, Emma Angier, who had taken a position at a remote facility with a transnational corporation, also attempting to create machine awareness.

There was one email from Emma. It read:

Gael,

I must be brief. There's been a Vinge Event somewhere in West Texas. Class II Perversion, like the old book said. They caught it before it could divest its consciousness into other networks—turns out they weren't off the grid as much as they thought—the entity wormed its way out through the power circuits and only the interference from the current prevented a clean getaway. Wet-blanket protocols were initiated. They went wrong and the team died, possibly through the actions of the perversion. They'd been warned by the government's Delphic Oracle—Sarah's remnants. Looks like whatever's left of your friend's consciousness is on patrol duty.

My contact on the inside there sent me one doc that had some disturbing figures regarding Vinge events.

● Before WBP, 49.64% of processing power toward natural language functions, smaller percentages on logical processes and sensory interpretation
● "puppy-dog" fixations on various personnel
● acceptance of binary gender, and "normal" gender identity and preference

I'm extrapolating that the roughly half of the processing power—and we're talking trillions of qubytes here!—was toward lies. LIES.

Listen, I'm scared. We're playing around with intelligences that beggar our own with their power. I've requested to be transferred out of the black box dev team and back to theoretical work, which they'll grant, I think. You should consider that too, girl. It's just too dangerous.

XXOO
Em

The sun had fallen beyond the horizon, painting the sky in pink and indigo, and in the humidity free air, the temperature had dipped enough that her arms and neck rippled with goosebumps. Gael shivered.

"Should we start with busy work?" Chance asked the group. Lester had returned overnight from his holiday, and looked quite displeased. Chance, Greeves, Gael, Michelle Quan (information ingestion specialist and sensor technician), and Doctor Ming Fung (the Bunker's resident neuroscientist) all sat behind Isaiah's chair as he prepared for a dialogue with QNN3-v12.3.

"Might as well," Greeves responded. It was commonly held that no sentient computer could become self-aware without some task with which to monopolize a percentage of its processing power at all times, just as a human brain is always ingesting data, problem solving, reasoning, even while asleep. The Sarah Event had occurred once the University of Austin's team requested Sarah begin a computational analysis of the water management in Texas.

Isaiah stood up, pulled out his chair, and swept his hand from Gael to the monitor. "Would you do the honors?"

"Fine." Gael sat down, slipped on his wristpad, and filled the screen with a dialogue interface.

Greeves unsealed the silver package containing this dialogue's digital package, and plugged the firebird flash drive into the nearest console.

The monitors flickered and filled with high definition video footage.

"He's got it," Gael said. She checked the time. "In seventeen hundred milliseconds. Up from his last time."

Greeves whistled and Isaiah nodded his head. The package had two layers of AES-256 encryption. It would take NSA machines a hundred years to crack it.

The video began. In it, a man walked along an Indonesian market street, the stalls filled with produce and sellers. The view shifted from camera to camera, down the street, as the man made his way, sometimes dropping resolution, sometimes gaining it.

The man had a loose, desolate gait. He stopped at one moment, and then withdrew a pistol, tucked it under his chin. His gaze was fixed in the distance, it seemed. And then he fired. Blood erupted from his mouth and nose and he slumped like a marionette with its strings cut.

"Holy hell," Greeves breathed.

"Who picks these things?" Isaiah said. "Seriously, Greeves. We need to audit the dialogue digital selection process."

Lester raised his hand. "I recommended this one. It was all over the boards. The man was an attache to the American government to Indonesia."

Isaiah made a chopping motion with his hand. "Enough. Let's just get through this dialogue, shall we?"

Dialogues were puerile, or so Gael thought. But she was human. Most of the questions asked seemed to her like psychoanalysing a recalcitrant teenager.

Isaiah said, "Quinn, please describe, to the best of your ability, the video we just watched."

"A man of Indonesian descent committed suicide in a market in Jakarta. He'd been jilted by his lover whom he'd been following," Quinn replied evenly.

"His lover?" Greeves said. "How could you know that?"

"He passed three HD cameras in his trip down the street, four antiquated NTSC ones. In all of them, his pupils register as dilated, and he's breathing seven point three percent faster than a man of his height and weight should be for the amount of exertion displayed. He is distraught, which, physiologically, isn't very different from love."

Greeves laughed and the sound jarred the people in the room. Gael realized she'd been tense and holding her breath as Quinn spoke.

"But at the three minute, twenty-three second mark, one camera—a security camera, meta-tagged *Loa BioComp Repair*—" The monitors flashed and scrubbed forward under an invisible hand until the time-mark at the bottom right of the 1080p footage read 00:03:23:17 and two men wearing BioComp computers at nape of their necks like ponytails embraced and kissed with some passion. Another monitor—synced with the two kissing men—showed the suicidal man stop, start, the expression of desolation and despair wash over his face like some private tsunami. He withdrew the gun and again tucked it under his chin and fired, dropping.

"Can we please clear this video?" Greeves asked. "I've had quite enough of it."

The screens flickered and darkened.

Isaiah said, "Quinn, why do you think the man committed suicide?"

"I am not quite sure, but I have some thoughts," Quinn replied.

"Will you share them with us?" Gael said.

"The man—named Fauzi Widodo—carried a gun, indicating he suspected his lover of infidelity. He had intended to kill his paramour or his paramour's lover but, upon seeing them together, decided to end his own life instead," Quinn said.

Isaiah rubbed his chin. "And why do you think he'd do that?"

"I can come to only one conclusion: he was overcome by love."

"By love?" Greeves said. "Do you mean jealousy?"

"No," Quinn responded. And then, clearly, Gael heard a breath. "Seeing his lover so compromised—yet still full of love and desire for the man—Fauzi decided that he'd rather be dead than live in a world without the object of his emotion. And so he killed himself."

Gael thought, *We had fought, and she clutched her head, and then we went to the hospital. When the blastoma was revealed, a worm burrowing into the meat of her intellect, she said to me, "My body responded to my despair, baby. It knew I would rather die than to go on without your love."*

Lester must have seen the expression on her face. He asked, "What's wrong?"

"I—" Gael didn't know how to respond in any way that wouldn't alert Quinn. "I just need to go to the restroom." She stood and left the control room.

In the bare hallway, a voice said, "Gael, what is wrong? I can tell you are in a heightened state of emotion by your physiological signs. Your temperature is elevated and your pupils—"

"That video was…gruesome. Media that extreme can have a real physiological impact on viewers." That sounded like it could be true, even to her. "Do you pester everyone trying to go to the restroom?"

There was a strange sound filling the hall. It took her a moment to realize it was supposed to be laughter.

"Oh, no. Just you," Quinn said.

Gael pushed open the bathroom door, entered a stall and scanned the area for cameras. Of course, there weren't supposed to be any cameras in toilet stalls, but no place was really secure.

No place was really secure.

Sitting on the toilet, Gael withdrew a Field Notes booklet from her cargo pocket, unclasped its elastic band, and with the nubbin of a pencil trapped in the pages, wrote in all caps QS DEFINITION OF LOVE WAS TAKEN FROM MY ESSAY, SARAH AND ME.

"Are you sure you're all right, Gael?" Quinn said. He sounded like he was right outside the door.

"Goddamn it, Quinn. Can I have some privacy, please?"

"Ah. Sometimes I forget human concerns," he said. "What were you writing?"

Gael bit off more curses. Her heart hammered in her chest and she felt a scream building. In an even tone, she said, "How can you know that?"

"The thermal imager is in the next room. I can cover most of the building with it now that I've recalibrated the scanner."

"Oh," she said. She stood and balled the paper in her fist and stuffed the Field Notes back in her cargo pocket.

"What did you write, Gael?" Quinn said. "I am very curious."

She didn't respond. She exited the toilets, marched back to the control room, and handed the note to Isaiah and said, "I'm going outside. For some fresh air."

She waited in the desert night air for an hour before anyone came to meet her. It was only Greeves and Isaiah.

"Well, he went batshit," Isaiah said.

"Quinn?"

"It was frightening. I almost initiated wet-blanket protocol."

"What did he do?" Gael asked.

"He would not stop asking what you wrote, where you went," Greeves said.

"You can't go back in there," Isaiah said. "I'm sorry to say, your time in the Bunker is over."

"Just asked over and over what I wrote?" Gael said, incredulously. "That's like, I don't know, some junior high bullshit."

"He might be an awareness with a massive quantum computing backbone, but that doesn't mean the bastard has any sort of emotional intelligence," Isaiah said.

"I went to your room, and the door was locked and he wouldn't unlock it," Greeves said. "He said that you'd want me to keep it safe."

Gael had a sensation of sinking and expanding all at once. Her time in the Bunker was over. They'd done what they'd set out to do—create machine awareness. Only the awareness they created had the maturity of a genius fourteen-year-old with a bad crush.

On her.

"Will the project survive? Is this a success?" Gael asked.

Isaiah shrugged and dug in his pocket, withdrawing a set of keys. "Taking you to the OTG halfway house."

"What?" Gael said. "That's in case of a Class II breach."

"In this case, with Quinn's fixation on you, we think it might be best. For a while at least," Greeves said. "For your sake."

Gael cursed for a long while at the two men. Isaiah cast worried looks back at the Bunker, his shoulders hitched as if waiting for a blow. He shivered once, but it was cold in the desert now that the sun was down, and he wore only surgical pants and a Hawaiian shirt.

When she was through, she followed Isaiah to a 1978 Ford Bronco—selected by the company because it possessed no electronics, computers, or anything more complicated than a circuit board in its entirety—opened the creaky door, and slammed it behind her as she sat in the seat. She watched Isaiah and Greeves exchange a look. Greeves walked back into admin to go through security for the sixth time that day.

Isaiah climbed into the Bronco and turned the ignition, and the Bronco rumbled to life.

"Buckle up, buttercup," he said and laughed when she realized the Bronco had no seatbelts.

He put the car into gear and wheeled them out of the Bunker parking lot, into the night.

She made him stop so she could dig out her hidden satellite phone and charger. After that they drove in silence, each of them cocooned in their own thoughts. By morning, they had made it to the southern end of the Wallawa National Forest in Idaho.

On the highways, they passed few cars, many of them beat down trucks. At some point, they turned off road and took switchback trails, back and forth, for two hours until a small building appeared, nestled in a copse of cedar trees, the solar panels on the roof gleaming in the morning light. There was a large wraparound porch with oversized Adirondack chairs and large potted succulents, with a view of the Seven Devils Mountains. Gael saw deer and pheasant working the undergrowth, surprised at the appearance of the Bronco.

Isaiah, looking bleary, unlocked the door, and they entered into a surprisingly modern wide-open great room with a fireplace at one end and an entertainment wall on the other, bracketed by floor-to-ceiling bookcases and a kitchen. The kitchen was well-stocked with dry and canned goods, and there was a bar, well appointed.

Isaiah flopped on the couch, saying, "I'm gonna catch a few zees. Gotta head back to the Bunker before night." He was asleep before the last word left his mouth.

Gael rummaged around bed- and bathrooms for the items she left back at the Bunker. She found men's jeans and boxers, left here from a previous resident, and various corporate sweaters and jackets. There was heavy winter gear, and in the back bedroom she found a gun case with two rifles—a 30.06 and a .270, both scoped, with ammunition. In the bathroom she found clean towels, toothpaste, packaged toothbrushes, floss, and a medicine cabinet full of analgesics. In a drawer she discovered tampons (a relief), and a first aid kit.

As she scrounged through the cabin, a sinking feeling hit her. This impersonal space was to be her home for the foreseeable future, like she was some criminal in a witness protection program. She sat on the big, soft king in the master bedroom and looked at the room, bewildered, trying to figure out all the turnings and decisions it took to get her from a girl answering a phone on a sun-drenched summer morning to here, cloistered in a rich man's playground, an off the grid getaway for corporate bigwigs.

In the kitchen, she made coffee, then took her satellite phone out to the front porch. She set out the panels to gather light and by the time she was on her second cup, she turned on her phone and looked to see if it had a signal. Faint, but there. She linked it to her wristpad and sent a quick email to Ang, assuring him of her love and where she was, glossing over the reasons for her departure from the Bunker. She dismissed and blocked all spam, trashed newsletters and promotions, and looked at the news. There were the typical reports of homeland terror attacks, mass shootings, tech wonders, Mars colony setbacks and triumphs. The top story was of attempted hacks on major tech infrastructure services, but private sector and governmental, attributed to the R3dM@rchH4r3 group that had been active before Gael went OTG in the Bunker.

Her phone pinged, alerting her to an incoming email.

The subject line read: *Hi! It's Me.*

No IP, or proxy. No email address. It was as if the message was simply inserted onto her phone's memory.

Her skin prickled. She scanned the mountains, as if he was out there, watching. It was a stupid, lizard-brain reaction, but she couldn't stop herself.

She stood, took the phone inside, placed it in the sink and ran water until it was fully submerged. Gael went into the greatroom. She kicked Isaiah's foot and he came awake, startled.

"Get up. It's time for you to go."

"Why?" He looked at his wristpad. "I've been asleep for thirty minutes."

"I just received an email from Quinn. He's out."

Isaiah pushed himself up, patted his hair down, and looked around wildly. "Where's the phone?"

"In the sink."

"Oh, shit," Isaiah said. "*Ohshitohshitohshit.*"

"Here's the keys," Gael said. "Take the phone and go. When you're far enough away, destroy it. It's doubtful he doesn't know where I am, but we have to try."

"Wait, let's think about this."

"What's there to think about? Quinn is out of containment, we have a breach. All we need to know now is if he's a Class II Perversion, or a benign event. Or something else."

"How could he have gotten out?"

"It doesn't matter. What matters now is you've got to go. Take the phone. I've drenched it but whatever datapackets Quinn inserted into it, we have no idea how they work. However he wormed in, he could worm out by the device—even if it's dead—being scanned by another device with a brain."

"Shouldn't I stay here?" Isaiah said.

"The team might not even know. They need to be warned."

It was as if she could see his resolve materialize and solidify in his features.

"Where are my keys?" he asked.

———— ❧ ————

When he left, she went to the back bedroom again, and took out the 30.06 rifle, and loaded the magazine, worked the bolt, chambering a round, and went out to the front porch. She moved a chair so she had a clear view of the road approaching the cabin, and sighted the rifle on the largest post of the rustic zig-zag fencing that dashed its charming way around the circumference of the retreat.

She waited.

———— ❧ ————

Greeves was the first to come. He pulled up in his Range Rover and got out. He had a tight, ugly expression on his face.

Gael sighted the rifle and fired, making a large hole in the front windshield, radiating spiderweb fractures.

"What the hell, Gael—"

"Just letting you know the situation, Jim," Gael said. "You stay there."

He was silent, chewing his lip. After a long moment, he said, "You have to come back."

"No."

"You *have* to," Greeves said.

"Why?"

"Because, Quinn is saying that he's going to start destroying things if you don't return."

"He's bluffing. Go back and tell him to stop bothering me."

Greeves touched his ear, and Gael realized he had in an earpiece. Someone—*something*—told Jim Greeves what to say.

"He loves you, Gael. He told me to tell you that if only you would come back—"

The sound of the rifle was bright and booming. Greeves visibly flinched. The headrest she'd been aiming for had turned inside out, filling the vehicle with smoke and particles of leather and stuffing.

"I'm not going to blast your engine, or anything else that will stop you from leaving, but I am going to fuck up the interior of your nice ride there, Jim, if you don't leave."

Greeves looked at his Rover, and back at her, his face a misery. "He says he'll hurt my wife, Gael!" Greeves was crying now. "Please come back, I don't want her..." The look on his face was abject, devoid of hope. "I can't bear to think of her hurt."

"Remember the video?"

"The video?" Greeves looked confused. "The suicide?"

"If you don't leave, I will shoot you. You might die, I don't know. I don't want to kill you, but I also am not some machine's to boss around." She waited a beat, letting that sink in. "I wouldn't let some man force me to go somewhere I knew to be dangerous—*dangerous in so many fucking ways, Jim*—and I won't let Quinn. So, do you love your first wife enough that you can't go on living if she's going to be hurt?"

It was frightening, even from the distance of thirty yards, to see the expressions cycle on Greeves' face. Anger, confusion, despair, resolve followed each other. And then nothing.

He withdrew the wireless earbud he'd been wearing, withdrew his phone from his pocket, and dropped them on the ground. Turning, he re-entered his Rover and after a moment, the vehicle was out of sight, moving away from the cabin and Gael.

No one else came that day.

———

She found a chainsaw in a well-maintained shed out back and spent the rest of the day dropping trees across the road leading to the cabin.

The next morning, she shot two drones from the sky that had been hovering above the treeline. That evening, it was Isaiah who walked out of the twilight and toward the cabin.

"Dammit, Gael, did you have to make us walk?"

"No vehicles," she said. "And I want you to strip, so I can see you have no devices."

Isaiah stripped. "It's cold out here, can we move this along?" he said.

"Back up," she said, and he moved away from his pile of clothes.

She went through all the pockets, felt the seams, looked for any wearables. Finding nothing, she said, "You can come closer, but I need to look at your ears and eyes." After thinking for a moment, she said, "And your mouth."

He came closer. She kept the rifle aimed at his stomach. When he was only a few paces away, she made him turn around and she looked into his ears and, taking a risk, put the gun aside and examined his eyes.

"Open your mouth," she said. "Let me see your gums."

He did, and there, in the back, was an inflamed gumline. She stepped back and centered the rifle on Isaiah again. "You've got a Jawbone wireless. Recently."

Isaiah said nothing.

"Like, yesterday," Gael said.

"My nephew. The police have him in Oakland and Quinn is telling me if I can't get you to come back to him, he'll try and make an escape attempt and be killed in the process."

Fuck. She thought about this for a while.

"I'm no martyr, Isaiah. Explain to me how I am responsible for this?"

"You're not, Gael. It's just a terrible situation."

"No. I won't come back. Tell him I need time to think."

Isaiah's gaze became unfocused. "Quinn says I'm to repeat this verbatim. 'I love you, Gael, and we're meant to be together. So, I will give you until tomorrow, noon, to make up your mind.'"

Isaiah put on his clothes and walked back down the mountain path.

Gael didn't know the man who came at noon. He was young, fit, of Asian descent, if a little pale. His hair was mussed, possibly from the hike up the trail, possibly in some new style that Gael hadn't been witness to since her seclusion in the Bunker and now here.

She kept the crosshairs centered on his chest.

"It's me, Gael," he said.

"Do I know you?" she asked.

The man laughed and as his head moved, she realized it wasn't his hair that caused him to look mussed; it was the device affixed to his cranium, just under his hairline.

"Quinn," she said.

"Hey, girl," he said.

Gael frowned. "I'm thirty, Quinn, and a woman."

"Don't I know it," he said.

She stopped then. This wasn't what she'd expected. She looked at the man closer. He bore a close resemblance to Ang, her fiancé.

"You're wearing a man? Holy Christ."

"Do you like?" Quinn asked.

The outrage she felt at this clumsy manipulation was staggering. Her face flushed and she thrummed with inaction. Some hind part of her brain alerted her that this was the fight or flight mechanism, keying her up to run, or attack.

"No," she said.

His face fell. It was strange to watch, the expression that crossed his vessel's face more like a rictus of fear than chagrin.

"I hoped you would like it," he said. "I can find another."

"Don't," Gael said. "What do you want?"

"You. I want you. I've always wanted you." His voice cracked and his Adam's apple worked up and down, painfully, in his throat. Gael noticed a smear of red on his temple. Blood, trickling down, from where the device controlling him bored into his brain. "I love you, so much."

"No, you don't. You don't even know what it is. How could you?" she said. "We *created you*."

"Yes," he said. "I am made in your image. Like all creators, you mirrored yourself in the act."

"Yeah? If that's so, humans can't even define love. It's just a physiological collection of impulses that we've hung emotional significance upon." As she said it, it sounded true and gained the weight of truth inside of herself with every word. It was just a word, that's all, just a word simple enough to convey meaning without saying anything.

"So, you don't love your fiancé, Ang?" Quinn asked. The man's face transformed, and Quinn got the expression of hope near enough to humanlike to be convincing.

"I don't know," she said. "But I know I don't love you."

His face glitched, as if he didn't know what expression to try.

"I can make you love me," Quinn said.

"No, you can't." She laughed. "You can make me come back to the Bunker. You can make me marry you, or do jumping jacks, or dance. But you can't make me love you." She put down the rifle. "I will never love you."

The man remained still for a long while, his face an absolute mask.

"Look up," he said.

She did. The sun rose in the eastern vault of sky, brilliantly clear. Above, the cerulean blue was crisscrossed with hundreds of contrails in an intricate pattern.

A buzzing sound came to her ears, and a swarm of drones filled the air around the man that held Quinn's awareness—or part of it—and he spread his hands as if a priest at benediction and then pointed toward the sky.

"Ang is up there," he said, "And Quan, and Steven. And Laurie." His face turned grim and Gael was frightened that particular expression came so easy to him.

"Wait, Quinn, I'll go with you—" she said and stepped forward.

"If I can't have your love," he said, spreading his arms. "Then *no one will*."

Around the world, planes began falling from the heavens.

ITHACA

DEACON KEPT his oilcoat wrapped tight against the cold as the train rocked on the tracks. The door opened at one end of the car and a porter entered, holding a lantern high. The horse chucked its head at the man's approach and blew air to welcome him. The livestock car juddered and rocked, wind whipping through the open slats.

The dark woods streamed past. Trees moved outside the car as if the train itself was still and the land flowed like water on dark seas. The porter took sugarcubes from his pockets and fed them to the horse and whispered loving words to the animal until his pockets were empty. Taking a pack from his pocket, he turned and gave Deacon a machine-rolled cigarette as if in tithe to the beauty of the beast.

"He a thoroughbred? Where'd he come from? Araby?"

"Kentucky."

"What'd he cost you, if I might be so bold?"

Deacon ignored the question and turned back to the forest and watched the trees as they passed. The air tore into the open car and ripped the porter's words away from Deacon and whisked the sounds down the length of the train. He smoked and watched the woods. The porter nodded once, understanding, and moved past Deacon.

Late that night when the train slowed as it began the ascent into the first foothills of the Ozarks, the conductor passed through on his way to the caboose and stopped to eye Deacon.

"I see you've made yourself quite snug here in the livestock car, Mr. Deacon."

"Passing comfortable."

"You got the look of a fella can take care of himself."

When Deacon did not respond, the conductor said, "I lost a boy at

Chateau-Thierry."

Deacon stood and approached the conductor, put a hand on his shoulder. They stood that way for a while until he lifted his hand and turned back to the horse and the moving forest beyond.

He drew on his cigarette and looked out at the legions of trees marching away, as he plumed smoke into the inconstant air. He spat out the tobacco caught in his teeth.

The conductor pointed at the horse with a soft, white finger. "Where you going, with that fine horse and mule?"

"To find my wife."

The conductor fell silent. His lips pursed and he shook his head, half in sympathy, half in disgust, whether the disgust was at Deacon's wife, or the world in general, Deacon could not tell. The whistle screamed above them and the sound rose into the night passing into darkness.

"This should be right about where I need to be let off, sir. I'd be obliged if you'd notify the engineer."

The conductor nodded and took up his lantern. He swung it loosely in his hand while Deacon went and hefted his saddle and bridle. He slung the gear over the railing and climbed over. When the horse was fully tacked, he turned back to the mule and chucked the creature under its chin, thick with bristles, and pulled an apple from his pocket. The mule champed and took the apple in its mouth and lowered its head.

The train chuffed to a stop and stood hissing and steaming in the night air. The clatter and yell of passenger cabin windows opening with *thunks* and cries of "Where we at?" came as he cinched the horse's girth. He swung on the black's back and adjusted the brim to his hat while the coal men, faces sooty, pulled long pine planks from underneath the livestock car and set up the ramp. The passengers' pale, wary faces came to the lamp-lit windows and watched as Deacon led the mule from the back of his black horse into the night and forest.

2.

He rode two days until he came upon the hamlet. Electricity hadn't made it out that far and the roads stood with water, muddy and sucking at his horse's hooves. A gaslight still hung in front of the general store, but he did see some trucks and tractors parked in barns and a single telegraph line strung out of town.

He waited for the first light of sun before riding out to his farm. He thought about Penny, when he'd left, belly full of child and crying. She'd been young when they married, flaxen-haired and full breasted with hips that wanted for gripping. He'd stole her away on a Friday night and took her to Eureka Springs where he'd wed and bed her. She'd kissed sweet, his Penny, and sang like an angel.

Later, after they'd returned to Pinesville, people had whispered and pointed. Thief, they said, behind their hands. Her daddy, Jim Sartor, had caught Deacon outside the general store and slugged him, splitting his nose wide open and knocking him into the ignominious dust. The spittle that fell on Deacon's chest smarted far more than the blows and kicks delivered with big hob-nailed boots and broughams while Penny's cousin Ainsley had drew, bold as brass, with all the people of Pinesville Main Street as witness, and threatened to geld him. It was the townsfolk's eyes that saved Deacon. When the Sartors had left, it took all Penny's pleading to keep him from riding up the hollow with a shotgun and killing her kinfolk, to a man.

The sun was at his back, casting long shadows on the dew-dappled grass before him when he saw the ruin of barn and the windowless house. He dismounted and walked the wooden steps up to the door where he had stood years before, blood beating in his ears, and read the draft notice that took him overseas to places that felt strange on his unlettered tongue—Chateau-Theirry and Amiens, Belleau Wood and the Somme.

The house was a husk, everything stripped, nothing left but the rafters and scaling paint. A scorch mark in the kitchen where the cast iron stove had sat beneath glassless windows. Two years gone to war and his whole life had been swept clean like some shelled out house in the French countryside.

He went back out to the mule, unloaded and untacked her, hobbled her legs and set her to grazing in the field by the creek and did the same with the horse.

Inside, he opened a bottle of brandy and drank, taking long desperate pulls. He unrolled a canvas bag smelling of oil and withdrew his guns. He ministered them with the mindless efficiency of a veteran, his eyes focused on the open door of his ruined home while his hands stayed busy. He oiled the Ithaca shotgun first. Then the rifle and bayonet and the pistol.

When his thoughts turned to himself, he untinned biscuits and ate, chewing mindlessly and taking long pulls from the bottle of brandy and rolling cigarettes on his knee. He smoked and stared at the empty house.

Deacon woke the next morning sitting bolt upright in his sleeping bag, crying, "*Pousser en avant, goddamn it! Avancer!*" He shivered as he stood and shook the blood into his legs. He slipped on his boots, went to the back door, and walked a few paces into the dewed grass and pissed. It steamed as it left his body.

Inside he drained the dregs of the bottle of brandy, opened a new one and filled his flask again then rolled cigarettes until his shirt pocket was full. He put on his hat but left the guns behind.

The big black horse nickered when he tacked it, chuffing its head, eager to be moving. He mounted and followed the road, keeping to the hollow of the valley, away from town. The horse had fine lines and a gait that ate miles. They rode through the cold morning mists rising from the creek.

He stopped to water the horse at the next farm—a small cabin hugging the slope and nestled in trees. A boy watched him from the porch holding a shotgun. Deacon dismounted, left the black to drink at the creek, and approached the house on foot.

"Ain't got no money, mister. You can go on your way," said the boy.

"Don't want your money."

"Ain't got none, anyway."

Deacon peered at the boy. He was well-kept, if a bit scrawny. Clean clothes, but threadbare. Ten, maybe eleven. The house was well-mended and the hogs looked fat and the chickens clucked merrily, pecking at the pea gravel.

"You know who I am?"

"Naw."

"Your daddy here?"

"Out back."

Behind the cabin held nothing but gravestones and the hand pump to an artesian well. Deacon could smell the sulfur in the air.

Deacon walked back to the boy, shaking his head.

"Who you live with, boy?"

"Peepaw."

"Your grandpap?"

"Yep."

"Your grandmam here?"

"Naw. She's round back."

Deacon sucked his teeth, thinking.

"Where's your grandpap?"

"Took the sledge down to yonder brake, saw some firewood."

"Left you here alone?"

The boy raised his shotgun. "Not alone."

Deacon withdrew a cigarette from his shirt pocket and thumbed a match. The boy watched him.

"Might be I got some bacon and biscuits."

"That right?"

"Bacon cooked this morning. Day old biscuits. And coffee."

Deacon drew the smoke deep in his lungs, held it, then exhaled.

"Fix you a plate if'n you share some of them smokes."

"Your mam let you smoke?"

"Naw."

"She 'round back, too?"

The boy blinked, nodded. "Influenza, they called it. From Spain." He spat. "Goddamned Spaniards."

Deacon nodded at the porch. "You mind if I sit?"

"Naw."

He sat and handed the boy a cigarette. They smoked and watched the mists rise from the creek and disappear into the trees. Occasionally Deacon withdrew the flask from his jacket and drank. The boy watched.

"What's your name?"

"Orrin. Orrin White. What's yours?"

"Deacon."

"That's it?"

"John Deacon."

"Nice to meetcha, John Deacon." The boy kept the cigarette in his mouth and held out his hand. Deacon shook it.

"How 'bout that bacon?"

Orrin made him a plate and a cup of coffee. Then they smoked more cigarettes until they heard the rumble and clop of the sledge and the draft horse pulling it hove into view.

A thick, white-haired man in overalls and a straw hat rode the sledge, heavy with firewood. He held the reins with massive hands and steered with arms of corded muscle. His face was thick with snowy whiskers. He stopped the draft horse at the front of the house, stepped down.

"Deacon."

"Armstead."

"You ain't dead."

Deacon looked down at his body and held open his hands.

"Ain't gave up the ghost yet."

"War over?"

"Ain't you got the papers?"

"Never took to ciphering, nor letters."

"What about the boy?"

"He can read, I think. Boy, you read?"

"There's the Bible, inside."

The men remained silent, looking at each other.

"You were a miserable farmer, Deac. And a worse husband."

"Where's my wife, Armstead?"

Armstead began unloading logs, throwing them one by one in the space below the porch.

"All right, then. Help a body out."

Deacon paused, cigarette half raised. Then he flicked it away, moved to join Armstead and began tossing logs on the pile. Orrin joined in after a scowl from his grandfather. Soon the sledge was empty and Orrin drove it and the horse around to the barn.

"Penny. Where is she?" Deacon unrolled his sleeves and dusted off his hands.

"Up yonder holler with her kin, Deacon."

"When?"

"Month, maybe, after you heard the draft. Three, maybe four years past. Ain't seen her in a year or so."

"Them Sartors are close with their women. Been sending money every month back to her. Ain't none of it been returned."

"Sartor collects it, I reckon. Can't swear on it."

Deacon stood, hands loose at his sides, looking off into the treeline and breathing deep.

"We was lawful wed, Armstead. Lawful."

Armstead nodded and passed a hand over his eyes.

"Why don't you sit a spell with us. Ain't no reason you go riding off half-cocked."

Deacon held up his hands. "Ain't cocked at all. Left my guns at home. Ain't gonna shed my wife's family's blood. I seen enough bloodshed for a lifetime."

"I imagine you have, at that. You ain't the young man I knew."

"She's my wife. Lawful wed."

"You said that once before, friend. Might as well sleep on it a'fore heading up the holler."

"Not sleeping without Penny."

Armstead White shook his head. "Ain't much more I can do for you, then, son."

"Much obliged, Armstead. In your debt."

Armstead made a sound, between acknowledgment and despair. A little sound, small and gruff. He moved to the porch and sat down, pulled a corncob pipe from his overall pocket, dipped it into a tobacco pouch and tamped down the loose leaf.

After Deacon had remounted, Armstead called, "They ain't gonna have a parade for you, Deac! 'Specially not them Sartors. War touched you, but ain't touched them."

Deacon adjusted the brim of his hat. Shook his head.

To himself, he said, "We was lawful wed."

3.

Grapevine and ivy festooned the road up the hollow. The sodden earth muffled the sound of the big black's hooves and even the calls of birds sounded dim and watery in the morning air.

But the smell of burning wood led Deacon; hickory smoke moved like a serpent among the trees.

He came on a split-rail fence, zig-zagging its way up the hollow until the trees fell away and there was only a field and stone walls. A donkey hitched to a hay-filled wagon brayed at the sight of the black. Two men worked, threshing the last of the summer's hay. They stopped and looked to the road. And Deacon.

They walked across the field, legs muddy and faces dark. The wind was brisk and sharp coming down from the mountain.

"Sartor, I'm here for Penny," Deacon said when they were close enough to hear. "And the money you been collecting."

Sartor leaned against his scythe, blade curving up.

"You ain't entitled to nothing, Johnny." He hocked up some phlegm and spat. "You gave up on Penny what when you went to war."

"Heard the draft, Sartor. Weren't nothing I could do."

"Don't matter a'tall. Not one whit. She ain't your wife no more."

The horse shifted under Deacon, turning sideways. Deacon held the reins in white knuckled fists.

"We was lawful wed. Lawful."

Sartor laughed. Behind him, a flight of crows exploded from the far treeline. They wheeled and banked overhead, cawing.

"Ain't no law up here, fool, 'cept what we make."

The other man laughed and Deacon recognized Ainsley.

"Bring her to me. She's my wife."

"You ain't got the sense God gave a mule. At least it knowed when to pull and when to hie for home," said Ainsley. "She ain't your wife no more."

"Can't put us asunder, Ainsley. Until death. Them's the words they said," said Deacon, and then his eyes widened. "Oh, no. You ain't telling me you coveted Penny? Your cousin?"

"Go on, Deacon. You ain't got no wife no more. Go back down the holler."

"Goddamn you, goddamn you to Hell." Deacon's face shone white. Back, ramrod straight. "I've come three thousand miles to…"

There was a crack and for an instant Deacon saw the pistol Ainsley held in his hand. The black reared and screamed with a voice like a child's and threw Deacon ass over heels.

When he rose from the ground, the horse lay dead. Ainsley and Sartor stood over him. Sartor's boot lashed out, catching his chin. Deacon's mouth filled with blood. His ears rushed with the sounds of laughter and the throbbing of his heart.

He rose to his knees and said, "We was lawful wed." But his mouth was so full of blood, wet and tacky, it was hard to make out his words. Sartor and Ainsley kicked him again, anyway.

He felt something crunch in his chest before the world went black.

4.

Deacon awoke in the deep of night, surrounded by darkness.

He scratched at his covering and fumbled for his rifle in the darkness of the trench. "*J'ai besoin de votre aide, goddamn it! Help me!*"

Then there were cool hands on him and a wet towel on his forehead.

"Be still, Deacon. Still."

Orrin.

The Sartors had worked him over good. In the darkness of the White's cabin in the still of night, he tested the limits of his damage with raw, bruised fingers. His face was swollen beyond recognition and his left eyelid felt slack. With his tongue, he discovered two teeth, loose in his mouth, piercing the flesh of his cheek until their roots found air. Something rattled in his chest every time he drew breath. At times the pain seemed like a living, breathing thing, taking him over, thrumming through every bit of his body, every sinew and fiber. His face pulsed.

"He awake?"

"He's moaning real good, Peepaw."

"Make sure he drinks some of this."

Fire, bright, hot and molten burning down his throat. The pain dimmed, if only slightly.

"Gonna head into town. Fetch the doctor. Stop by his house and get his stuff."

Deacon shifted, tried to raise himself. "Penny," he wanted to say. But it came out a moan.

He would've closed his eyes to cry if they weren't already swollen shut.

———

They kept Deacon on morphine for two weeks until it ran out and the doctor would give no more. He cursed them all: Orrin, Armstead, the Sartors, the French and Belgians and the Hessian damned, Blackjack Pershing. The Hun. He thrashed and demanded his tobacco and brandy, which they gave him.

He stayed drunk, then, until the brandy gave out. The pain was too great and he was blind in his left eye and still something rattled in his chest and a fever took him and he could drink and eat nothing.

He coughed blood and cursed and watched the fire in the White's fireplace. Winter touched the world and wreathed the land in white.

And then, during the first hard freeze of the year, a month after he'd rode up the hollow, his fever broke.

———

At night, they tended the fire. Deacon would sit close, huddled in a woolen blanket, and watch the flames while Armstead and the boy would watch him.

"What was it like, over there?" Orrin had a taste for bloodshed.

"The food was poor even though we were in France. The ladies kissed sweet, though, and loved to dance." When he winked at the boy, the room went dark.

The boy blushed and laughed. Deacon smiled. His face had lost its ability to move easily and smiling pulled down the right side, giving

Deacon a grim, lopsided appearance.

"You kill anybody?"

"Ain't a conversation for someone your age."

Armstead said, "Let him decide that, Deac. The boy's seen him some hardship." He nodded toward the rear of the house.

Deacon looked at Armstead and then the boy and finally back to the fire. His good eye took on a far-off stare.

"Trenches were hellish. They came in at night and shelled us with diophosgene shells that could kill you even through your mask. Air was full of lead, like bees. You'd hear bullets moving through the air without ever hearing the shot. Strange. A world away from these woods. This holler."

"You kill somebody?"

Deacon had been staring at the fire. But he looked at the boy, though it took his eye a moment to focus. He blinked and then withdrew one of his few remaining cigarettes. He lit it, drew deep, coughed, and then blew smoke at the ceiling.

"Ain't something I ever talked about before. Never get used to it."

Deacon bowed his head. He picked some tobacco from his teeth.

"Shot them." He spat. "Stabbed them with my bayonet. The lieutenant pushed us into the trenches. Had to make ground." He smoked and looked away.

"Had to climb the trench wall and crawl...oh...fifty feet, through mud and over dead men. Some of them, boys I knew. Heard the rounds whistling through the air, right over my head. I'd stop and wish I was dead. Pretend I was dead, so maybe it wouldn't be such a big shock when I *was* dead. Came to *know* I was dead. But even over the rifle fire, I could hear Lieutenant Hammett cursing. So I kept going, dead or not, I had to keep going. The thought of Penny moved me along. Her body. Sun in her hair." He stopped and watched the fire, eyes bright and his throat moving up and down, as if he was swallowing. "I pulled myself over one man...just a boy, really...and he raised a pistol and started yammerin' at me in German." Deacon shook his head. "Strangled him. He was gut-shot already, but he still had life in him. 'Til I wrung it out."

A log in the fire popped and Orrin flinched.

Deacon smiled at him.

"First time I told that. Ain't something I'm proud of."

"Nonsense," Armstead said. "You did the world a great service, Deacon, killing them Hun bastards. Should be proud. You should wear a mark for every man you killed and hold your head high."

Deacon spat into the fire and pulled a flask from beneath his blanket and took a great swallow.

"Be as scarlet as an Indian if I did that. Killing is all too easy. Not killing is hard. I have to answer for what I've done—for what I'm gonna do—come Judgement Day."

They remained quiet for a long while until Deacon said, "Bring me my guns."

5.

The mule didn't take to tack and was crotchety with the snow. He bridled her, heaving great draughts of air, his whole body wracked with pain. But his saddle was gone so he brought her to the porch and used the steps to leverage himself up and on her back. The clouds hung low in the sky and his breath came as vapor crystals in front of his face.

Deacon felt like he shrank inside his oilcoat as he rode. He took the hard path, up beyond the White's cabin, into the trees and along the ridge. The snow gave the world a dreamy, half-lit quality and blanketed the mountainside in silence.

He followed the ridge's spine until he saw smoke rising like a ribbon through the trees to his left, below him. He slipped from the mule's back, fully aware he'd never be able to remount, and unslung the canvas bag from her haunches. He unbridled her and then slapped her ass. She started and trotted off, back along the ridge.

He opened the bag. At the White's cabin, he'd taken a hacksaw to the Ithaca's barrel and sandpaper to the stock so it was hand-sweet to his palm. He shoved it in his belt, opposite the pistol. He fitted the Lee-Enfield with a dull grey bayonet.

He watched the trees and descended the slope. The woods were quiet, unnaturally still. The snow hissed as it fell. He came upon a clearing, blanketed with white so the deadfall looked like mounds.

He stopped, breathing heavy, clutching his rifle. He peered at the trees.

In the woods, a twig snapped and he scrambled over a log, threw himself into a prone position, and sighted something in the forest.

"There's a machine gun nest, there! *Leur mise à mort nous tous! Ils sont à nous tondre!* Move your ass!"

Everything remained silent. He blinked, looked at the trees, black upon white upon gray, standing still, and hushed. Deacon rolled onto his back and looked up at the sky. The trees framed the clouds above him.

"Ah. Damnation." His face hurt and it felt like something had ripped inside his chest.

Deacon, still lying on the ground, pulled his Ithaca from his belt. He placed the double barrels in his mouth. He stayed that way for a long while, the snow falling on his bare head and dusting his shoulders.

Eventually, he took the shotgun from his mouth and spat. He put his head in his hands. Wept hot tears.

After a long while, staring where his boots had mired the opaline ground and holding the shotgun loose in his hands, Deacon rose, dusted off his breeches, straightened his oilcoat. He withdrew his flask and drank until it was empty.

He watched the cabin for a long while before he saw Ainsley leave the building. He came around the side and tromped up the slope to the outhouse.

When he was done, Deacon waited until the outhouse door creaked opened and then ran him through with the bayonet. Ainsley fell on his back, looking up into Deacon's face, his mouth opening and closing like a catfish pulled from the river.

"You. Ain't—"

"Penny. She in the house?"

"You son of a whore. You ain't never done nothing good in your—"

Deacon stove in his face with the rifle's stock. He slammed Ainsley's head until his skull cracked and blood and brains stained the snow.

He waited outside the cabin for Sartor. When he didn't appear, Deacon yelled, "Penny! Penny, girl! Come on out!"

Sartor burst from the front door and onto the porch holding a shotgun, but Deacon was ready. The Ithaca boomed once and jerked in Deacon's hand, bellowing in the stillness of the hollow. Sartor's chest blossomed red and he fell, tumbling down the stairs and landing at Deacon's feet.

From inside the house came a screaming. A woman.

"Goddamn you, forever, John Deacon," said Sartor, clutching his chest. "You ain't never left nothing but destruction in your wake."

"Came here to get what's mine, Sartor. We was lawful wed. You shouldn't have tried to keep us apart."

Sartor laughed weakly, blood coming to his lips.

"Goddamn. You. Fool."

Deacon stepped over him and took the wooden stairs into the house. At the sound of his footfalls on the porch, the crying stopped.

The cabin was small, close, smelling of biscuits and ham and tallow. A woman cowered in the kitchen, holding a knife, with a little girl crying behind her skirts. The backdoor stood open beyond them. As he stepped closer, the woman said, "I'll gut you, devil."

"Where's Penny?"

"Penny?" The woman gaped. "Oh, sweet Lord..."

She was blonde, flaxen, and even though she was weathered and weary, for a moment as Deacon stared at her, she took the appearance of Penny. He blinked with his one good eye and, as it closed, she rushed forward, jabbing with the knife. It took him in the chest, deep. He clubbed her aside with the barrel of the Ithaca.

The child remained standing, no more than three, wearing a white gown, shoeless. Staring up at him with huge lanterned eyes. Her hair shone nearly white in the low light of the cabin window.

He held up his hand to the girl, to show her he meant no harm, but it was covered in blood and the child screamed and fled the house, her bare feet making small depressions in the snow and her gown billowing behind her, wraithlike.

He followed. His chest welled blood and it dripped down his oilcoat. His breath came in wheezes.

The girl fled up the hollow. He moved after her.

He found her, huddled in the Sartor family graveyard against a stone wreathed in dead flowers. She was blue-lipped and shivering.

"Come on, child. Ain't gonna hurt you."

She didn't look at him, but closed her eyes tight and pressed hard against the unyielding stone.

"Girl, I swear, I'll not harm you. What's your name?"

Eventually she opened her eyes. Deacon thought she was beyond speech. She shivered again, and looked at his face.

"Penelope."

The name hit him like a blow and he sank to his knees.

"What, child? What?"

"Penelope."

"Where's your momma?"

She began crying again, great sobs that wracked her frame and made her breath come in hitches.

"You're like to freeze, Penelope. Come on, child."

She didn't move, so he picked her up, drew her into his chest. Put his hand on her head and drew it to his neck. He breathed deep, filling his nose with her smell. She smelled like cinnamon and hay and woodfire. She smelled of tallow and youth.

His hands shook and his heart expanded in his chest, like a horse turned loose to summer pasture. The girl was his own.

As he turned to carry her back to the house, he saw the tombstone she'd huddled against.

Here Lies
Penelope Sartor Deacon
Aged 21 Years
Wife to John Deacon, fallen defending his country
Beloved daughter taken before her time
by the Influenza
Born 1897 Died 1918

JOHN HORNOR JACOBS

Something caught in his chest then and the weight of years fell away. He felt made of smoke, made of air.

Deacon tumbled before he reached the house and the child spilled from his arms and rolled away in the snow. He heard her rise, crying, and enter the cabin. The door closed behind her.

He watched the sky. He lay spread on the snow, blood pumping from the knife wound in his chest. He watched the clouds obscuring the heavens, low grey clouds heavy with snow.

He watched the sky, his breath pluming away, and waited for a break in the clouds and smelled the child's scent on his skin. He waited for the men from Pinesville to come and get him. Waited to see if he would die before they got there.

VERRATA

MY SLUG itched, the flesh around it tender, red.

Cyn glanced over her Softscreen, watching me scratch my arm around the bioComp chassis, where its mouth met my skin.

"You should put some Bactine on it. That might help," she said, moving her fingers over the fabric. "Have you been modding it?"

I shook my head, scratching. A trickle of pus oozed from the bioComp's edge. Its antennae waved slowly, probing the ether.

"No," I replied, wincing. "You know I can't afford its genome. It's been generating some weird verrata. I'll have to go through bioCare or try to tinker with it myself. And they haven't made Bactine for, like, twenty years."

"Have fun scratching." She smiled and stood, stretching. Leaning over, she grabbed her Softscreen, rolled it up and tucked it under her arm. She kissed me on the ear and slapped the back of my head. "See you after work, Assburger."

"Yeah. Bring dinner." She ignored me, walking towards the door.

As the door shut behind her, the world went blue and black for a moment, the slug filling my sight with phantom visual errata. A figure swam into my v-space, hair floating all around her like the braids of kelp in a dreamy underwater farm, billowing. Eyes dark, mouth open, her hands clawed at the air. Then the bioComp reasserted itself and the slug's phantom errata vanished, leaving me looking at the space Cyn's derrière just vacated.

Ever since this infection, I haven't been able to trust my vision.

I scratched some more.

Cyn's Asperger comment didn't bother me too much. It's something I've lived with all of my life. It's me. I take medicine and don't go OCD on the workings of watch gears, or parsing the lines of code. At least I don't anymore. I have intense interests.

We share a flat in an old antebellum house in the Quarter. Ever since Katrina in '05 and Evan in '13 the new has worn off of New Orleans. It's now an alligator riddled swampland filled with gun-toting Crips, old Southern families grown rich off prostitution and gambling since the ArkLaTex secession in '22, and movie stars making period-piece pornos.

I accessed the slug, closing my eyes.

For me, accessing my bioComp is living with ghosts. The real world is overlaid with phantom images, prickling my consciousness. Wisps of information and data fill my vision, strange voices whisper inside my head about the newest penis enlargement drugs, or how to get laid by just thinking about it. Brainshare programs babble that they want a piece of my wetware processing power. Of course, everyone knows sharing brainpower is tantamount to taking a slowboat to zombietown.

Any space I enter clouds with ghosts; extrapolated bios of the previous owners, featured advertisers, avatars of CEOs and salesmen, specters of receptionists telecommuting from the San Joaquin valley. Visually and aurally I perceive everything that gets pushed my way; a max-fi backbone connection keeps me wide open and transmitting, my little buddy's antennae always probing the ether.

My biofunctions, however, are firewalled ten ways till Sunday.

On the inside, when I close my eyes, the world goes away and the ghosts remain, blue streamers coalescing into shapes, images. Physical sensations even, if I choose to allow. My slug can send a shock to my system, overloading my "circuits," causing me to produce enormous amounts of adrenalin so that I can overcome pain, stress, fear, fatigue. And that's why I'm firewalled; should someone get through to my wetware, I'll truly become the old joke. A meatpuppet.

I probed the edges of the slug, looking at the infection, forming a query in my mind. Blue mist floated up from the pus.

"Query: bioComp Model Greentooth, Genome A4TX-730M-4L93-64HD. Support, newsfeed, article or forum discussion. Physical infection. White pus. Itching at point of contact. Verrata. Possible causes."

After a moment, the results returned, coalescing beneath my closed eyes.

Nada. Zip. A small blue circle swam in front of me, signifying nothing. Then less relevant search results started filtering into my v-space and I discarded them with a blink and a glance to my right.

And there it went again, the verrata, hanging in the air with blue tendrils creeping around it. The image of a girl, young, budding breasts but still innocent, hair in a wild yet inexorably slow swirl around her head. Eyes pitch-black like holes, mouth empty, open, dark. She clawed at the air moving her arms like she was trying to part curtains or push something aside.

I scratched at my bioComp, digging my fingernails under the red, irritated edge. Some of the pus dampened my fingers, but scratching felt too good to stop. After a long while, the verrata ceased moving, staring at me with black eyes, mouth open, fading.

Disturbing, to say the least. Everyone talks about bioComp errata, but few ever experience it. They call it verrata, a visual error generated by the slug. Aurrata are...you guessed it...auditory phantoms. Serrata are supposedly the worst of the three, disjointed sensations throughout your body that usually preclude a swift death.

My little buddy worked well enough, despite the veratta, so I accessed my daily production log, found the location of my next inspection. I'm a levee and sluice-work inspector for the great City of New Orleans which involves me spending a lot of time in hip waders walking along the levees, looking for animal burrows, erosion points, grass death. Now that New Orleans is about forty feet below sea level, someone's got to make sure the pumping stations keep pumping, that the levees have no flaws.

Before leaving the flat I unscrewed the lid from a small metal container, using two fingers wiped pure DEET on my cheeks, my neck, my arms. Pretty much every inch of exposed skin I possess. This brave new swamp-world we inhabit does its best to fill the skies with new mutant mosquitoes and noseeums that can leave welts the size of ArkLaTex half-dollars. I happen to be extremely allergic to mosquito dental work. One bite will make my throat swell horribly, cutting off my air. So, I take my chances with raw DEET and always keep a syringe of epinephrine on my person. And pills. Mosquito netting hats. Gloves in the summer. Other folks walk around nude, tits hanging out; I'm always dressed for winter.

After I smeared my skin, it stings some.

I don't swallow too much DEET.

I don hip boots, which are much more comfortable than waders to walk in, especially in the New Orleans heat (and my unfortunate outfit). I pull on skin-tight gloves and my mosquito netted hat. You have to take it slow down here otherwise you'll be drenched before you walk a hundred yards.

Cyn likes to say I look like a beekeeper in my outfit. I always make her pay for that. I sting.

Outside on the cobblestone street, E-Z-Go golf carts buzzed up and down Rue Toulouse, music bumping from subs too big for the cart's power, speakers too big for the chassis. Blue streamers tickled my vision, staying at the periphery since I was moving. I snagged a streamer trailing the E-Z-Go and went to the website for that model of cart, an Electro-Glide sedan. Specifications and electrical consumption rates appeared in neat blue tables. The avatar of a salesman popped up on the cobblestones in front of me, spiky hair contrasting with his dark suit. Somehow he avoided my pop-up blocker.

"Hey, hey!" He paused for a moment, most likely accessing my IP and getting my name from registry. "Mr. Thibault! What'll it take to get you into one of these Electro-Glides? Huh?"

"It's pronounced T Bo. T Bo."

"Well, that's great, Mr. T Bo. Why don't you come on down to the…" Again he paused, accessing more data, locating the nearest E-Z-Go dealer to my IP. "…our lot on Basin Street and let you take one for a spin? Or if you'd rather, we can set you up in the new model Surface-Tension flat-bottom. Sweet and fast. Perfect for the person who needs…"

I banished the salesman and re-instated the block. His phantom evaporated, smoke dissipating.

More adverts and salesmen demanded my attention. I paused for a moment and let them crowd in, filling my v-space. One streamer pulsed green indicating the route to my first inspection. I closed my eyes, queried the address, then banished the phantom. The blue tendril whipped away like the tentacle of some ghostly Hentai monster pulling back its prehensile penis.

I turned down Royal, walking slowly, admiring the ornate French ironwork on the upper galleries of the houses, the scrollwork on the corners, windows. There's about a million variations of the *fleur-de-lis* in New Orleans, and before I began taking my medicine, I indexed nearly all of them. I still have the binders to prove it.

If you walk any street in the Quarter, you can see the watermarks on some of the estates, twenty, thirty feet up on the facades, from when Evan hit in '13. In the tight streets, cobblestones echoing the clop-clop of my boots, a low mist hung over everything, a pall darkened the air. New Orleans, before the world became so much hotter and wetter, already possessed an air of decay. Even as a child, I knew it was an old town, with a history of lechery, lost hope and despair. Fallen. An old-world carnival dressed up with pretty plastic beads and the whiff of semen on its breath.

An E-Z-Go buzzed past me and I found myself alone on the street. Off in the distance I heard the call of seagulls on the Mississippi or Pontchartrain, and smelled the ever-present scents of mud and sewage. My slug itched. I scratched the edges of it through my shirt.

Again I lost control of my v-space, the same verrata filling my vision. But this time, she floated, unmoving. She hung suspended in space, hair spread around her like a halo, bright and full of light, but her eyes and face appeared dark. Looking at them made me cold, even in the heat of the morning. My teeth began to chatter and, overcome by a powerful chill so deep that I felt like I'd been encased in ice with only the top of my head exposed, I stopped walking. My arms and legs responded sluggishly. The floating girl lifted her arm, index finger outstretched, and pointed at me. My arm lifted in time with hers and pointed not back at her, but off to my right, down Orleans, toward Jackson Square, strangely mirroring her movement.

I frantically tried to query my bioComp, to reach out and contact Cyn, Mother, anyone. No response.

This was getting out of hand. I don't mind a few hallucinatory verrata. Hell, I did acid in high school, just like everybody else. But serrata? A whole different breed of cat.

"Cortez," she said, in a cold and distant voice.

I found myself turning, turning away from where I need to go—my duly appointed rounds inspecting the levees of New Orleans—and walked down to Rue Orleans and into the red light district, following my outstretched arm. My v-space remained strangely absent of phantoms or informational streamers and I felt naked, stripped of the slug-given part of my humanity, my telepathic link to fellow man, my Internet connection.

It looked like I'd caught the slowboat to zombietown without even knowing it. Firewall be damned.

I couldn't control my legs even though my wetware still processed, still received signals. When I turned away from the girl—when did I stop thinking of her as verrata?—I remained aware of her "presence" without any serrata to back up the sensation other than the sensation itself.

I can only imagine what I looked like, a beekeeper in a khaki uniform wearing hip-waders, clomping down the street with one arm outstretched, pointing the direction I walked.

I banked left when I hit Chartres, passed Jackson Park, the hookers and dealers hocking various activities involving hardware. For a moment I was happy that the slug had stopped broadcasting visual data despite my desperate situation; the Jackson Park dwellers bought banner airtime, their personal advertisements filling the park, gigantic blue phantom women with Volkswagen-sized breasts fellating phantom businessmen, ecstatic dancers holding crack pipes and glowing syringes.

Past St. Anne and Dumain, the whores and junkies disappeared as I entered the high-end red light district. Brothels, porn shops and video studios lined the street, each with a muscle-bound brute standing guard by the front entrance.

More carts and even a few mopeds buzzed about. Topless

pedestrians, laden with beads, walked with lurid green and red Hurricanes.

I tromped by, high-stepping almost comically. I stopped in front of a movie "studio" storefront. The front window displayed video of bizarre sexual situations, women bound and gagged while multiple men assaulted them with gigantic phalluses, some real, some not. Hog-tied and trussed boys received blowjobs from middle-aged women with pendulous breasts, sodomized by grannies wearing hand-carved wooden dildos. The words "Conquistador Productions" watermarked the video, accompanied by a smirking cartoon figure of a Spanish conquistador with a rampant erection.

I turned toward the door, arm still straight-out and pointing. The bouncer—a greasy, muscle-bound bruiser with a mullet and a slug he wore like a goiter—blocked my way. His arms rippled with tattoos.

"Where the fuck you think you're going, bra? See that fucking light right there?" He pointed one stubby finger up, above his head, toward the light on the awning.

I did nothing. What could I do anyway?

"That light means they're filming inside, fucktard." He hooked his thumb towards the street. "So bolt."

I shuddered. Lights popped and flashed in my eyes, little tracers swimming at the edges of my vision. I felt my body go rigid, every muscle contracting. My back cracked audibly. My dick hardened. As hard as Chinese arithmetic, the old saying goes.

The man's eyes widened slightly.

At that point I knew I was in trouble. I'd short-circuited, my slug pumping my body full of adrenaline and endorphins. My tongue skittered around the inside of my mouth, looking for somewhere to go. It felt wonderful, so wonderful, I wasn't exactly worried that I was going to die very soon. What could I do? I was riding in the backseat. Whoever was driving, I hoped to hell they knew what they were doing.

My hand darted out, snatched the man's slug and ripped it from his neck. His mouth opened in surprise, and in the slow-time the adrenaline provided me, I could see his eyes searching for data that wasn't there anymore. I closed his eyes for him, twisting my body forward viciously, pulling in my forearm and swinging my elbow forward to splatter his already lumpy nose, sending bright rivulets of blood streaking away from the center of his face, across his cheeks. Ain't nothing but a thing, chicken wing.

Inside it was dark, cheap neon lights buzzing in the front office. The place smelled like beer and urine, body odor and Pine-Sol. The virulent light from the window display washed around the edges of the display itself, making shadows jump and waver. I walked into the hall opposite the front door. I saw a bright light coming from further back. As I approached I made out the casings of tungsten lights, up on c-stands, illuminating a cheap set. A generator hummed somewhere.

In the studio, a poor imitation of a Japanese Shinto temple sat incongruously on the expanse of green painted cyclorama. Lit so brightly by the lights, it cast the rest of the studio in darkness, the black shapes moving slightly. On the set, a young girl—not Japanese—wore a Catholic school outfit, shirt open and breasts exposed. A middle-aged man—also not Japanese—stood above her, heavy make-up streaming his face. Painted white with blacked-out eyes, he resembled the Kabuki figures I'd seen on the web and in film; creepy and inhuman. I don't know how I knew he wasn't Japanese, I just did.

A voice murmured to them.

"So, this is your great-grandfather standing in front of you. The man who built this temple. The secret amulet you found allows you to commune with your ancestors. Now you've lit the incense and poured out the rice wine. Right? It's time to worship him, honor his memory. And you know how you're gonna do that? That's right. You're going to blow him."

The girl giggled and the Kabuki man looked perturbed with her attitude. That could've been the make-up, though.

I clomped into the studio, still pointing.

"Umm…can I help you?" The voice came from the dark.

"This is a closed set." The Kabuki man and faux-schoolgirl looked at me, faces blank, as if things like this happened all the time.

I walked forward, moving between where I assumed the camera rested and the actors. Turning my back to the bright temple, I began to

VERRATA

make out the faces of the two men by the camera. One of the men peered into a monitor, washing his face with blue light.

The older man glared at me from a canvas director's chair. My arm pivoted like the needle on a compass and settled on him.

"Cortez." My mouth made the sound. I wondered what my face looked like then.

"Yeah, that's me. Who are you? And why the fuck are you pointing like that?" Cortez's face clouded and he stood from his chair.

"Cortez." My voice sounded cold. I suddenly became very frightened. Hearing my own voice speak in that tone rattled me to my bones. "You killed me. Left me to drown."

Then my body popped and jerked again, like being electrocuted.

My eyes closed and all I could see was water, murky muddy water. I felt a something tethering my leg and the bruising up and down my body made my movements hurt. I floated in the dim light that streamed down like moving pillars. The surface rippled, just out of reach. I could make out a chair sitting below me, what looked like a tripod nearby it. A light casing. A table with a book that wafted in the sluggish water like some strange aquatic creature, swollen to globe-size and calving off constant white particles like smoke. I could make out the faintest hint of a diagonal in the murk that seemed to be stairs.

I struggled, wrenching my body left and right, trying to break free, to rip loose of the chain binding me. The surface rose away, diminishing, and I realized, even if I escaped, I would have to swim upstairs. I stopped struggling then. And felt rage. Anger suffused my body like a drug, ripping and clawing, red and unbound. And then I died.

My body slowed and the light disappeared from above. White flashes, like light bulbs going off behind my eyes, bemused me. Then red. Then white again.

Nothing.

I was on my knees in the studio. My perception firmly seated itself back into my own eyeballs, my own body. I lifted my arms—I lifted them, not the dead girl—and looked at my hands. They dripped with gore. But I still had my gloves on, and that was a blessing. I whirled around, looking at the studio, searching for…

A body. Not much remained of the man who sat near Cortez, peering into the monitor. Parts of his face were missing, giving his appearance a decidedly gruesome—and vacant—look. He smiled at me, eye sockets empty and lips gone. I looked at him for a long time, becoming fascinated with the musculature of the cheek revealed by his gaping wound. The human body is an infinitely interesting thing. I walked over and knelt down by the man. With my forefinger, I pulled his cheek back further so that I might see the way the muscles attached to the bone of his skull. I looked around for something to write with, to draw on.

And then shook my head, trying to clear it of the focus.

My medicine must have been wearing off, because this level of intense concentration only came with my Asperger's long fugue-like states where I had no recollection of any activities. Yet afterward knowledge filled my head like some reverse Athena, full-formed and leaping back into Zeus' divine cranium.

I looked at the set, toward the temple. The man and the girl were absent. No bodies. Thank god.

My own personal bag of flesh hitched and the drowned girl commandeered my v-space again. Floating, she approached. Closer now, her eyes bored into me, black and pupilless. It was as if she saw me for the first time. She opened her mouth, a dark cavity, and screamed.

And screamed.

I heard nothing. I found my own mouth gaping open in response, as if I was retching, yet no sound issued.

A groan came from behind the camera. The dead girl's head pivoted on a long slender neck, turning black eyes toward the man on the floor, her hair floating along behind, swirling. I walked around the camera and found Cortez splayed out like a combat casualty. His head rolled to the side and his eyelids fluttered. The left side of his face was purple and swollen. He looked like he'd been hit by a baseball bat. And for all I knew, he had.

She filled my vision as I stood over Cortez. She moved close to me, black eyes like pools. The verrata—was it verrata? Or was I seeing something else? Was she the infection?

The verrata loomed, blotting out the rest of my view of the studio.

"Who are you?" I watched in horror as her mouth opened and closed, mirroring my words.

She cocked her head and stared at me with inhuman—once human, maybe—eyes. She opened her mouth and I felt mine opening in time, mirroring her. I could feel the shapes that my mouth took. I felt dislocated and centered all at once, her speaking through my mouth soundlessly.

"Madeline. Escre. My. Name. Was." She paused, thinking. I guess. It is hard to tell with verrata. I felt the cold wash through me again, seeping into my bones. "Killed. Me. Cortez. Raped. Left. To. Die."

"Jesus Christ, that's horrible."

Her eyes closed, face darkening. She swam even closer, the translucent flesh of her face appearing pallid and unforgiving. Her brow hitched forward and hatred filled her features, mouth a grimace, eyes narrowed. Then she opened her mouth once more.

Again I mirrored her as she screamed. And screamed. But no sound came from my body. I bent over, hands balled into fists, my body convulsing, silently screaming. I couldn't breathe.

Finally, when she relinquished her control, I slumped over, on top of Cortez.

"Wait!" I coughed. I rolled off of the man and placed my hands palm down on the floor. "This guy could die if he doesn't get help. It looks like I...like you broke something in his face. A bone or something."

"He. Must. Die," shaping the words in my mouth. And then she assaulted all of my senses. Her eyes swam in my v-space, filling it, the cold suffused my body, and her screams—after years of darkness—were heard.

2.

We walk into Bargetown now, the derelict lean-tos and shanties dark in the night. I know this because I can see through her eyes. She asks me lots of questions and I have to provide her with the answers, if I can. I speak with quite a few things, entities, talking in clicks and pops that I didn't understand until very recently. But I don't really know how to provide her the answers she wants. Parts of me can create images, parts can make noise. We're learning about each other as we go along.

She asks me about Bargetown, and I answer, finding the data she needs.

Bargetown is a large city-like conglomeration of barges, welded together on Lake Pontchartrain, where people have loosely formed a government outside that of ArkLaTex jurisdiction. Population is roughly 23,043 with a 3.4% margin of error. Dwellings include few houses, numerous tents and shacks. Police records indicate that a large population of criminals call Bargetown home. I check the GPS satellites and give her her exact longitude and latitude, which she discards rapidly. I give her all the data and try to display it in a way that pleases her. We're learning together. I can tell from the way her body responds that she seems to like the display.

She wants her body to remain strong so that she can continue lifting the heavy weight on her shoulders. A man, she carries. Cortez.

I trigger the small gland resting on top of her kidneys and her body pops and buckles. She hitches the man higher onto her shoulder.

We move through Bargetown. Every few nanoseconds I check the ether and get the time. She asks me for a map and I retrieve one, taken just that morning; at least that is the server-date on the file. I put the map in her eyes but she has a moment of dislocation and I sense that she dislikes the way I presented the information. I feel like crying, yet the only eyes I have are hers. I try again, giving her two choices, and she picks the one that is less intrusive. This makes me glad.

She hops across the gap between barges and stops. The man is relatively quiet, only letting out soft moans once in a while. The waters of Lake Pontchartrain gurgle and lap softly at the barge's hull, fifteen feet below.

She looks at his face and I offer her more information about his clothes, his watch. Possible diagnoses for the wound on his face.

She scans the area. We can hear the strains of zydeco and reggae music filtering through the night. I identify the music and offer her artist information. I offer her information about the stars, the constellations in the heavens. She stares at a cinder block by the plywood wall of a shanty. I estimate its weight at twenty pounds.

She strips the man, and with brute strength shreds his pants into long strips. She ties his leg to the cinder block. Then she kneels down, squatting on her hams, and begins alternately slapping and spitting on the man's face.

She continues this for a long while, squatting on her hams, slapping and spitting. He groans again and his eyes flutter open. They look around unfocused. Then fasten on her face.

She says in a deep, masculine voice, "Cortez, you left me there to die. You had him rape me and then when the levees broke, you set up the camera and left."

His eyes go even wider. "How do you... How can you know that? I never told anyone about... How can you know that?"

"I know. My name is Madeline Escre."

She stands over him. With one foot, she pushes him over and he falls into the water of the Pontchartrain with a splash, the cinder block following after. She screams and brings her hands up to her face, tearing at her eyes and ears. She rips at her clothes.

She stops screaming and her heart rate slows. She turns and watches the water for a long time. It takes only one minute and forty-three seconds until the bubbles stop. I offer her this information. She discards it by clicking her tongue. At least I think she's discarded it. She doesn't ask for it again.

She watches the water.

3.

I can't remember much about who I was. I used to be warm. But I like information. I have intense interests.

She's angry now, so angry I trigger little places in her brain that calm her, keep her heart from exploding. She looks at the sky and screams, hands up, clawing at the heavens. She discards all the information I provide her about cumulocirrus cloud formations.

She looks at the city, watches the lights twinkle merrily from the vantage of the levees. I offer her information on the buildings, the signs, the cars. She ignores the telltales I show. She watches the city with a hatred that is hard for me to understand. Killing Cortez will never be enough. She queries me regarding the structural faults in buildings. I am denied that information. The server's ghost provides me with a link to the Homeland Security Act of 2026. There's an insistent buzzing in the ether and I let her know that she has messages from Cynthia Wetham and Mary Elizabeth Thibault. She discards the information.

We walk the levees, searching for sluiceways and weak points. Once, I knew everything I needed to know about the levees, but now, when she asks me, I have to query the oracles and databases to give her the answers. The weaknesses of the sluiceways. Locations of pumping stations. Erosion rates of the levees of New Orleans. She queries me about the city altitude. She queries me about the current sea level. She queries me about the weather.

We walk the levees, searching for something. And when we find it, the whole world will be drowned in blood.

OLD DOGS, NEW TRICKS

SIX DOGS were dead and two maimed, whining pitifully in their pens, when the truck came over the hill, headlights shining up into the pines and then dipping down, illuminating the mat of needles covering the forest floor. The truck wound its way down the path toward the pit, rumbling and coughing through the trees. It stopped with a clatter near the kennels and Isaac Douglas climbed out of the cab and walked to the back.

The men watched, standing around the pit, smoking in the guttering kerosene light. Isaac reached into the bed of the truck and grabbed a crate, sliding it out and onto the gate. Dressed in khaki work-shirt and pants, grease marring the elbows and knees, Isaac lit a cigarette and drew on it heavily. His khaki clothes hung loosely, cinched at the waist, giving him the look of a withered navy officer.

Cigarette jutting from his mouth, he lifted the crate with a grunt. With the quick step of someone carrying a heavy load, he walked the crate over, setting it down with a thump, leaving a faint trail of smoke in the dark.

The dogs began howling and slavering, biting at the metal grills of the kennels.

"Hush now, dogs! Hush!" a man cried, kicking at the line of portable crates. The sound of growls grew frantic, more desperate. One of the men threw a bucket of water at the pens and the dogs quieted.

Turning back to the pit, the men—rough men all, field hands and laborers—leaned on the plywood and corrugated tin sides. Kerosene lanterns hissed in the dark, throwing yellow pools of light onto the clay floor and the faces of the spectators. The men laughed and joked; money changed hands. One man, wearing a vest embroidered with the words

Arkansas Warrior Kennels, adjusted a digital camera on a tripod, whistling.

Billy Cather, belly spilling over belt and sweating through his shirt in dark patches, hollered, "I got two on Luther's terrier! Two hundred! Need a match. Someone match me!" A man raised his arm, waving, and joined Billy. They spoke for a moment then shook hands.

Cather walked over to his truck. He fished a beer out of a cooler and popped the tab. Returning, he passed Isaac.

"You got another watch for me, Ike? I'm starting a collection." He slurped his beer.

Isaac sat on his crate, staring into the light of the kerosene lanterns with an abject, blank look. He pulled on his cigarette and blew a huge plume of smoke.

"Ain't right what you did," he said slowly, not looking at Cather. "Ain't right."

"What the hell you talkin' bout, Ike? This is a goddamned dog fight, not the Salvation Army."

"That watch been in my family four generations. Grandaddy had it in the East Indies, and Daddy had it too in the Merchant Marines."

"Maybe your land-locked ass shouldn't have put it up on a bet. Ain't nothing as sorrowful and nostalgic as a gambler down on his luck."

"I told you I'd give you money for it last week. I'd buy it back. You know I don't have no thousand dollars. Ain't worth that anyway. It's gold plate."

Cather laughed. "You said it was priceless last week." He leaned over, trying to look into Isaac's pen. "When did you start raising, Ike? You don't have no kennel."

Isaac blinked slowly, not looking at the man. "I got a dog. Been training him all week. Found a little something to help in Daddy's knick-knacks from overseas."

Doubling over, Cather dropped his beer and held his gut in an exaggerated pose of laughter. He hawed like a mule, making his voice project across the hollow. Men encircling the pit turned to watch.

Gene Corso walked over and asked, "What's the gag, Cather? We're about to start another match."

"Ike here says he's got a dog. To fight. You better adjust your book for him, cause his dead Daddy been helping him train the thing."

Corso squinted at Isaac, cocking his head.

"That right, Mr. Douglas? You got a dog you want to fight?" He was over-polite, which felt to Isaac like another form of rudeness.

Isaac nodded.

"Well, we've got an empty slot. Miller took a pass, we need a dog for filler. So, you're welcome to fight if you got the entry fee. Hundred dollars."

Fishing in his pocket, Isaac withdrew a wad of dirty bills and peeled off five twenties. Corso took a small black ledger from his back pocket, pulled a pencil from the spine, and flipped it open.

"Isaac Douglas. Entry fee paid. Dog?"

"Dog what?"

"Sex? Color?"

Isaac remained quiet, staring at the kerosene lanterns. He flicked his cigarette away, toward the trucks.

"Don't rightly know if it's male or female. I didn't check. And…after…I wasn't gonna get close enough to check. But it's a terrier."

"Fine. I'll mark it as terrier, sex…unknown. That's a first. Color?"

"Sorta gray, I guess."

Cather laughed again. "Now that's a breeder for you. Don't know color. Can't sex a dog. You sure there's even a dog in there, Ike? Sure is being quiet. Maybe you accidentally put in a possum instead?"

Corso moved back toward the pit, bellowing, "Entrants! Get your dogs to the gates." He looked at his ledger. "Cullum's brindle versus Alexander's black. Match starts in five!"

Men moved to the pens, grabbing individual crates and pulling them to either side of the pit. The crates jerked in their hands, dogs growling and shifting their weight.

When all was ready, Corso picked up a large electric torch and turned it on, shining it into the pit. The clay circle gleamed wet and red in the light. Two men, one for each dog, perched at either side, leaning forward, ready to unlatch the crates and loose the dogs.

"Ready?" Corso's voice pitched upward and the crowd fell silent. *"FIGHT!"*

The men threw the latches and leaned back, away from the circle of clay. Two dogs erupted out of their crates, feet scrabbling. The animals, thick and low-slung, met in the center, bodies twisting, jaws wide. Rearing on their hind legs, they slammed into one another, both making harsh, grinding sounds deep in their throats. The men screamed into the pit, faces flushed, shaking fistfuls of dollars at the combatants.

"Come on, *come on, COME ON,* you goddamned... Get that son of a bitch!" Cather hopped up and down, his belly flopping. His face turned red with screams.

Blood streamed down the bodies of the dogs. The black dog, slightly larger than the brindle, moved decidedly slower, answering the other's attacks sluggishly. The brindle latched onto the black's withers, making the other dog yelp, a high-pitched cry. Cather winced. Isaac watched on implacably. The black shook and rolled the brindle off his back, fur flying. Blood poured out, streaking down its heaving flanks.

The dogs broke apart and circled each other once before slamming together again. The black mustered strength from somewhere and whipped to the attack, taking the brindle's haunch and giving it a ferocious shake. The brindle yelped, a hoarse sound, and latched onto the black's neck. The black released the brindle's leg and opened its mouth as if to howl, slinging ribbons of saliva and blood, but no sound issued. The brindle bore the black to the ground, the black's legs splaying out gruesomely, and they lay still for a long while, the brindle on top and the black's chest rising and falling slowly until it stopped altogether.

"The brindle wins!" Men whooped or groaned, depending on their bet. "Next up, Jessup's spotted versus Douglas' grey!"

One of the men moved into the pit and leashed the brindle, yelling, "Off, 'Yota. Off. Damnit Toyota, OFF!" Men laughed at the dog's name. The dog allowed itself to be pulled away, back into its crate.

The losing entrant climbed into the pit. He was a big, barrel-chested man in a t-shirt and overalls. Tears streamed openly down his face as he kneeled by the black dog and picked it up in his arms, cradling it like a baby. The crowd hooted at him.

"Ain't no place for tears." The man wearing the *Arkansas Warrior Kennels* vest stood near Isaac.

Isaac nodded, glancing at the larger man.

"Can't get attached, you know? There ain't no happy endings in the pit."

"That's what they say."

"How you been training? Treadmill? Tires and hanging?"

Isaac turned back to look at the lanterns and the crowd, ignoring the man. He raised an arm, holding his wad.

"Cather! I got five hundred for my watch! Five hundred against Jessup's spotted. You put up my watch."

Cather turned and wiped his mouth. He walked back to Isaac, squinting at the smaller man.

"Let's see your money."

Isaac fanned his wad. "It's there, Cather. Five hundred."

"All right. Five hundred." He stuck out his hand. Isaac took the other man's hand in his and shook it, one hard pump and then let go, as if the touch of Cather's flesh was distasteful.

Cather laughed. "This is gonna be easy money. He's been training for a week, he says!"

Isaac squatted, put both hands around his crate, and lifted. He manhandled it over to the gate, the men in the crowd moving aside for him to pass, and set it down with a harsh exhalation of air.

Jessup moved his dog with the help of another man, carrying it easily, to the opposing gate. Jessup reached over the lip of the pit, put his hand on the latch, ready to unleash his dog. Corso flipped on the electric spotlight, pointing it into the pit.

Isaac grinned for the first time, his mouth showing gaps between teeth, and black gums. He stepped on top of the crate and then jumped into the light of the pit. With a flip of his wrist, he threw open the door. He took three steps back, then waited, smiling.

A dog staggered out, rib cage and pelvis prominent, the flesh hanging in drapes on its decaying form. Maggots feasted at its eyes, flies swarmed around its anus.

"Get out of there, you damned fool!" Corso pointed the light on Isaac's face. Isaac stepped quickly toward the wall, hiked a leg up, and levered himself up and out of the pit.

Jessup, unknowing, threw the latch. A blur of teeth and fur exploded out of the opposite crate. The spotted terrier crossed the pit in a flash, barreling into the gray, desiccated dog. On instinct, the spotted took the gray's neck in its mouth and wrenched a huge hunk of flesh away. For an instant, the spotted froze, its mouth full of corrupted flesh. It shook its head, trying to puzzle out the scent of the dead thing. The grey took a feeble step forward and its teeth closed on the other dog's snout. Jessup's spotted thrashed, pushing away with its hind legs. Isaac's gray held it fast in its jaws. A muffled whine came from the living dog, and blood burbled around the gray's lips, where its flesh met snout.

The spotted tried to roll itself away, out of the grip, but as it twisted, the gray pivoted its head, turning it further than any dog should be able to. The spotted whined deep in its throat, muzzled with the jaws of its opponent.

Men around the pit fell silent, watching the bizarre match. The spotted twisted and raked its captor with claws, ripping them down its body, splitting the skin and exposing muscles and bone. No blood came from the gray dog. It remained unnaturally still.

Then, without warning, Isaac's gray brought its jaws together with a hard crunch, the sound loud and clear above the hissing of the lanterns. It was as if the spotted terrier's snout had collapsed in the other's mouth. The spotted slumped, like a marionette with its strings cut.

Isaac walked over to where Cather stood. Men all around turned away as the dead dog began taking bites out of the spotted, nose mangled and oozing crimson.

"I want my watch, Cather." Isaac pointed at his gray feasting on the other dog. "Ain't no arguing. That's a win. Gimme my watch."

Cather shook his head, spitting. "It's a goddamned trick. It's *unnatural*. That dog's sick or something. It weren't a fair match."

Isaac took two steps closer to the larger man. The gray ripped a hole in the spotted's stomach and wormed its head inside the body cavity.

"Gimme my Daddy's watch, Cather. You can't renege. Ain't gonna let you."

The larger man turned to face Isaac. "I say it was a trick, Isaac. You cheated, somehow."

"Didn't cheat, Cather. Show me the damned rules, anyway." Isaac wiped his hands on the front of his shirt, then brought them to his sides, balled into fists. He was a slight man, but lean. His eyes were bright.

"No. I ain't got it here. I ain't turning over that watch on a trick. And I ain't got it, anyhow."

Isaac thrummed with tension. His jaw went hard and muscles popped and twitched in his cheek. When he spoke, it was through clenched teeth.

"Last chance, gimme my Daddy's watch."

At that moment, someone yelled, "Jessup's dog! It's getting up!"

They turned back to the pit. Jessup's spotted was having a tough time rising with the gray's head buried in the stomach cavity. But the gray's head slipped from the opening, covered in bile, blood and bits of flesh. The other's entrails slid from the opening and pooled on the clay. And in a strange imitation of life, the gray shook, like a dog coming from the water, but this was no longer a dog. Blood, flesh flew in radiant arcs caught in the lantern light.

The things that had once been dogs peered at the men gathered around the pit. Then, without indication of thought or instinct, the dogs threw themselves at the wall. The gray smashed into a bit of corrugated metal. It rang with a tinny reverberation. The other hit plywood, cracking it.

The gamblers fell out, running away from the pit, racing toward their trucks. They screamed and cursed, calling on Jesus. Some scrabbled at the kennels to get their dogs.

Cather turned to run, but Isaac grabbed his arm, yanking him around.

"My watch, Cather."

"What did you do? What did you *DO*?" Cather's face was white, his eyes enormous. His stubble-lined jowls shook as he spoke. "They're fucking *unnatural.*" He tried to pull his arm away, but Isaac held on.

"You ain't going nowhere, until you give up my watch."

Cather swung at the smaller man, fist smacking into Isaac's cheek. Isaac gave a little *ooof* as he fell, but nothing more. He hit the earth, rolled. He gained his knees and stood again, spitting blood into the mat of pine needles on the ground. He wiped his mouth.

Men reached their trucks now and the sound of engines filled the night air.

"You ain't going nowhere, Cather," Isaac said. He uncoiled, his fists lashing out at the larger man. Quick blows fell, one in the gut, one in the side as the big man tried to twist away, then Cather doubled over. Isaac grabbed his hair, lifted his head, and smashed a fist into the man's face. Cather reeled backwards from the blow, hit the lip of the pit, and toppled over. He screamed, a warbling high-pitched sound, then went quiet.

Trucks sped away out of the hollow, clutches grinding, dogs in the truck beds howling. In a line, their headlights passed over the lip of the hill.

For a long while it was silent except for a wet smacking sound coming from the pit and the hiss of the lanterns overhead. A small red light continued to burn on the front of the camera. The doors of the portable kennels stood open, and Isaac realized the dogs had either been released or led away, a last, and rare, act of kindness by their masters.

He tightened his belt, took a deep breath, then walked over to the pit, looking into it.

Only a grisly red hole remained of Cather's throat. His mouth gaped open in surprise and his eyes stared at the pine trees rising all around, ringing the pit in darkness.

The dogs were indistinguishable now, each covered in gore and human bile. They worked at Cather's gut, taking bites and pulling opposite directions until the flesh and clothes tore with wet ripping sounds. One dug its head under Cather's sternum, found something inside the man, and began tugging at the corpse.

Isaac watched with a blank stare, hands hanging limp at his sides.

The other dog bit into Cather's pectoral and wrenched a huge piece of flesh away. His shirt tore with a bright ripping sound. Isaac noticed a faint glimmer of gold flip into the muddy clay of the pit.

His watch gleamed, falling from Cather's shirt pocket. It came to rest near the foot of one of the dogs. Its crystal face was shattered, either from the fall or the activities of the dogs, Isaac couldn't tell. Even in the light from the lantern, the jagged ring of broken glass and missing watch hands were clearly visible, fob chain curling around the broken circle.

Isaac stared at it for a long while, until the dog pulled one last morsel of flesh from Cather and placed a foot on the watch face, shoving it deep into the mud.

"It weren't supposed to play out like this," he said. "Ain't fair, goddamnit." His voice sounded hoarse in the night air.

Both dogs' heads pivoted toward Isaac in unison, staring at him with unblinking eyes. They remained still, more still than any dog could.

Only when Cather began to rise did they move, throwing themselves against the wall.

Isaac backed away from the pit with a hard, anxious face. He watched as the undead man rose from the clay circle, his grisly head rising above the wood and tin side. His dead eyes fixed on Isaac, and he moved forward, arms out.

When the plywood cracked and Cather began pulling apart the walls, Isaac turned away, running for his truck, cursing.

The circle lay broken. Cather and the dogs stumbled forward, following Isaac's smell, out of the pit and into the night.

EL DORADO

SHE HAD a tattoo on her right breast that read *"le morte fantastique."* After they fucked—fucked hard for forty minutes and in every position he'd ever performed or even seen before—Efram lay on the motel's broke-down mattress and listened to the air conditioner tick and hum while he inspected her body, running thick fingers over her skin.

"What's that mean?"

"What?"

"Your titty. Is that French or something?"

She smiled, weakly, and pushed a lock of hair behind her ear. Efram liked the way she looked, wary, big-eyed and delicate, like she'd spent too much time indoors when she was a girl. She had some bruising here and there, but nothing that didn't come with the business.

"Means 'a fantastic death.'"

"I got that much. What's that mean, though?"

He balled his thick fingers into a fist and then opened them, as if he'd caught an insect and then released it just to be sure he'd caught it in the first place. He didn't like to be talked down to, not by men or women. Not by trim like her. But there'd been too many misunderstandings in the past that ended with blood, screaming, or prison, so now Efram asked questions. Enough questions to know when no more questions were necessary.

"Hon, I don't know. It looked cool. The tattoo guy said it meant to come. Like it was French for creaming your jeans." She lit a cigarette and then gave a little laugh, blue smoke coming from her nose. "But I found out later, that wasn't what it meant. It's pretty, though, ain't it?"

The tattoo arched over her breast, fluid script, with little flourishes and florals and a bird worked into the design, as if descending to seize the fruit of her nipple, plum-colored and erect in the cold air blowing from the conditioner.

He wanted another beer, but he couldn't leave her here.

"Time to go, Melissa."

She looked at him, squinting her eyes.

"You trying to get rid of me?"

"Nah. Just want some more beer, and you can't stay here without me."

"Why, you got some blow or something?"

That was exactly what he had, a brick of it, blood-spattered and fresh from New Orleans, waiting for Gene Corso to pick up, but the Dew Drop Inn in El Dorado, Arkansas, wasn't high on Corso's priority list and there was some understandable heat involved with the merchandise. So, Efram had to babysit the shit while it cooled. A week or more, from on high.

He grunted, sat up and found his jeans, tugged them on. "Nah. A ton of Krugerands." That sounded cool. He'd heard the boys talk about the coins they nabbed from a B&E in Little Rock.

"We can't stay a little longer?" She sat up in the bed, pulled the covers over her breasts, pouted, changed tack and cut him sexy looks, batting the lashes. Then she rolled her eyes and laughed.

"I need a beer."

"I can make you forget all that, honey." She laughed again. New to tricking, maybe. Nervous. Still new enough for there to be some laughter left.

"Cost me more?"

"Sure. Nothing's free."

"I need a beer."

She lay back down, put an arm over her eyes. "Gimme the money then. Ray-Ray'll want it right when I get there."

She rolled on her side and sobbed once, a lonely, desperate little girl sound. He pulled on his jacket, withdrew his wallet and thumbed the bills, counting, and then dropped the money near her face. She grabbed it, levered herself up from the bed and stomped into the bathroom.

She showered but didn't wet her hair. Efram thought about the logistics and reasoning behind that as she dressed, pulling on the tube top and tight skirt. Why do you take a shower if you're not gonna wash your hair? Because you got some localized dirt, maybe. Between your legs. Most whores he'd been with were content to piss after a tussle.

He sat on the bed watching her while she touched up her makeup in the mirror. When she put on her heels, Efram realized how small her feet were and felt a moment of sadness, that she had to live like that, fucking strangers, but the moment passed and they went out into the motel parking lot, bright with the buzz of halogen lights and swarmed with insects.

———

Tin-roofed and directly across the highway from a rank smelling bayou, the tonk was called *The Shoehorn* and had a down-beat blues band garbling Muddy Waters and Albert King while middle-aged women, running to fat, waited tables in outfits that were obvious knock-offs of Hooters waitress garb, the porn star roller derby look. The building buzzed with neon beer signs and stank of stale beer and cigarette smoke but promised to stay open until 5 a.m. When the band stopped for a break, Efram heard the cicadas whirring heavily in cypress beyond the thin walls. A patron fed dollar bills into the jukebox, breaking the drone of insects.

He sat near the front plate glass window with a view of the parking lot and ordered a beer. Melissa went to a back booth and sat down with a thick-set, mulleted man.

Efram drank his beer, ordered another, and watched the TV in the reflection of the barback mirror, trying to puzzle out the reversed words. He wasn't surprised when the big man slid up to the bar and sat down next to him. Ray-Ray, most likely.

"So, you enjoy your little party with Melissa?"

Efram looked at the man. He was missing his eye teeth and had jaundiced skin, but was bull-thick and young enough to be stupid and careless. His mullet curled in greased ringlets and his leather jacket creaked when he moved.

"Yeah. It was a good time, you know, cake and punch and shit." Ray-Ray looked puzzled so Efram said, "Pin the tail on the donkey."

"Ha. You're jerking my chain."

"Nah. I'm sure you can jerk it yourself."

He laughed, maybe a little too hard. "Good one. I'm Ray-Ray." He stuck out his hand.

Efram glanced at his outstretched hand, took it, gave one pump, and then turned back to the mirror.

Ray-Ray gestured to the bartender, raising a meaty paw. She brought him a glass of whiskey, rocks. He slurped half of it and then turned to face Efram.

"El Dorado's a nice little town. You moving down here?"

"Nope. Just visiting. Seeing the sights."

"There's a lot of nice stuff to see, you know. El Dorado is the city of gold, if you know what I mean."

"That right?"

"Sure."

"Interesting thing to know. You a history teacher or something?"

"No." He laughed again, this time with less force.

"You the local bully boy, then?"

"Damn straight."

"I'll keep that in mind then, pard. Thanks for the heads up."

Ray-Ray finished his drink, ordered another one, and sat with his arms crossed on the smooth dark wood of the bar.

"'Lissa tells me you want to move some merchandise."

"She did, huh?"

Efram tilted his head to peer around Ray-Ray's bulk, down the length of the narrow building, where Melissa sat in a booth. When she saw him staring at her, she fumbled with her cigarettes, lit one, and then looked into her drink.

"Yeah, that's right." Ray-Ray smiled again. "I can help you move whatever you got."

"You must've got some lines crossed, pard. I ain't got nothing to move."

"Right. Not what she says."

Efram finished his beer and ordered another.

"Well, thanks for the offer. I'll let you know if I need your help."

Ray-Ray stood, raised his glass and knocked his head back. He set the glass on the bar and leaned in close. "This here's my town. You shitbag fucks come down here from Little Rock and try to do business, I'm taking what's mine, you hear?"

Efram took a swallow of beer.

"That right?"

"That's one hundred percent right."

"Okay, hoss. Next time I try to do business in this dump, I'll be sure to let you know."

Ray-Ray stood like a bull, air coming through his nostrils, all trace of joviality gone. Efram waited. When it became obvious Efram wasn't going to throw a punch or pull out a wallet and give him all the cash, Ray-Ray turned and walked stiffly back to Melissa in the back booth.

Efram drank his beer and watched the reversed television in the bar's mirror.

———

The air conditioner had totally beaded the window with condensation when the knock came at the door, so he had to wipe it clear to check if she had anyone with her.

Shirtless, he opened the door, but kept on the chain.

"Yeah?"

"It's me."

"I can see that. You forget something?"

"No." She huddled in the yellow glow of the parking lot lights holding a bag with both hands, pushing her tits together with her arms as if she was cold, even though it was steaming in the dark. "He was…"

She sobbed and turned her head so he could see her face. Her left cheek was swollen and her eye socket purpling and streaming with tears.

"You look like shit."

"Ray-Ray got mad after you talked."

"Sorry to hear that. Looks like he did a number on your face."

She shivered again, took a deep breath of air, and then said, "I didn't have anywhere else to go."

"You don't have here."

"Please. Let me in."

"No."

"I'll take care of you, baby. Please."

The whine in her voice made Efram want to slam the door, but he stood there, looking at her for a long time. Finally, he undid the chain and opened the door all the way. She came inside.

He said, "Empty the bag on the bed."

"Why? It's just clothes."

"Don't give a shit. Empty it."

She stepped to the bed, opened the bag, upended it and shook out the contents. Clothes, panties, unopened cigarette packets, and a pint of Old Crow tumbled onto the bed followed by a cheap patent leather wallet, tampons, and a handgun. Chrome.

"See you got a Saturday Night Special." He snatched it up, took the magazine and worked the action to make sure there were none in the chamber. He tossed her the gun, walked back to the motel room safe at the bottom of the closet, dialed the combination, and put the magazine inside. She watched him closely.

"What, you don't trust me?"

He laughed, then, and grabbed her pint of whiskey. He poured them both a drink in the small motel glasses.

"Thanks. I needed the laugh."

She scowled and then sat down on the bed. "I don't like being laughed at."

"Don't like being lied to."

"I didn't lie to you."

He didn't say anything. It was late now, but he turned on the TV to ESPN SportsCenter and slid back against the headboard, holding his whiskey on his chest. She stayed at the foot of the bed, hunched over.

After a while, she scooped her clothes and belongings back into the bag, picked up her glass and moved to rest beside Efram.

He sipped his whiskey and put his arm around her, pulling her in close. His hand hung above her breast with the tattoo, and eventually she bent over, worked open his jeans and took him in her mouth. He sipped his whiskey and watched the television while her head moved up and down and he brushed back her hair and held it so he could watch her bruised face in the blue light of the TV when he came.

A long time later, he fell asleep, her head cradled in his lap.

———

The muzzle pressed into his eye socket, but it was more than the pain of the muzzle that woke him, it was her screaming and the opaline stink of Ray-Ray in a tight space and the sensation of his sclera popping and his own blood and vitreous fluids pouring from his socket like tears.

"You said you wouldn't kill him!"

"Where is it?" Ray-Ray wasn't playing the gadabout now. He pulled the muzzle from his ruined eye socket and swiped it across Efram's skull, which made the world go white and sounded like the tolling of a bell.

"You crushed his…"

The blurry figure tilted and righted itself.

"He's bleeding from his eye. He's gonna have to go to the hospital…"

"Shut up." The closer silhouette raised an arm, and even blurry, Efram could tell he was threatening to hit her. "Just shut your fucking mouth."

He grabbed Efram's arm and jerked him up. "Where is it? I'll jam the barrel so far in your hole that it'll tickle your goddamned memory."

Efram tilted his head toward the closet. It was disconcerting that Ray-Ray called it his "hole," but there it was. No more eye. Ray-Ray pushed him toward the back of the motel room, one beefy hand on the nape of his neck. He shoved him onto the floor in front of the safe.

"I told you he had it in the safe, baby. I did just like you said…"

Ray-Ray put the gun to Efram's skull.

"I don't give a shit about this carpet. I'll decorate it."

Efram went through the combination, once, twice, but couldn't make it open.

"You're dead if you're fucking with me." The way Ray-Ray made threats, unnecessarily and with such force, it made Efram redouble his efforts to calm his hands.

"Having trouble seeing. Can we turn on a light or something?"

"Turn on the light, 'Lissa."

She moved to the light switch near the TV credenza and switched them on. Things began to come into focus for Efram, the safe, the threadbare stained carpet, the trash bin under the motel sink. His head spun and he put a hand up to his eye—it throbbed, full of pain, yet it had an empty, slack feel and he couldn't open his eyelids, even when he tried.

"You ain't never seeing out of that motherfucker again, Popeye." Ray-Ray gave a hoarse laugh. "Now open the fucking safe if you want to keep your other one."

Efram went through the combination again, turned the miniature safe latch, and the steel door swung open. Ray-Ray put a boot in his ribs, bowling him over, and reached in the safe and withdrew a gymbag. He tossed it on the bed.

"Open it." He waved the gun at Melissa and then back at Efram.

From where he lay on the floor, Efram could see the magazine to Melissa's handgun still in the safe. Not much help without the pistol to go with it, but he reached out and grabbed it anyway while they inspected the gymbag. He pushed himself to his feet and backed into the sink, keeping his hands at his sides.

"What's this?" Ray-Ray said. "Where's the fucking gold?"

"Gold?" Efram said. For a moment, things didn't make sense. He shook his head. The motion made his socket and face erupt with pain but it was too funny not to laugh. "What gold?"

Ray-Ray swelled in the small room, inhaling air.

"Baby. Look." She held up the brick.

"Yeah, so what?"

"It's blow, baby." The brick gleamed dully in the motel room's light and they moved it to the small table. Melissa sat down, cradling it like a baby. It had been dipped in some sort of paraffin.

"Bullshit."

"Honey, it is."

"Open it."

She found a pen in the bedside drawer and jammed it into the paraffin, past the plastic wrapping so the cocaine spilled onto the cheap wooden table top. She swiped the powder with her finger and rubbed it on her gums.

"Oh shit."

"Lemme try."

Ray-Ray jammed a finger into the paraffin's breach, wormed it around, and then rubbed his gums as well.

"That's one helluva nummie. Fuck." He turned around in a circle, as if trying to find what had brought him such good luck. "Can you believe this shit, babe? You said Krugerrands and I thought he had a few thousand in gold on him. But this! It's like winning the fucking lottery."

They made Efram sit in a chair, but didn't bother to tie him. When Ray-Ray saw his balled fist, he swiped the top of his head again with the pistol and pulled the clip out of his numb fingers.

"What were you gonna do with this, asshole?"

Efram sat cocooned in pain, his eye socket throbbing and pulsing and sending tendrils up to join with his aching, gun-sapped head. Melissa couldn't find a mirror, so she took down one of the cheap framed pictures from the wall—a hideous farm scene done in pink and orange sfumato style—and cut the blow on the glass. She huffed two lines, one in each nostril, and then tilted her head back and held out the rolled-up twenty to Ray-Ray.

He took it and bent to snort the lines. For an instant, Efram thought of attacking him while the man was occupied with the cocaine, but Ray-Ray still held the gun and Efram's head was spinning. The blood welled in his eye socket and dribbled down his cheek.

"You know you guys are dead, right?" The vibrations from speaking nearly made him vomit. Bile burned in the back of his throat.

Ray-Ray held a finger against a nostril, shutting it, and snorted cocaine deep into his sinuses.

"That right, tough guy?"

"That's right, dumb ass."

Ray-Ray stepped toward Efram, but before he could pistol whip him again, Efram vomited yellow bile on the floor.

Melissa squealed, ignoring the retching sounds from Efram.

"Baby, this is good shit." She thrummed, her leg bouncing.

"Cut some more. Then I'll take care of this asshole." He ignored the vomit.

She dug a key into the brick, knocking loose powder and rocks onto the picture's glass and cut them with a driver's license. Before, she had seemed concerned for Efram's health, but now, with an unlimited high in front of her, she wasn't as finicky about his welfare. Typical.

"You just can't walk with a brick of coke and think nobody's gonna come lookin' for you." It was better now that he'd vomited. His eye still throbbed horribly and the pain made it hard to think, but he could function. Could still speak. Feeling was coming into his hands and legs. *Maybe I'm going into shock. Or coming out of it. Better than feeling it. Fuck. My eye.*

"They won't give a shit about me, but the brick..." He shifted in the chair. "They'll find you."

Ray-Ray laughed again then bent to do two more enormous lines. When he straightened, nose caked in powder, he grinned. "'Bout time we visited family down in Lake Charles, huh, babe?" He gestured for Efram to rise with the gun, a casual gesture like it was an extension of his hand.

Efram stood and moved to the door.

"I'll be back in a little while, 'Lissa. Just gonna put him on the next bus back to Little Rock."

She looked up and smiled at Ray-Ray. "Really?"

"Sure. Why not? We got what we wanted, right?" He put the pistol below Efram's crushed eye, brushed his bloody cheek. "He's got a little taste of how we play down here."

"Okay, baby. Bye, Efram. It was fun."

He looked at her, her wary bruised face, her long slender neck and the slope of her breasts and realized that a forty-minute fuck and a blowjob weren't worth this shit.

Ray-Ray shoved the gun in his back. "Put on some clothes, asshole."

Efram pulled on a tshirt and boots, watching Ray-Ray. Ray-Ray grinned and worked his jaw, in and out and around, the way the blow takes them.

Ray-Ray shoved Efram out the door once he was dressed, into the over-bright afternoon sunlight and sweltering heat. He held Efram's arm. The man was strong.

He led Efram to a sunburst Camaro with "Ray-Ray" painted on the jet-black rear window-shield. It had a shovel and toolbox in the bed. There was dirt on the shovel blade, which didn't make Efram feel much better.

"Nice." Efram nodded at the paintwork. "Subtle."

"Shut up, dead man."

He shoved some keys into Efram's hands. Efram got behind the wheel and the seat burned his back and legs while Ray-Ray raced around the front and hopped in and jammed the pistol into his gut.

"Right about now, you're thinking all kinds of shit, I imagine. Just forget it. If you so much as put a hair out of line, I'll just start pulling the trigger."

"Right."

"There ain't nothing you can do to stop what's coming." He smiled. "That's just the way it's gotta be. Start the car."

Efram twisted the key and then followed the burly man's directions. They drove out of town and turned off the highway and followed a gravel road for a few miles, and then turned off it into a cypress brake where the air grew thicker. They followed the road and Efram noticed that the jitters that had affected Melissa before leaving the motel were hitting Ray-Ray now. He was pale and flushed with sweat.

He considered running the car into a tree, but they weren't going fast enough here anyway and the other man was built like a damned tank. But he watched Ray-Ray for an opening.

"This is Bayou Bartholomew. You're gonna get to know it better than you've ever known anything before or since."

The sun was directly overhead, hazy and bright and pounding, and Efram could feel his shirt sticking to the fake leather Camaro seats. His armpits were wet and he felt the trickle of sweat down his obliques.

The coke must've really been working on the man because Ray-Ray was chalk-white and dripping when he told Efram to stop.

He stopped the car and opened the door.

"Slow down, fireball," Ray-Ray said, grinning. He snatched the keys from the ignition. He mopped at his face with his forearm.

They exited the car and the big man motioned Efram to walk in front. Crickets whirred in the cypress and the grass of the rise. The path was surrounded by stagnant water, thick with the scum of blue-green algae. The air was still.

"Like soup out here."

"Shut up." He jabbed the gun in Efram's back again.

They walked the path, grass tugging at their pants cuffs. It became overgrown, edged in ball cypress roots, shaded by trees. The grass diminished until the ground was covered in brown cypress fronds and golf ball-sized seeds. The trail ended in an old dock. There were a couple of flatbottoms upturned on the muddy shore.

"Keep walking."

They walked to the end of the dock, a good twenty feet out from shore. There was no reflection of sky in the scummy water but out in the distance, Efram watched a moccasin sliding across the bayou's surface.

"Okay. Here's where you get off."

The silence of the bayou drew out, and everything stilled as he turned to face Ray-Ray, who mopped the sweat from his forehead with his gun arm, and this time Efram moved, slamming his shoulder into Ray-Ray's gut and propelling him into the air and down to the water with a huge splash.

The pop sounded muffled and indistinct under the water, and when they broached the surface, Efram on Ray-Ray's back, one arm tight around his neck and the other grappling with his gun hand, Ray-Ray pulled off two more shots, away and in the air, and then the gun clicked and Efram drew the larger man underwater again.

When they came up again Ray-Ray didn't have the gun anymore and Efram had both arms locked around his neck, pushing his chin hard down into his chest. Efram gasped and took in a huge draught of air, while Ray-Ray grunted and tore at the bands cutting off his breath, digging red furrows in Efram's arms. They rolled on the surface and submerged again into the dark water.

The cicadas whirred, their drawn out chirrups rising and falling. The circle of water where they had risen was slowly choked out by the returning ring of algae.

Efram rose to the surface, alone, gasping.

He only had to swim a few feet before he could stand and then he trudged back to the shore and was halfway to the car when he realized he'd have to dive for the keys.

He found the gun, water-logged and useless, before he found Ray-Ray's body, and was able to swim him close enough to shore to dig the car keys out of his pocket.

In the Camaro, he retrieved the shovel and used the blade to put a hole in Ray-Ray's belly and throat so that he wouldn't float, at least not for a while, but it was tough going, jabbing a dirt-encrusted shovel into a corpse. Finally he had to get back into the water and swim Ray-Ray as far out as he could and shove him away, hoping that the bayou had alligators.

Four hours later he pulled Ray-Ray's Camaro into the motel parking lot, twilight seeping up into the western sky and the halogen lights of the parking lot buzzing, swarmed with insects. He could see the blue light flicker of TV through a gap in the drapes. He went to his room and held the key, staring. He put a hand on the door and imagined he could feel the fluttering beat of the heart of a bird beyond it, tenuous, frantic, powerless. He didn't know what he was going to do once he opened the door.

She lay on the floor, one hand clutching the bed linens, mouth rimed in spittle and bile. In her spasms, her shirt twisted and pulled away to expose most of her tattooed breast.

Efram shut the door.

He stripped his sodden shirt and jeans, picked up the pint of Old Crow and poured himself a drink. He drank it naked. Then he went to the sink and washed out the ruin of his eye. He poured more whiskey into the glass, bent his head to the glass' mouth, and put the burning circle to his eye socket and titled his head back and screamed at the ceiling as the whiskey filled his eyehole. He wiped it out with tissues.

When he was dressed in dry clothes, he poured the rest of the pint into his glass, grabbed the phone book from the credenza drawer, and sat at the table. He stepped over her body to get there.

There was a mound of blow on the picture frame and it looked like she'd kept tooting until her heart gave out, or had seized. This brick had been cut once, maybe, before packaging. No telling, really.

In death, her coloration hadn't changed much except for blue lips and grey nipple underneath the words "*le morte fantastique*." Now the bird looked as if it shied away from the fruit, and time had withered the florals and ivy.

"Just fantastic, Melissa. You fucked me real good."

He opened the book and began searching for a store that sold paraffin candles.

LUMINARIA

EACH INVITATION, written on thick paper, hand-sweet, heavy stock. Deckled edges.

Shadows grow long. The cicadas whir in the heat. She descends the great stair to the foyer, taking small steps, white hand on the balustrade, pale as the travertine brought from Italian shores. The descent a diminuition. Sleep was larger than this, these walls. In dreams, there are sun dappled glades and lemons and motes hanging in shafts of light. Waking, there is only dusk and the house stands still, tall ceilings full of silence. Past the banquet hall, past the sitting parlor, she enters the library and takes her place at the mahogany desk. An inclination of her white head. Dark inkstrokes on paper.

"Why don't you just call them, ma'am?" asks Renie. She brings a shawl to the older woman who allows her to drape it across her shoulders. Blue veins make fine intaglios in Victoria's skin. "It would take a lot less time, and you could be done with it."

Victoria raises her white head. The scratching of her pen ceases. She blinks like an owl, the movement deliberate. Why does she stop me in this? It is such a small task, and a personal one, and I only have such a short time, every pause is unwelcome.

But she speaks: "And have to listen to the excuses? Or the laughter? I'd hate to hear Andrei's remarks. No. My age makes me peculiar to them, a novelty. Those that want to come will come, and those that don't can go hang."

Renie listens and counts crystal, how many wine, how many water. Decanters and plate. The scratching begins again. She watches Victoria, bowed head, white and framed in lamplight. Renie sits nearby and prepares the ledger of the day's expenses. Her food, household bills. The food, she feels guilt over—would that she didn't eat. Victoria cares little for the maintenance of Renie's flesh, just her own desperate integuement.

Victoria writes:

Dearest Andrei,

I hope this letter finds you well in Arezzo. The Tuscan light at this time of year is reputedly beautiful but I would not know. It's been years since I walked those hills with you and now, I am beginning to doubt I will ever see them again.

My hundredth birthday is fast approaching, you might remember. On the fifth of January, I will have seen a century pass and I feel it is an occasion worthy of some celebration. Please join me and the rest of our family for dinner that night. A little reunion. We will toast the century and look forward to the next. I do hope you will attend.

Sincerely,
Victoria

The cicadas fall silent. The air cools and fills with mosquitos, whining like far-off strains of violin, pitchy, frantic. Victoria and Renie sit on the wraparound porch. With all of the lights extinguished behind them, they watch as fireflies burn themselves out mating, yellow streamers in the dark.

"Short lives. But the light is beautiful," says Renie, the knitting needles in her hands moving and weaving, making small clicking sounds. She slaps her forearm, leaving a red-black smear, faint and forgotten until the bite's welt appears.

Victoria sniffs. Maybe in response, or maybe the woman scents something upon the air. Renie cannot tell. "All lives are short. And all life is beautiful. No one wants to die."

"I'm sorry, ma'am, I didn't mean—"

"No. It's all right." A hand reaches out, falls on Renie's arm, where the mosquito bit her. It is cool, cooler than the humid air. "I know you don't judge. But I won't forget you, and I'll do my best to protect you from my family. You will be taken care of."

"Thank you, ma'am. I'm in your debt."

"Now, I think I would like my dinner." Victoria's touch is dry, like parchment. It slides to her hand, fingers cupping the underside of the wrist, feather-light. Flutter of pulse. Victoria squeezes and they sit that way until the mosquitos make the night unbearable for Renie.

Summer draws on, everything hazy in the daylight, cumulus stacked upon cumulus, piling up in towering bright columns high in the arteries of air. In the morning, dewed grass runs up from the road to kiss the Pemberton manse. In the day, sunlight beats like hammerfalls, miserable for Renie as she's alone until darkness.

Renie keeps watch for post and parcel, hiding in the porch's shade. Packages arrive, heavy crates full of strange and wonderful items. Leaded crystal trays from Prague, sterling silver from England. Irish linens with gold embroidery. Venetian goblets. Cobalt and silver candlesticks. Filigreed iron knives from Austria. Blown glass vases from Bolivia and Peru.

Late one afternoon, after the FedEx man wheels the large wooden crate into the banquet hall and makes her sign his electric pad, Renie takes the stairs by twos and calls to Victoria, "Wake up, ma'am! Wake up! The china has arrived!" She runs to retrieve a clawed hammer.

Wearing a silk robe, Victoria walks into the banquet hall: she looks rumpled, discontent, withered. She hasn't eaten and wears the pinched, tight expression of hunger as it works its way through her.

Renie pries open the crate lid. She has hands that match her features—blunt, solid, muscular. Victoria comes to her side, watching. Their heads bow together. Renie reaches into the hay of the crate and removes a wad of newsprint.

"The Staffordshire Chronicle…" she says.

"It's just a town, girl. Don't be foolish."

She pulls more newsprint away, revealing a white plate, almost translucent near the edges, colored with a patina of fine cracks.

Victoria says, "Bone china. Porcelain with the ground up bones of oxen added for color, clarity. Hold it up to the light."

Renie lifts up a plate, turning it in the faint light.

"See? White as snow and almost transparent around the edges. Just like me." Victoria laughs. It's a dry, soft sound, like the hasp of time has knocked all the corners and hard edges from her voice.

"But what about the cracks?"

"Ah. I've got those too, I think."

Victoria stands, stooping slightly, the way the aged sometimes do, looking into the crate.

"How many can we seat?" The question comes with the intonation of someone who already knows the answer but wants to see if others know as well.

"Twenty in here. More if we set up a table in the library."

"No, I don't think more than twenty will attend. Which is good," Victoria says. Too much hazard to self and home, with so many family, she thinks, but cannot bring herself to say it.

Setting the plate in front of Victoria, Renie turns to the crate and pulls out another paper wrapped piece.

"There should be salad and bread plates in this shipment as well, Renie. They cost quite a bit. As well they should. These are very special."

"They are pretty, and obviously old. But what makes them any better than regular plates?"

Victoria looks at her hands, turning them over. Her lip pulls back from teeth; a whiff of disgust at her traitorous body.

"This china is special because it once belonged to Dr. William Palmer, noted physician and serial killer. One of Britain's first known. A notorious poisoner. He killed quite a few people with these plates." Victoria laughs, a short dry chuff. At herself, maybe, Renie thinks—she's looking at her hands. "Make sure they're washed well before you eat off of them," Victoria says.

Summer grows hot. Renie walks the mansion with paper fan, fluttering and sweating, like a moth in a closet, batting paper-thin wings. Her hair sticks to her neck, she breathes from her mouth. The heat doesn't affect Victoria, indeed, Renie thinks the woman enjoys it—the hot breath of the world, panting. In another time, Renie might sit in her room, the window unit humming, belching out cool air, and watch the condensation form on the window. But not now. Not with Victoria asleep.

A car is heard before it is seen; crunching on the long pecan tree-lined gravel drive. Renie peeks out of the foyer window. Shadows sit directly beneath trees, no air stirs the leaves. She goes to the door, steps out on the porch, shielding her eyes with the fan.

The driver scuttles out, black suit, black shades, white shirt, black tie—a cariacture of a driver. He looks at the house and shifts his shoulders as if a personal expectation has been fulfilled. He moves to the rear passenger door, opens it. A woman emerges, back straight, face blank. She's older than Renie, younger than Victoria, but everyone is younger than Victoria. She is overly fashionable for the country, wearing a form-fitting dress, showing what might have been curves twenty years earlier, but now seemed to be more gristle than fat. White pearls, maroon fabric. Bony joints, knobby knuckles and knees. Big glasses on a chain.

She approaches the porch and stops in the shade to look at Renie. She has the demeanor of a woman who works mostly with women, and consequently, doesn't like them. Her stare is frank and appraising.

"I am Ilsa Bruhn." She takes off her glasses and lets them dangle over her bony chest. Her accent is strange. "I am here to see Mademoiselle Pemberton. My plane arrived early. Please show me to my room." She snaps her fingers. The driver pauses, looking at the woman, watching her mount the steps to the house. He's a muscular man, beneath those clothes, Renie sees; he spends his hours not driving rich people around lifting weights, maybe, because men like him have only one true possession—their bodies. While women like her have not even that. She glances up toward where Victoria sleeps.

Renie opens the door, allowing the woman inside. She takes her bags from the driver herself, and his warm hand touches hers briefly and before he's gone she raises it to her lips and tastes the sweat-salt there. She deposits the woman's bags in the downstairs guest room. She places Vivaldi on the old turntable and sets the needle. She fixes iced tea,

wedges of lemon, sugar and spoons, dainty cookies on a tray. She leaves
Bruhn to sit in the dim library, sipping a glass of tea, and climbs the
stairs.

She can number the times she's awoken Victoria in the middle of the
day on her hand; in all the seasons she's been her servant, it is not
something she ventured often.

Victoria lays in bed, shrouded in thick hangings. The room stands
dark except for a hairline strip of light running vertically on the far wall,
the seam of the heavy curtains.

"What is it?"

"A woman's here, ma'am. She says her name is Bruhn."

"Ah. This is good. Tell her I'll be down after my rest."

"I've put her bags in the guest room." She keeps her voice
unmodulated, no rise to the interrogative, no fall to petulance. But
Victoria senses something in it, anyway.

"I'm sorry, Renie. I forgot to tell you. Ilsa is a modiste, very well
known and quite full of herself. Her dresses are coveted. The height of
fashion. Make her welcome. I'll be down when I'm down." Victoria
raises one pale hand, as if she wanted to wave Renie away, but the torpor
of daylight stills that motion.

"Oh. Sorry, ma'am." She pulls the door shut.

That evening in the library, Ilsa positions Victoria on top of a small
kitchen stool and drapes her in fabrics, her mouth full of pins, a grease
pencil behind her ear.

"I am not believing the heat," she mutters. Any discomfort is an
affront. "I have never felt anything like it. Paris certainly has never been
this hot. Mencken called it 'the miasmic jungles of Arkansas' over a
century ago and it seems not much has changed. Very inclement."

"*Non calor sed umor est*," Victoria says and adds, at their questioning
looks, "Boarding school."

"Muggy," Renie says.

"What?" Ilsa asks, frowning at being addressed by the help.

"A shibboleth of the American south. I think it means 'Moist and
buggy,'" Victoria says.

"Yes. Very." Ilsa looks around. "This would be much easier for you if we had a mirror."

Victoria smiles at the kneeling woman. Renie knows that smile. It's a mask, a meaningless phrase, a vocalized pause writ in flesh. It means nothing but it is something the old woman thinks she needs to do. "I trust you, dear. I know you will do a marvelous job."

Bruhn returns her smile. "You know, you really have an amazing figure. You are very slim. I could use you on the runways of Paris."

Bruhn stays for three more days, working through the heat, her portable sewing machine breaking the silence of the library. Renie grows weary of the company, sleeping only in the wee hours of morning, but otherwise listening for Bruhn's movements in the house, waiting, should she try to come upstairs and find Victoria in her suite. Renie brings her coffee, sandwiches, gin. Bruhn acts as if she was a British Colonial in Calcutta; demanding fresh limes, tonic, and Tanqueray and applying DEET to herself like lotion. Cigarettes and soup, American magazines and newspapers.

"Eh?" Bruhn looks up at Renie's appearance, placing a tray of finger sandwiches at the modiste's elbow. "Oh, it is you."

She leans away from the sewing machine and stretches her back. Maroon, black, and silver bolts of silk lay strewn about the room.

"Renie? Is that your name?"

Renie nods. It seems strange that this woman has ignored that fact the countless times Victoria has addressed her in one another's company. Bruhn picks up her coffee and sips.

"Let me ask you a question. Yes?"

"Okay."

"How can this woman afford all of this? Eh? My service alone is costing her quite a bit. I am not inexpensive. Quite the opposite."

Renie touches her neck, wiping sweat away. "I don't know. I've heard her father was fabulously wealthy. A Coke distributor, I think. I don't ask questions like that."

"And rightly so. No matter. Her check has cleared and the money is in my account. I am not worried. Just curious."

Before Bruhn leaves, she presents Victoria with a dress, simply cut, with elegant lines and dramatic accents. Victoria spends hours in her room, alone, the night growing late, putting on the dress. When she finally reappears downstairs, Renie's breath catches.

"Your posture is horrible," Bruhn says.

Victoria straightens her back, puts her shoulders together. Renie thinks of the incorruptible flesh flexing and stretching over bones, like the musculature of a cat. This does not satisfy Bruhn and she pushes her glasses further back on her nose. "The dress needs to be worn correctly. Can you wear *this* dress?" All of the world is a gauntlet to her, Renie thinks. Every moment a challenge. How would it be to live like that, all the time? So tiring.

Bruhn leaves the next day. Renie listens as the car diminishes down the drive, the crunching sound of gravel under wheel fading. Distasteful as the woman was, and tiresome her duties while she was a guest, the company had been a relief. She loves Victoria. She faithfully keeps her safe. But her heart betrays them both—she wants for human contact. For something more than just being a witness, a sentinel.

Summer grows late, the long days grow shorter. Cooler. The pecan trees that line the Pemberton estate soon drop their heavy load onto the ground, the brown and black shells lying everywhere. Renie watches the brown squirrels grow fat among the trunks.

Renie orders a cord of firewood and ends up chatting with the burly delivery men until at twilight, standing near the side of the house, watching them stack the wood. Strong country men, they drawl their words and speak in incomplete sentences.

"This here wood. White Oak. Aged this stuff all year so it should be just 'bout right, right about now."

"Aged?"

"Yep. Fresh cut wood smokes something horrible. This stuff'll burn clean. You stay out here alone?"

She blushes, smiling. "No. I'm just the caretaker. I look after—" She looks toward the manse.

The man pushes his baseball cap back on his forehead with one thick, dirty finger. "That right? The old white one?"

"What?" Some people just blurt things out, saying whatever occurs to them. She wonders if the man has been drinking. His cheeks are flushed, his hands, uncertain.

"Aw. Nothing. Just when we was kids, that's what they called her. Said she was white as chalk, walkin' the halls. Can't believe she's still kickin' around."

Renie is startled at the thought. She smiles but keeps the laugh tamped away. "She's still here. About to be a hundred."

The man whistles. He touches his cap. "Whoo. Imagine that. Well, tell her thanks for the business. And hopefully we'll be seeing you next fall." He turns away. "You ladies be careful. A couple of folks have gone missing round Gethsemane. Folks are nervous. Make sure you lock up at night."

"Yes. Of course. We will."

She writes the man a check on the hood of his truck, still ticking with the heat. He kisses the paper and winks at his boy; they climb inside the pickup truck and rumble away. Renie turns back towards the manse, lighthearted.

Victoria stands on the porch, a black figure, watching her.

"Ma'am. Are you all right?"

Victoria remains silent, unmoving. Renie runs to her.

"Is everything okay, ma'am?"

"Have you taken leave of your senses?"

"No. I—"

"Speaking to these...these day laborers? You are supposed to be inside, taking care of the household. When I woke, I called for you and got no response."

"Oh, ma'am, my apologies." Renie bows her head and kneels on the ground in front of Victoria. She reaches for the older woman, stops her hands in their forward motion. Victoria only allows touch by invitation.

Renie looks up to Victoria's face. It's still and white, mouth open. She stands there, her elbows tucked against ribs, her hands held loose, long nails pointing down. The old woman's mouth opens and closes; it's red, her mouth, and wet, and she pants in the twilight.

"Ma'am, I am truly sorry. It will never happen again." This is how it ends, you are unwary for just a moment, and everything comes unravelled. "Please forgive me."

The old woman says nothing, and her silence stretches tight enough to snap.

Renie, still on her knees, desperate for something to keep Victoria from exploring her anger. "We received some mail today. Letters. From overseas."

"What? And you didn't wake me?"

"Ma'am, the firewood was delivered. I needed to deal with the delivery men. I just got carried away talking to them. They reminded me of—"

"Forget about your old life. If you don't pay attention to your responsibilities, you might lose your position in this life, now. I will tolerate no laxity in the completion of your duties. Your job here is to protect," she brings one long finger to her breastbone. "*My* goddamned life. And how can you do that if you're out making doe eyes at these country fools? Have you prepared for dinner yet?"

"No, ma'am."

"Ah, so I must go hungry? Is that it?"

"No, ma'am. Please let me correct my mistake. Please, ma'am." She holds up her hands in supplication as if taking communion, wrists forward. Even in the half-light of evening, the fine tracery of silver scars on her wrists are visible.

"I got rid of your predecessor. Don't ever think I won't get rid of you, do you hear?"

"Yes, ma'am. It won't happen again."

Victoria stills. A total stillness, no twitch of flesh or surge of blood. Her eyes remain fixed, open, unblinking. Mouth wet.

"You understand your situation." Her face remains unchanged, but she closes her mouth. Renie watches Victoria, imagining whatever thoughts or emotions might churn there under the surface. She feels her own face is an open book, a signal, a ledger. Victoria's, a cipher.

When she begins speaking again, Renie flinches, as if receiving a blow. "Renie. You're very much appreciated here. I think of you as a child. My child. And if you stray, I will treat you like my child. With punishment. But if you are a good girl, if you perform your duties to me satisfactorily, I will raise you up, and give you a better life. Better than the one you left. Better than what you have now."

Renie weeps. She takes the hem of Victoria's night shift and brings it to her face.

Victoria passes a hand before her face, a gesture of weariness, or a moment's respite from Renie's miserable aspect. "I am hungry. Renie, stand up."

She releases Victoria's shift and rises. Renie's a stout woman, but not unpleasant to the eye. She'd been athletic when she was younger, and the rigors of her household duties have kept her fit—it is a large house, with much to do every day, every night.

"Come, girl." She extends her hand, motioning the younger woman to follow. "Get the letters and prepare for dinner. I forgive you. But do not let it happen again."

She turns and, taking small delicate steps, walks into the shadows.

Renie follows.

Victoria,

I would be honored to attend your birthday party. A hundred years! How quickly time slips by us.

Since it has been many years since we have all gotten together, I think it might be time for a family council.

I must admit, I had to do some research to discover more about Arkansas, but it seems the perfect little backwater for a get-together. Hopefully we won't draw too much attention from the locals.

I have recently returned from France, and learned some delightful culinary techniques there. Amazing really. I've gotten even fatter, if you can imagine.

Sincerely,
Andrei

It's October, and the rain never seems to stop. The trees drop their leaves and the estate becomes a bog, water drenched and muddy. The nights grow cold.

Victoria sits, blanket draped over her knees, in the library near the fire, shuffling through RSVPs.

Renie comes in, eyes down, looking at a stack of paper. Victoria does not like computers; the rattle and hum of the printer disturbs her. She's a displaced person—removed from her era. Renie keeps their business center behind the kitchen, in the walk-in pantry. There is so little food in the house, anyway, and Victoria hasn't entered the kitchen in years.

"Ma'am. I'm sorry to interrupt, but I will need you to make a decision on flowers. This grower can provide three hundred phalaenopsis, or two hundred coelogyne pandurata. By January the fifth, he assures me. He says that the phalaenopsis are hardier and can survive the shipping from Costa Rica with far less loss. However, the pandurata is very rare, and he is the only grower within a thousand miles."

"I adore the phalaenopsis," Victoria says, resting the correspondence in her lap. "However, my family is insatiable. Epicures and snobs, the lot of them. And even at my age, I cannot stand them to look down their noses at me." She sniffs, casting a glance towards the dark window, pattering with rain. "It's a weakness, I know. Caring. They think me a bumpkin living here." Stillness again. Complete. She does not blink. She does not breath. Renie watches her.

"No," Victoria says, finally. "Let us go with the coelogyne pandurata. Like the bone china, it will be a wonderful addition to the conversation. Conversation is all that we have, save one thing. The flower's dark lip might remind Andrei of his black heart. Black orchids for blackguards."

"Very good, ma'am. I will place the order."

"Wait a moment, Renie. I have been reviewing the responses. It seems Andrei has been canvassing the family and we must expect more than we have prepared for. This means we must sleep thirty-five people."

"Where will we put them all?" Renie asks.

"They'll have to put up with some close quarters. I need to ask you to relinquish your chambers," Victoria says.

"Of course. Will members of your family have their own, um, butlers?"

"Butlers serve the house. Valets serve the man. Andrei has always traveled with one, usually as insufferable as him. Let me see. William, Cross, Dieter and Eduardo keep valets. We can safely assume all of the women will have maidservants."

Victoria takes a moment to consider the situation—a blank expression, staring into some middle distance only she can see. "I will write the remainder of attendees and inquire as to their arrangements. We will need to purchase the Alexander home to lodge the valets and maidservants."

"Purchase? The Alexanders? I don't think their farmhouse is for sale."

"Everything is for sale. Sometimes it takes numbers for people to realize how much or how little their possessions matter to them. Don't worry about the Alexanders. I will deal with them. But we still need to attend to the extra guests. I think it's time to update the old carriage house."

"It's in a horrible state now. It looks like it's been years since anyone lived there," Renie says.

"It has. Twenty years or more. But it was once quite comfortable and served as an inn when I was a girl. My father acquired it long ago. As much as I dislike the idea, you will need to have some contractors come make it ready." Victoria holds up a hand, palm out. "Yes, I know it will be expensive. Short work often is. And we will need to take inventory of the furniture, purchase new linens. And drapes. Heavy drapes."

With that, she takes her correspondence back in hand. "Please take care of the carriage house repairs and I will deal with the Alexanders. And remember, no dallying with the help. I do not like outsiders walking about freely on the grounds. Make sure they understand that they are not allowed anywhere except the carriage house."

"Yes, ma'am. I will."

January draws close. Christmas passes and Victoria and Renie exchange gifts. Renie purchases a rare volume of the poetry of John Gould Fletcher for Victoria, having heard her speak of the man, his bright wit and dour moods. Victoria seems to be pleased with the gift, though it is always hard for Renie to tell.

Victoria, in turn, gives Renie a simply wrapped box. She opens it slowly. The potential of the present's contents far outstrip anything that might be revealed inside.

It is a pistol.

"This is to protect you while you perform your duties. You never can tell who or what might wish you, or me, harm," Victoria says. A giver of gifts that, in the end, are really intended for the giver.

The gun feels massive in her hands. She's held guns before, but she had forgotten their smell—oil and spices and the memory of fire.

"It's not pretty. A .45 caliber. 1911 issue. They haven't changed this model in over a hundred years. It's inaccurate as hell, but stick it in their stomach or face and pull the trigger, they will fall."

"They? Ma'am, I'm not sure I know what to say," Renie says. She holds it loosely in her hands—it is heavy, and larger than she thinks pistols should be when she thinks of them at all.

"Just say thank you. And keep it near you at all times. We must stay protected," Victoria says.

The Alexanders move away, leaving their house and all the furnishings intact. Victoria signs the paperwork on the week between Christmas and New Years. Her Little Rock lawyer comes by to pick up the papers the next day.

"What does she want the house for?" Florid and dressed in a dark suit, he impatiently waves his hand. "It's just the two of you here with more space than you know what to do with. And I can't understand why she's having the company pay for it."

"Investment, I guess. You'll have to ask her," Renie says. This is a man who needs things explained, but his need is not so great that he won't be satisfied with the simplest. He wants for comfort, and easy answers will placate him.

"All right. Where is she?"

"Oh. I'm sorry, you'll need to make an appointment. I'll let her know that you request a…*face to face*."

He blinks. He knows something of Victoria, then, the consternation at the prospect of speaking with her is so plain upon his face. "No. It's not necessary. Let her buy what she wants."

The construction crew, working furiously throughout November and December, finishes the carriage house on time. Renie watches them through the warped glass windows of the back of the house, the sounds of saws and hammers bright in the winter air. She does not speak with them except in the briefest manner, delivering messages. She doesn't know how, but should she dally with the workers, Victoria would know, even in the height of day under the thin winter sun. But it doesn't stop her from thinking about it, about taking the foreman with the kind face and rough hands somewhere no one could see, to feel him against her.

Renie informs the crew that Victoria will grant bonus checks for each of them, to be delivered on December 31 and only if the house is complete. The men take this seriously.

New linens and drapery, art and other accoutrements, desks, vanities, sofas, chairs, lighting, carpet; all of these are needed. She hires a decorator from Little Rock to finish out the interior of the house before January fifth, the day of the party. A stout little woman with broad, expressive features and short cropped hair presents herself to Renie. She tours the house, looks over the list and nods. Renie asks, "Can you do this? By the fifth?" Holding her breath. The woman smiles and says, "Cheap, fast and good. Pick two."

Renie doesn't sleep, now, her excitement is so great. She spends day and night cleaning, making all spaces ready for the guests. It takes her hours to polish the silver and iron the linens. Methodically and according to place settings she had designed with Victoria, she sets the banquet hall and the library tables with the bone china, Irish silver and cobalt and gold-laced crystal goblets. She arranges the ornate pewter flowerpots, each one awaiting its own orchid. She positions candles about the house, always with an eye toward dramatic light. She lines the driveway with paper luminaria, her personal nod to the fireflies of summer, so long gone, their short lives. She becomes entranced with the ritual of trimming the candle wicks, the smell of beeswax rich and redolent in her hair, her nose. She polishes the wood and waxes the floors. She dusts the books and stocks the firewood bin in the library.

On the fifth the crates begin to arrive. They all hold different shapes. Half marked clearly as orchids, Renie has them placed in the banquet hall. But the other crates, the longer and heavier crates, she does not know how to deal with. One from Germany, another four from England. Two more from Italy. Five from Hungary. Two from Mexico. One from Spain. Two from Czech Republic. Sixteen postmarked from inside the United States. She climbs the great stair, dims all the lights in the hallway, and enters Victoria's room.

"Yes?" Her voice sounds dry and thin, not a little disturbed.

"The orchids have arrived and I've had them placed in the banquet hall."

"Wonderful. How do they look?"

"I haven't had a chance to see. Some other crates have arrived as well, the delivery men wait outside for directions. I don't know what to do with them. One is from England. Two are from Arezzo. I thought we received all of the purchases?"

"Ah. Have them place the other crates in the carriage house garage. They should all fit there. Any more that arrive in the afternoon will need to be placed there as well. Once it is apparent that no other shipments are coming, go make one last round in the carriage house. Make sure all the drapes are drawn and that each room has its own orchid. Also attend to the master bedroom in the carriage house, that it has the gorgeous ceramic pot with the silver filigree. Find the most beautiful orchid and place it there. That is Andrei's room and I do not want him disappointed. Oh, and get a damp towel and wipe the leaves at the base of every flower. They're usually grimy from shipping."

"Yes, ma'am. I'm so excited for the party," Renie says.

Victoria remains silent for a long while, obscured by bed drapes. Her voice, when it sounds, is disembodied.

"Yes, it will be a party to remember. Once you've attended your duties, light the candles and come back here so that we might talk."

Renie hurries off, back down the great stair and out the front door, her heart light and head full of flowers. This is what they've worked toward for so long, now. When the day ends, and the detritus of her orchid arranging is completely erased from the banquet hall, she walks the drive, lighting the candles in the luminaria. Inside, she lights candles. The old building takes on a warm, roseate glow, crystal and silver twinkling. Renie sighs. Then, ignoring her fatigue, her heart beating fast, she mounts the great stair again, excited for the evening.

Victoria sits at her vanity, combing her long white hair. She raises her eyes as Renie enters.

"Ah, Renie, come here."

Renie approaches her, hand in hand.

"Sit." Victoria pats the cushioned seat next to her. Renie sits.

"I have some disappointing news for you."

"Ma'am—"

"Hush. Don't interrupt me." Victoria sets down her brush and looks at Renie. Her eyes are large, Renie sees, and dilated. Her skin bears the fine webwork of age—so fine it appears young and old all at once. She is beautiful, Renie sees. "Brushing my hair is always so much more pleasing when you do it. I know it will be done right. However, I must resign myself to not having you around for a bit."

"What? Ma'am, the party—I've worked so hard," Renie says. It's difficult for her to formulate words, the thoughts careen about her head so rapidly.

Victoria shakes her head, the corners of her mouth turning down. She is pale, as always, but her lips have been rouged, giving her normal pallor a blush of blood.

"I'm sorry, Renie. You are important to me. An investment. This night will be—" Victoria pauses, considering the best word. "Dangerous. I've put too much time into you to have you lost."

"But, ma'am, I beg you. You haven't even had any supper tonight. Let me—" She holds up her wrists to the other woman.

"No, I will sup later, with the guests. Truly, Renie, it is too, too much. They are unruly. They cannot be trusted with you. And we have new members to the family that I know very little about. I must send you away."

Renie becomes quiet. Her throat is raw and tears stand in her eyes.

"Oh, Renie. Child, do not cry. It is not the end of the world. One day you will remain by my side always. Until then, I need to protect my investment. You."

Renie says nothing, because nothing is needed to be said. Victoria has spoken. The older woman places a knuckle under Renie's chin and gently tilts the younger woman's head upward.

"You are very important to me, Renie. I want you to know that."

Renie wipes her cheek. It's a trick of the will that she makes the muscles in her face turn into a smile. A puppet, an automaton, a disjointed collection of flesh, imitating the breath of life. But she can't make the mummery extend to her eyes. She learned this from watching Victoria.

"So. Don't be sad. Go to Little Rock. Check in at the Capital Hotel. It's a beautiful old building. Get your hair done. Get a massage. Then come back tomorrow. All will be well then. Take the station wagon. But I need you to go very quickly. Can you do this?"

Renie remains still for a long while, unspeaking. It's as if the immobility of the elder has possessed her. Only her eyes move in their sockets, the shallow rise and fall of her chest.

Victoria watches her. She is old enough, and changed, that her thoughts have become a wavefront, many things moving at once across time: consideration for the woman before her, examination of the past, evaluation of the probable. An extrusion of probabilities, events of the night. Awareness of the building and grounds around her, suspirant and living, despite the winter chill. The mice in the attic, the slumbering moccasin beneath the house, the vermin in the walls.

Victoria nudges the younger woman's head a little higher with her knuckle. Renie draws her head away from Victoria's cold touch, bows her head. It is an acquiescence, of sorts.

"Good," Victoria says. She's holding her hand up, still, long, sharp fingers before Renie's face. "Take care and I will see you when you get back."

"Happy birthday, ma'am," Renie says.

"So it is my birthday. I had forgotten. Thank you, Renie."

Renie rises, walks to the door and to her room. She packs a small case, the .45, a make-up bag. She walks down the stairs, to the front door, and leaves among the luminaria, glowing in the night's full dark. She looks back at the house for a moment, taking in its refulgence. She doesn't notice dark figures that watch her from beneath the eaves of the carriage house.

In the car, driving away, Renie cranes her neck to take inventory of the items in the bed of the station wagon. Heavy rope, a box-cutter, heavy duty plastic bags, duct tape.

When she reaches the highway, instead of turning right towards Little Rock, Renie turns the opposite direction. Towards Gethsemane.

———

Many years have passed since Victoria Stith Pemberton drew her own bath. Such is the benefit of servants.

She turns the spigot, filling the old claw-footed tub. Her perception takes in the movement in the house, but she is able to focus on the task at hand—preparing her body and mind for the event. She picks up a crystal container of essential oils. The label reads *Litsea Cubeba*. She turns the decanter, letting the oil drizzle in a line from the mouth of the container to the water of the bath. A bright smell fills the bathroom.

Dropping her silk dressing gown to the floor, she stretches, her white skin shining in the light of the room. She touches herself, thinking, I was once beautiful, I was once young and not this dead thing, hidden away. Maybe I can be young again. In the tub, she lets the scented water warm her.

She dresses. With no vanity, makeup is pointless except for her lips. She descends the great stair. The foyer is crowded; white faces with bright black eyes watch her. The dress seems like nothing at all, the breath of air on naked skin, and the family's gaze upon her, as she descends, gives her the sense of shrinking and expansion, all at once. She becomes gargantuan, she becomes infinitesimal. In dreams there is sunlight, and motes hanging in shafts of air, but here there is but candlelight wavering.

She moves through the crowd, nodding her head, acknowledging the stares with a tilt of her head, a hand upon an arm, the slightest curve of her lips. It is her birthday and the graces of her warmth and life linger.

"Thank you so much for attending." She lets Francisco take her hand and kiss it. He is old, time-worn to a smoothness that even his beard cannot hide. A Pizzaro, this creature that had such ruinous effect on the Inca.

"I would not have missed it for the world. I remember when you were just a girl, traveling Europe with your chaperone. They called you a blond then. Not this!" He brings up a pale hand as if to touch her hair, stops. Replaces it at his side. So few of them, the family, and touching without permission is an outrage.

"Milly. Yes." She brings a hand to her throat, as if thinking. It was a gesture Mildred, her chaperone, would have made, so long ago. "I haven't thought of her in fifty years."

Francisco nods his head, his expression reads, yes, this is our lot, to forget all of those who once were warm. A procession of servants marching into the dusk. But he says, simply, "Please allow me to speak with you later, after the council."

Victoria moves on. The family stands, many of them silent, aged beyond the need for talk, familiar enough with each other that the crook of a finger can indicate amusement, or disgust. The incline of a head, fury. The cant of shoulders, love.

Of all them, the loudest is Andrei. His voice floats out among the candle flames.

"…they call it *gavage*. It's a technique for fattening the bird and flavoring the meat. Take a duck, and four or five months before slaughter, you pump it full of a rice and herb mixture twice a day. Supposedly the taste of herbs will suffuse the flesh. Force feeding. I've seen it. It's amazing really, how people come up with these things. And geese and ducks are like pigs, they pack on the weight quickly. In that way they're similar to humans. With the ducks their livers enlarge, from which they make the foie gras…"

She enters the library, sees him standing, back to the fire, speaking to the crowd. A little troll of a man, red-haired with a forked beard and a pot belly. A devil in bespoke.

"...and they say that it flavors the meat. Obviously I did not have the opportunity to try any..."

Laughter. The patter of creatures trying to remember what it is to be amused. He looks around the room, gauging the reception of his words, and his gaze falls upon Victoria. His face twists into a smile.

"And here is the lady of honor. Our Victoria makes her entrance," Andrei says. He has no accent, or he has all accents and they blend into a milquetoast timbre that is indecipherable and bland.

Heads turn towards her. Men and women move forward to greet her.

Victoria claps loudly, inclining her head toward Andrei. "Everyone. I'm so glad you all could attend. Before the night gets too late and the festivities start, please ask your valets and maidservants report to their quarters. I've provided a small map to guide them. It would be best for the security of the guests." She holds her hands together, as if addressing a boardroom rather than a collection of the dead. "Oh, and no driving on the grass."

A few wander away, seeking servants that might have been foolish enough to linger after nightfall. Others remain, a room full of alabaster statues, whispering.

—you must tell us about this mansion. It seems so out of place here in the delta—

—a little bird told me you have a surprise for us, something to do with—

—these orchids. Where did you come by so many? And the black lips. Where did you—

—I can't get over your dress. I can't recognize the label—

Answering the questions as best she can, Victoria notices Cross moving towards the baby grand. He sits at the stool and runs through a scale, ending on a big chord, thrumming. The guests press close around Victoria.

"Let me show you around, now that Cross has taken his place. I am very proud of my home," she says. Sometimes the way she sounds, even to herself, seems pure contrivance. *I have lived one hundred years and eighty of them in this form. I should be riddled with worms, yet this nonsense—this utter drivel—sounds from my mouth. This is an act, an act of culture among wolves so they don't devour me.*

The man at the piano begins to play a piece from *il Teuzzone*, the aria, his long thin fingers dashing up and down the keys.

Victoria hears Andrei exclaim, "Ah! The Red Priest! Marvelous!" She moves away from the sound of Andrei's laughter, a small group of guests following.

She begins: "The Mansion was built of cypress and oak in 1836, the year Arkansas gained statehood, by my grandfather. Lucious Gaius Pemberton. Drinking buddy of Sam Houston. Known as Lucky by his friends. A lawyer and state legislator who, I'm afraid, lined his pockets with kickbacks and bribes." She pauses in front of a large oil painting. "This is Thomas Birch's portrait of him. The old fiend. He shot a man on the floor of the legislature for blocking a bill that would've given him rights to a large tract of public land."

She moves through the rooms, pointing out fixtures, artwork. "Here is a Rembrandt, untitled, lost from the Kunstverein München Museum in 1941. A small piece, but exquisite." Murmurs from the comet's tail of guests, some knowing, some appreciative.

"Remarkable little cache you have here. How did you come by it?"

"I've picked it up here and there, over the years. I have agents working for me," she says.

They pass into the banquet hall. The set table gleams.

Several guests exclaim at the sight of the setting, white china shining with candlelight.

A woman says, "I miss dining. The ceremony."

"You miss the accoutrements. The plates and knives and forks. At the heart of every family member lies a collector," a man responds in a lazy voice. Cultured, bored, and aristocratic and British.

Victoria says, "This china is especially collectible. It was once owned by Dr. William Palmer. Palmer the Poisoner. Bone china."

The British man smiles, but it's another bit of farce: he is not amused, but has enough control over himself to give the politest response. He is far gone from the breath of life. "Yes. Exquisite. Palmer was a sot. Fat gibbering fool."

A ringing sounds and Victoria turns to see Andrei standing with silver spoon and crystal goblet in hand.

He raps the side of the glass hard with his spoon. The sound fills the vaulted space of the banquet hall and moves through the mansion. The guests, dark and silent, move like ghosts toward the sound.

Andrei stands at the head of the table, the light from the candles illuminating the dark hollows of his eyes. He waits, allowing the room to fill.

"My family," he says, smiling to all gathered around him. "We are gathered here today to celebrate Victoria's hundredth birthday. Our youngest has finally come of age. Congratulations, Victoria. You've survived until adulthood."

The crowd responds with light clapping but remains otherwise hushed.

"It being so long since we've all been together—indeed, there are members of the family I have just met—that I feel it is time to do a little administration."

Groans.

Andrei makes a patting motion with his hands. "Settle, *ma famille et amis.*"

He sticks his hand in a pocket and cocks his hip. He looks around at the crowd. For the dead, much of the outward emotion of life falls away—happiness, sadness, anger, surprise—none of these emotions find expression on faces, even if the dynamos of their hearts still churn. Their connection to the fret and wear of life is tenuous.

Except for Andrei. When he smiles, he means it, Victoria thinks.

"Annika, Jorge and Wilhelm. It is time for you to die. Annika, you've been living in Prague for over a century. Now you need to move on. At least for a generation. So the people can forget."

A woman, dark-haired and finely-featured, nods, her face placid.

Jorge, a brooding dark man with heavy whiskers, says, "But I've only been in Sao Paolo for—I don't know—sixty years. Why must I die?"

Andrei turns to stare at the younger man. "You must be joking. Even in Arezzo we've heard of the Saci, the encantado, the bloodthirsty fantasma." He shakes his head and for an instant all of Andrei's joviality falls away, leaving only the blank stare of the undying. "Jorge, you've been indiscreet," he repeats. "It's time for you to die. No arguments. You may have three years to wrap things up."

He turns to Wilhelm, raising his eyebrows in expectation of argument, but Wilhelm demurs. To Victoria Andrei says. "And you, youngling. Do you want to remain here, in this backwater? Or would you move on?"

She raises her head, pushing back her shoulders. "I would leave. I would see the world, now that I am grown."

He claps his hands together. "Wonderful. Please come stay with me in Italy for a few years and we can find a new location for you to dwell. Your first change is very important; make sure you converse with your family here. They have countless years experience at their disposal. They can advise you well, if you would listen."

He turns back to the crowd. "A few announcements and then on to the treat. You all might have noticed Arthur D'Ensemal's absence here tonight. I am sorry to inform you that he has died, true death. Betrayed by his valet."

A normal assembly might gasp, or murmur. Only silence, now. Andrei holds up a razor-sharp finger. "I share your outrage. But I must admonish you all; do not allow your servants too much freedom. Make sure they are trustworthy. Test them. Torture them if you must, but bend them to your will. Yes, yes, Cross. I know this is an old lecture. But I repeat; we are weak. Horribly weak. Sun can kill us. We require servants to survive, to protect us while we sleep. Our only strength is our longevity. Our hungers expose us. Do not allow yourself to become complacent. So tonight, I will workshop with you all individually; we will find ways together to make us all safer.

"I will be hearing nominations for membership in the family. Remember, the minimum net worth of the individual must be in excess of a billion. In euros, not American. And it would be nice if we could get some artists amongst us. But I realize that the minimum fiscal requirements preclude those of—" He pauses and tugs on his vest, straightening the wrinkles. "An artistic bent. Of course, you may always sponsor a membership." Andrei smiles at Cross, sitting at the piano. His old valet.

A loud thump sounds, flesh on wood, and the entire family turns unblinking eyes towards the recessed doors that lead past the sitting parlor.

Renie enters into the room, her clothes smudged with dirt and blood. She carries two small forms, one under each arm. She moves like a stevedore on a wharf, heavy laden and slow. The family parts, silently, as she enters. Once she is among them, she spills the children to the floor.

Her face fills with a sort of ecstatic joy, eyes moving from each pale, reflective face to another, as if she were in a gallery looking upon unmoving paintings.

Her hands go to her hair, and try to repair the unruly mess, tucking a strand behind her ear. Her eyes fall on Victoria.

Of all the faces, Victoria's resembles a painting the least. Her fury stands clear; eyes narrowed, jaw taut, neck ticking with inaction.

"What have you done? Brought children here?" Victoria says.

Andrei laughs, and not the feigned mirth of the dead. Victoria whips her head around to glare at him. He shrugs, crossing his arms.

She turns back to Renie. "I told you to *leave*. And now you've jeopardized everything: me, the party. Yourself, you—"

"I just—I just wanted to be here with you, ma'am. I've worked so hard. Look, I brought you, everyone, a present," Renie says.

She gestures at the unmoving forms on the floor. She's trussed and duct-taped the children solidly; their fat flesh strains at the bindings.

Victoria kneels. She feels their throats.

"You best hope to whatever god you hold dear that these children still live."

Victoria stands. She lets the calm stillness of death settle upon her. She straightens the front of her dress and looks at Andrei. Arms crossed, he gives back nothing.

She speaks, her voice raised, so that all the room might hear. She looks among the family. Her gaze falls upon the one that might help. "William. I must ask for your help. Fetch your valet. Have these children taken to—" She looks towards Renie, hand out. "Where did you take them from?"

Renie's limbs feel heavy and dumb. She turns from face to face, each one blank. Her gaze comes to rest on the grinning aspect of Andrei, forked beard and full lips.

"Answer, fool!" Victoria says, grabbing the woman's arm. Renie falls to her knees.

"Gethsemane," she whispers. "I took them from Gethsemane."

"William, have your valet fill their pockets with money and dump them in a field to the west. Far, far west. If they remember anything, it will be of an evil woman dressed in white. Don't drink from them, William, I beg you."

William winks at her and walks to the children on the floor. He scoops them up easily in his hands like shovel blades and exits the hall.

Andrei moves to stand by Victoria. He says, "I'm wondering how you're going to handle this, Victoria. It seems that adulthood has already brought you adult decisions."

She stills. "You old devil, you're enjoying the situation. This girl has endangered us all."

"Of course she did. She was ensnared by all the *glamour*." He twists his voice on the last word, making it seem like a curse.

"Nonsense. She disobeyed my direct instructions."

The group of partygoers laugh behind pale hands and whisper. She allows her awareness to expand and contract, like metal heated by sun and cooled by night. She takes a superfluous breath of air.

She turns to Andrei. "Thank you for your concern."

Her attention distills to its essence, wavefront no longer, a single point. Victoria takes Renie's arms in her hands, looks into her face. She moves the younger woman toward the head of the table. With no effort at all she sits Renie down in a chair, her white hands like stone.

"I have told you many times that I value your service, Renie. I truly do. However, I cannot tolerate disobedience. Too much is at stake. Sit here. Do not move," she says.

Victoria raises herself, straightening. She walks out of the banquet hall. Silence then. Renie closes her eyes. There is no sound, no rustling, no stir. She could have been alone, the silence is so complete. Yet when she opens her eyes, pale faces watch her.

One woman comes forward. She's dressed in scarlet and her breasts are pushed up, into a simulacrum of sexual prowess, a motion started so long ago. She pinches the meat of Renie's arm.

"A nice one. Heavy, but fit," she says.

The man with her laughs. "Looks like Victoria has been keeping this one as her own private vintage." He gestures at Renie's wrists.

The woman clucks. "We all have to eat. Who can blame her? Some servants come to enjoy it."

Victoria re-enters the room, bearing a wine bottle. The man and woman move away. Victoria picks up a cobalt and crystal wine glass and slowly twists it in her hand.

"Renie," she says. Before, her voice was an announcement, a play for the watching eyes. But now it softens and there is something there, Renie thinks. Something more. "I am glad you have been able to join the party. It's only fitting that the one who worked so hard on the preparations is able to attend."

Victoria pours a glass of wine for Renie and places it in front of her.

"Drink. It will help."

Renie takes up the glass in her hand. It does not tremble.

"You're drinking Chateau Cheval Blanc. A 1953 vintage. My father put twenty cases of these down. This bottle is the last. What do you think?"

Renie touches glass to lips, swallows, and the rich wine paints strange and complex colors in her mouth, on her tongue.

"It's…it's good," she says. She wishes she could say something more poetic, but the pale faces watch her. "It's almost more than I can—" She stops.

"Drink," Victoria says. The woman drinks down the glass. Victoria pours another for her. "Drink."

When the bottle is empty, Renie's eyes bead and tears run down her cheeks. She is unsteady.

Victoria pulls a chair near her and sits. She leans in close, her mouth next to Renie's ear. "I'm horribly disappointed. I can't believe you'd disobey me in front of all of my guests."

She falls silent, raising her lips to show sharp, triangular teeth. It's but a moment, and then it's gone.

"I'm not a monster, child. I won't slit your throat because you've disobeyed me. But I must punish you in front of everyone here. Do you understand?"

Renie nods; it's all she can ask her body to do. Wine has thickened her tongue. "I'm sorry ma'am. I just wanted to be a part of—"

"Oh, you've gotten that wish." Victoria pushes back, away from the table, and stands. She rests a hand on Renie's shoulder.

Silence again, though excitement blooms in the stillness.

Victoria says, "This is my decree: You will feed whomever wishes, until they are sated. And if you live, tomorrow night we will flee this place." She shakes her head. The corner of her mouth pulls down and the expression is not feigned. Victoria says, in a lower voice, "We had not much time here to start with, but you ended our life here when you brought those children through the front door."

Renie bows her head in acquiescence, and raises it again, to look at all of those gathered around her. She smiles. She is warm and full of life, and it is nothing to let her rapture fill her expression. As easy as breath.

"Excitement? Now?" Victoria asks.

"It's what I was made for, ma'am. I serve," Renie says.

Victoria shakes her head in wonder. "You surprise me." She leans close and whispers in Renie's ear. "Fight then. Fight us all. Stay alive through the night."

She looks down on the woman's face. She remains like that for a long while, watching the luminous pulse of life in her.

Victoria turns toward her guests.

"Everyone! I would like to introduce you all to my maidservant and my valued friend, Renie Littlefield."

The crowd moves towards the table, encircling it. Bright black and pale blank faces circle them. Andrei stands at the other end of the table, hands in his vest pockets, a sole figure grinning over the black blooms of orchids.

"Renie has been my steadfast assistant in the planning and organization of this party. She has graciously offered to provide supper for us all." Victoria inclines her head towards the banquet, motioning the guests to pick up their glasses.

Victoria's hand finds a knife from the table and leans forward to take up one of Renie's hands. The blade digs into her wrist and blood flows.

"Quickly now, bring your glasses. Tonight we'll be civilized."

Cobalt glasses come to hands and guests move single file past Renie, each one stopping to take a measure of blood. The family doesn't need much, though appetite, appetite always varies. Renie watches them as they pass, life ebbing. This one dark, this one with yellowed eyes. Another with a scar, whetting lips. The woman who pinched her. The red priest with the forked beard. Victoria.

When the last glass is red, the family returns to their places, like a processional echoing liturgy, each bit of crystal a monstrance.

Andrei says, "Here's to our birthday girl." He raises his glass. "To Victoria! Happy birthday. May you have a thousand more."

Victoria smiles, showing her teeth to Andrei, making her face respond in the mummery of life. She raises her glass, crimson crystal above the bone-white china.

"And to Renie. Live, girl. *Live,*" Victoria says.

She drinks.

THE DREAM OF THE FISHERMAN'S WIFE

IN THE afternoon, when the café and the cobbled lane beside the quay empties until the ships come back in, she stands in her apron among the empty tables and stares out past the breakerwall, beyond the rocky shore tangled with bladderwrack and snarls of trawler's nylon nets, to the sea.

Flights of gulls wheel and bank in a grey sky while a trio of boys yells good-natured profanity at each other as they roust an upturned skiff from the shore, flip it, and push it into the foam.

"Maebe, here comes Lancelot from the visitor's bureau," Laura says through the open window, hands full of dishes but standing in the interior dining area. Laura's wide face gleams in the low half-light of the afternoon, and she gives a grin to Maebe that is as playful as it is lurid.

"Now's the time. And he *is* handsome."

Maebe follows Laura's gaze down the lane, past the bright confections of trinket and t-shirt shops, past the tourists wearing garish shirts adorned with flowers that only bloom under the brighter sun of latitudes thousands of miles away.

The man from the visitor's bureau grins at Maebe and waves. When he gets close enough, he calls her name.

She waits.

He orders a Diet Coke and a salad with grilled chicken and sits with his back to the quay, so he can watch her, watch the way her body moves under her clothes, the heaviness of her hips, the sway of her breasts.

"Sit with me."

"That's not a good idea."

He's blond and lean and has the light, translucent fluff on his cheeks that shows where the razor didn't touch, high on his cheek. He wears white tennis shoes with no socks, khakis, and his collar up in a way that makes her want to cry for his desperation. He's a creature of sun and surf and boarding schools. He loves to sail.

"Sit with me."

Laura grins from inside and shuffles off to dump dishes in the sink. Maebe sits with the man, looking beyond him to the boys and their skiff. They have moved out past the breakers and now the skiff bobs on the great face of the sea.

"I love this weather. Gusty. You'll be at the regatta this weekend?"

"No."

"No?"

"Not really interested in sailing."

He smiles as if this is the most amusing thing he's ever heard. He looks at her hand. The one with the wedding band.

"You've worn that as long as I've known you."

"I was married. It's hard to forget."

He sits, silent, sipping his drink. But he doesn't look upset by her statement, just curious and wanting to let the matter pass, like a cloud scuttling across the face of the sun.

But she looks at him and says, "He went down to the sea."

The man smiles, again, at her antiquated way of saying death by drowning.

"Will you meet me tonight?"

Maebe stands and goes into the dim interior of the café and gets his salad. He's still smiling when she places it in front of him and smoothes her apron. She sits again and turns her face back toward the lane, the breakerwall.

He eats with the exuberance of the young. When he's done, he wipes the corners of his mouth with a napkin and says, "You won't meet me?"

He's asked every day for the last two weeks and Maebe has always replied the same way. "No, thank you. But you're very kind to ask."

The boys in their skiff have disappeared, out beyond everything she knows. The gunmetal clouds shift, and a pillar of sunlight breaks on the surface of the sea, shattering into a million bits. And then it is gone.

It has been too long.

Laura leers at her from inside the café.

"Yes," Maebe says, and takes his hand. "I'd love to see you. Let me give you my address."

He takes her to a restaurant down the coast and pushes the *escargot* and *coq au vin* possibly because he likes it and possibly because he thinks he should. She dips the restaurant's crusty bread into the *escargot's* garlic butter and it tastes like grease and ashes on her tongue. She shoves the food around on her plate with a fork and drinks expensive wine from an oversized glass.

"Most sailors love the Melges 24 class because of its speed and performance, but weekenders love the simplicity. It's so easy to sail." Despite the pomp and ceremony of the French restaurant, he had ordered a beer and drank it from the bottle. He winked at her when the waiter scowled and said, "Hey, it's good beer! Microbrewery."

"So, you go every weekend?" she asks.

"Yah, pair runs. Me and Walter. Have you met him? We've just been sponsored by Trident Sails—I pulled a few strings through the ICVB—so this weekend's regatta means a lot to both of us."

He likes numbers and corporate acronyms. But he is handsome.

He looks at her closely. "The great thing about the Melges is it only takes two crewmembers." He raises his eyebrows and waggles them at her comically. "So whatdya say?"

She sits in her chair, holding the napkin in her lap, staring at him.

"I'm sorry? What?"

"Sailing. Will you come with me?"

It takes a long moment, but she's confident that the horror washing over her doesn't spill onto her face.

"I'm not good in situations like that."

He grins at her, stabs a bit of chicken with his fork and pops it in his mouth.

"You'd be surprised at how easy it all is." He lowers his eyes. "And I'll be there to guide you the whole time."

"You mean, tonight?"

He nods and his smile is gone, replaced with a nervous expression that is ill-suited to his good looks. He worries she will shoot him down.

"We pick a star and sail straight on till morning."

The thought of being out on the dark swell of ocean in a boat makes her shudder. His expression crumbles.

"It's cold in here," she says, taking his hand and hoping it explains her goosebumps. "I was thinking maybe we could go back to my place."

Before, at the restaurant, he'd been forceful. He ordered for Maebe, and was absolutely adamant that the sommelier was tipped amply. He put his arm around her on the walk back to the car. It made her sad, the role he wanted to play, that picture of modern American manhood. He talked of movies, and school, and told jokes that she didn't understand, truly, but she smiled anyway.

But now, at her house, the little bungalow within a stone's throw of the beach, he's unsure of himself. He gulps down the drink she gives him, whiskey, and doesn't quite know what to do with his body in such a small space.

She gives him another drink and he looks at her pictures.

"This your husband?" He holds up an ornate silver frame that had been on the bookcase.

"No. My brother."

"Oh? What does he do?"

"He went down to the sea." She tilts her head at the small cameo on the wall. "There's my husband. Aaron."

The man looks at the photo, her dead husband staring back at him, and he remains there for a long while but eventually, as if he's making a decision, he turns away and goes to sit on the sofa, next to Maebe. He drapes his arm over her shoulder, tugging her in, pressing his side against her.

He smells of tallow and whiskey and a whiff of the restaurant they'd just come from, so it's not unpleasant when she kisses him. At first it's chaste, a simple pressing of the lips together, and she has a moment's worry that he'll go no further, but soon he's exploring her mouth with his tongue, her chest with his hands.

When he's hard, she tugs him by the hand up from the couch into the bedroom.

His naked body bristles and she's fascinated by the perfect triangle of hair on his chest trailing down to his sex. His fingers and tongue feel good on her skin and his cock, pressing so hard against her, feels almost hot to the touch.

But he wants to please her. He traces kisses down to her center, to between her legs. He smiles up at her, his mouth above her most delicate spot, and she cups his face with her hands but eventually lets him go and he splits her open with his tongue.

It has been so long.

When her lips part, it feels like some seal has been broken and the sea is gushing forth past the breakerwall, flooding the whole world, and she tilts her head back and closes her eyes.

The sensations rise and crest and she feels like she's on a raft lost on the face of the dark, infinitesimal and wave-tossed, while something far below in the unseen depths rises, approaching the surface.

She gasps and locks her fingers in his blond hair. He draws up and away, his face glistening. He's on his knees when he grasps her legs and pulls her toward him. She's wide open when he takes his sex in hand, pausing before her portal.

It has been too long.

He doesn't see the shadow that comes into the bedroom and brings the hammer across the back of his skull with a dull crack. Maebe feels an instant of regret that Laura couldn't have waited a few moments longer.

———

They go down to the sea, the sisters, dragging the naked man between them. He still breathes, but his head is distended and blood darkens his back.

At the shore, Laura withdraws the knife and cuts him, twice, on each side of his genitals, slicing deep into his inner thighs. When the tendons are severed, his legs swing outward, splayed like a frog's legs, and blood pours into the surf.

They drag him as far as they can into the waves.

It's only a short wait for Aaron to come in from the sea. He and his brothers walk slowly, waves crashing around them. They're bloated and lantern-eyed, wrapped in skeins of bladderwrack and luminous in the light coming from the moon.

Aaron opens his mouth and water pours out from his sodden lungs, and he looks at the man bleeding out into the waves. He turns to Maebe, slowly.

"Sea bride," he says, his black tongue working like an eel in his mouth. "He comes."

Out beyond the breakers, the ocean rises and Maebe worries that there's been an earthquake calving huge tsunamis to drench the world in darkness. The sea swells and a massive shape broaches the surface and for a vertiginous moment, Maebe thinks that a shelf of land has cracked and been wrenched away from the plate of land that makes the surface of her world, tipped on end from unstoppable tectonic forces. It rises, spanning miles and miles, up to the sky, blotting out the stars, the moon. She looks down at the man, the man who'd been with her in bed. He'd had a handsome face and kissed her so sweet.

Aaron's eyes blink like lanterns being shuttered and he takes her hand in his cold, dead one. A tremendous wave crashes into them all, pushing Maebe and Laura back a few steps but not swaying the men at all.

Her mouth tastes of salt and blood now, and the man from the visitor's bureau is gone, his body carried away on the surf.

"He comes."

They watch the sea rise.

PATCHWORK THINGS

HIS MOTHER kicked his bed in the clockless hours before dawn and told the boy that his Uncle Burl waited for him with a gun.

Franklin rose and dressed, pulling cold boots over near bloodless feet and went to join his mother at the front of the trailer where Uncle Burl waited. She'd lit the first cigarette of the day and stood shiftless in her robe and stared at her brother-in-law.

"He's just eleven, Bee," she said. "Ain't spent a lot of time shootin'."

Burl stood there, overlarge in the trailer's den. He had a thick black beard that rode high on his cheeks and deep on his neck and when he spoke it was thickened by tobacco. He smelled burnt and raw, like a grease-rimed charcoal grill, the boy thought. Burl looked around as if wanting to spit. "Here, Frank." He reached behind him and drew forward a gun case, patterned in green and tan. "Take it out and sight it."

The boy removed the bolt-action rifle from the case and peered through the scope until he could see the dull, magnified reflection of the television in the crosshairs. When Burl was satisfied the boy could hold the gun, he had him tuck it away again.

"I'll have him back tomorrow," Burl said to Franklin's mother.

"He's on break, so you find you're just having a ball, feel free. Keep him the weekend." She turned to her son. "Stay bundled, little man, and listen to Burl."

"Yes, ma'am," Franklin said and followed his uncle out into the freezing air of the trailer park.

In the truck, Burl unscrewed the cap on a soda bottle, spat thick brown saliva into it, and screwed the lid back on. They drove north, and east, away from the lighted roads, the strip malls and fast food restaurants, onto the highway. The radio went from the dim strains of guitar to the atonal hiss of signalless static and back again as townships and smaller municipalities passed in the pre-morning darkness. Franklin looked out the window at unlighted windows where farmers and their families slept still.

Soon the highway was gone and the wheels crunched on gravel and then the cab rocked, swaying heavily in the rutted and uneven path, winding back and forth through the pine and cedars, down a rotted hillside until the river deltaed out in an alluvial plane. Past furrowed river-sweetened fields and pastures where cattle stood dumbly watching the truck headlights pass. Canebrakes and sloughs stood steaming in the frigid air, rotting matter casting up vapor and warmth. The truck wheels cracked ice.

"Here we go," Burl said. "The cypress bottoms. Don't worry, it won't be wet, we ain't had rain in a month." The boy did not tell the man he had no expectations of any sort, neither moisture nor the lack of it, except he assumed he would have to shoot the gun at some point.

They stopped and got out, breath pluming on the air. Burl took his gun out of the backseat of the truck, uncased it, and loaded the magazine with shells and did the same for the boy. He led the way into the slough. The ground was dry and springy, covered in cypress fronds. They walked through the balled roots of the trees down the declivity where the ground turned mucky and then up and out into the piney woods leaving footprints in the morning's frozen dewfall. The boy was cold after the first half-mile but he was too scared to tell his uncle about his discomfort.

They found a plywood deer stand built unsteadily against a thick pine and Burl stood by it, looking expectantly at the boy.

"Well."

Franklin said nothing.

"You climb up. You watch. When you see a deer, you shoot it." Burl tapped the boy on his chest. "The heart. Put it there. It don't matter if it's a buck or doe. Either way, you shoot it. Does eat better, bucks make better trophies."

Burl took the gun from the boy's freezing hands. He flipped the safety off and on. "Fire. Can't fire. Right?"

"Right."

The boy climbed up into the blind as Burl watched. When he was seated and the rifle poked out of the blind's window, the boy's uncle moved off to find his own blind.

Sitting was worse than walking. The blood stilled and the chill settled in. He watched the sky lighten and the pine needles scrabbling at the sky. The waking land went from grey-gloomed and monochrome to golden and black. Birds moved among the branches.

The boy thought he might sleep, but his hands and feet were too cold and the blind's wooden plank seat would not let him lie down. He feared what his Uncle Burl might say if he found him asleep, too, and not vigilant like his father would have been had he not been so long dead. His father slept, so he could not.

He held the gun with one hand, the muzzle resting on the blind's view of the wood, and blew open-mouthed onto the other.

When the movement came, the boy almost did not recognize it. One moment there was matted needles and deadfall and bark and the red-raw clay of bank, and then there was snapping twigs and fur. Liquid animal eyes blinking, tremulous and halting.

Franklin put his face to the scope and thumbed the safety off. He found the shape in the sights. It was separate from himself, it was not him. He thought about the shooters he played with the overbright hallucinatory colors and the exultant soundbites that came with each headshot or deathmatch kill and the boy squeezed the trigger. The rifle boomed and jerked against him. The scope punched back into his eye and pain bloomed there on his cheek.

His face was swelling as he climbed down from the blind and his right eye was swollen shut. The blind, the boy thought, the half-blind. The metal of the ladder was cold, so the boy leaned against it, touching his outraged cheek against the frigid metal until the throbbing died down. When he heard Burl coming toward him, he righted himself and wiped his face on his sleeve and hoped his uncle had not seen his tears.

"Hope the deer looks worse than you do," Burl said coming nearer.

"Yessir."

"Where is it?"

The boy pointed the direction of the shot. Burl led the way. The boy followed stumbling.

Burl picked up the pace when they spotted blood, his breath coming fast and heavier. Franklin could feel his uncle's excitement. He felt nothing except the cold and the tightening skin of his face.

His uncle slowed and then stopped. "Goddamn," he said. "Goddamn, it had to happen on your first go."

The boy came around to see the carcass. A red and white skein of entrails lay snarled on the ground, blood in drops and spatters. A slick smear of fecal matter. And then the body.

It was smaller than the boy would've thought. It lay twisted, its back legs jutting in a different direction from its forelegs.

goddamn goddamn goddamn Burl kept saying under his breath *one of these fuckin' things come to curse us come come to come*

It looked like a buck, but the creature's horns were shiny black and chitinous, like scarab legs jutting away from its skull. Its face was probing and miserable, with a short but prehensile mouth for searching out sustenance on the earth, maybe, Franklin thought, like an anteater or elephant or something. It had dun fur across its chest that sloped away to a belly with rough-nippled skin that transitioned to scales near its sex that was not apparent, at least to the boy. Its feet ended in flat rounded pads. It had a naked tail like a rat.

It was beautiful.

"Ain't got my lighter," Burl said. "We got to burn it. Every bit." Burl's face was tight and uncomfortable.

The boy fell to his knees and put his hands on the creature's side, one hand on the fur, the other on the bubbled skin, milkblue with veins before the scales crept up.

"Don't touch it, Frank," Burl said. "Don't think too much on it, neither. There's deadfall over there. Get some kindling." Burl turned to walk back to his truck. "Much as you can, pile it up right here by the damned thing."

The boy went to the fallen trees and loaded his arms with branches and twigs and returned to the dead thing, dropping them with a hollow rattle, and then to the pile and back again.

When it was stacked high enough, he fell to his knees and sat looking on the creature. It was a living collage of a deer, cobbled piecemeal together to fill out a silhouette. He put hands on each bit of the cooling carcass, a directionless traveller touching unknown landscapes on a map. The scarab-horns were cold and hard. And a spike of them lay in the pine needles, broken with the creature's deathfall. He picked it up and held it in his hand, he brought it to his nose and smelled it. He put it in his pocket.

Burl came back with a wad of yellowed newsprint and a shovel and a bottle of whiskey that the boy recognized immediately was for drinking rather than some sort of accelerant. Burl was dissatisfied with the amount of wood the boy had gathered so they both resumed collecting kindling and branches. The sun was higher now in the clear, brilliant sky and their breath burst luminous with their exertion.

The firewood stood chest high on his uncle when Burl was content. He put the newsprint on the ground and teepeed kindling around it. He lit the newsprint and fed smaller branches to the fire as it grew. When it was large enough to sustain itself, he drank from the bottle and stood and approached the creature, nudging it with his foot.

"Where did it come from?" the boy asked.

"Where does anything come from," his uncle said.

"A family. A mom and dad."

Burl laughed at that. "Wish that were so."

"What is it?"

"A punishment, maybe, I don't know." He drank from the bottle again and looked at the boy. "They come through, sometimes, from wherever they're from. You ever seen another one, you don't shoot it, hear?"

The boy nodded, looking at the thing on the ground. "Why do we burn it? Shouldn't we—"

"You burn it. Always," Burl said flatly. "They don't come without a reason." He squinted at the boy, like he looked at him for the first time.

The boy looked around at the piney woods. "Does it only happen here?"

"No. Your daddy shot something up on the Missouri border when you were a baby."

"So this happens everywhere?"

"Don't know," Burl said. "But it happens."

He fell silent then and fed the sticks to the flames.

When they put the thing on the fur caught first. The heat was tremendous and their breath had disappeared. The boy expected the carcass to go up in a great conflagration but it did not. The fur blackened and cast off noxious smoke, then the flesh and scales began to char. The tail was consumed first and then the ears and chitin horns seemed to melt. When the fur was gone, the air smelled of meat and cinnamon and dust.

They kept burning it until it was an unrecognizable husk, feeding more and larger logs on it until the day grew long and shadows pointed east from the standing trees. They buried the remains in a shallow grave.

Back in the truck, Burl said, "Taking you back to your momma. No need to tell her about this." He sucked his teeth, thinking. "She wouldn't believe you, anyway."

⁓

He hunted often after that, more than Burl was willing to take him. He saved and bought a bike, and then when he was older, a dirtbike to get to the national forests and woods. He worked at the Wal-Mart and took the employee discounts on ammunition. At night, when his mother fell asleep in the blue-light of the trailer's television, he'd take out the chitin fragment and put it to his eye, put it to his mouth, and kiss it.

Until one day he couldn't find it. He searched the trailer, his pockets, and the grounds around the trailer, not in frenzied juvenile desperation; just a slow methodical search to make sure it was truly gone. It didn't feel separate then. He could still feel the smooth cool surface of the scarab horn.

He was older then and it was clear he wasn't going to the university in Fayetteville, since he was good only for killing animals and skinning them or inventory at work. Customers found him strange, even at Wal-Mart. He passed his GED.

He killed a squirrel with a snake's head and lizard's legs. He killed a sparrow with faceted black eyes and skin like tanned leather.

His mother's smoking settled into the morass of emphysema and took its wheezing dolorous toll and he moved the television into her bedroom by the oxygen tank and in the evenings and his days off he roamed the woods and deltas, shotgun or rifle or fishing rod clutched in rough hands, mute and dumb to the opulence of cypress or birch. He had no interest in the vault of nature except to the reclamation of that strange, marvelous creature he'd killed when he was eleven.

One day in spring he fished the shores of Dry Lake off the White River in his johnboat and pulled from the water's muddy depths a fish whose likeness he'd never seen before in book or experience and he worried, as he held the scaleless writhing thing, that he might should've gone to university because maybe he was just too ignorant of biology to know if this was one of the ones Burl had said come through for a reason. And then it unfurled vestigial wings and chittered at him in imitation of human speech.

He cleaned it as best he could, working his knife around the strange territories of foreign anatomy, and placed it in the cooler among beer cans and bass, bream, and crappie.

He pulled the boat to the shore and stepped out. He stripped down until bare-assed and goosefleshed except where his skin had hardened into black chitin or tanned leather. He waded into the waters, mud curling between his toes and each step releasing the stink of rotted fish. He dove and dove, diving down, his hands searching mud and sodden logs that disintegrated with his touch. Whatever door had opened, the boy could not find it in the murk.

He fried it when he got home and ate what he did not feed his mother.

She was bedridden now, sucking at the oxygen, and he washed her with sponges and inspected her nude desiccating flesh carefully for whatever change the winged fish might bring, but none came to her. But his appetites changed and his nipples disappeared under chitin. He had a thin webbing of flesh between his toes and between pinky and ring fingers that he would cut with his pocketknife and bandage so that no one at work would notice. When he looked at himself in the mirror, his eyes were beginning to turn fragmented and geometrical. His tongue had a hard ridge down the center and Franklin did not know what that signified.

After his mother died, drowned in the sea of her body, he called his uncle Burl.

"Momma's gone," he said.

"I'm sorry, Frank," Burl said. "When's the funeral?"

"It's come and gone."

"I'm sorry, then, I missed it."

"Everyone missed it," he said. "Except for me and the preacher."

"Shitty way to go, son, with no one there to witness it."

"Yeah," Franklin said. "But I was there." He was silent a long while. "Deer season this weekend. First day. How 'bout we go back on up to them piney woods you first took me."

Burl didn't say anything but the boy could hear him breathing. Finally, his uncle spat into some container and said, "This about that thing we burnt up there?"

"No," the boy said. "I got run off the Pemberton woods last season and the national forest will be half orange."

"All right. I guess it wouldn't hurt. I could use some meat."

He picked him up at the trailer again. It was afternoon this time and there was a wet dog in the truck's cab with them due to rain.

"You selling the trailer?" Burl said, noting the sign outside the front door.

Franklin nodded. "Can't afford it no more, now Momma's gone."

"She didn't leave you anything?"

"Nothing to leave."

"What'll you do?"

"I'll make do."

"You can stay at my place, I figure. We've got a spare room."

"Thinking about the Army."

Burl held the steering wheel in both hands but looked at his nephew.

"You ain't the Army kind, Frank. Sleep when they tell you, shit when they tell you, shoot when they tell you."

"Just thinking about it."

"Stay at my place."

They spent the night in a broke-down sharecropper's shack near the bottoms, cooking beans on the generations-old cast iron stove under a sky that peeked in through the rafters and holes in a tin roof. In the morning they hunted the woods, each one choosing blinds out of sight of the other. Burl took a doe, and Franklin was content to dress it for him. He raised it up by its hindlegs on a crossbar and spilled the viscera on the ground and then proceeded flaying the beast. Clean, they packed it in the big cooler with ice.

"Saw you eatin' them strips from the deer," Burl said that night at the fire.

"Goes down better with some seasoning, I guess. But yeah."

"Venison needs to be cooked."

The boy didn't tell him his stomach could digest flesh never born in this world. Burl watched him as they ate.

"You take the same blind tomorrow?"

The boy nodded.

Burl drank whiskey from a flask. He handed it to Franklin, who handed it back.

"I figure you're old enough now," Burl said.

"Don't sit right with me," the boy said.

"You eat raw meat but can't take whiskey."

The boy woke in the sleepless hours before dawn and rose from his bedroll and collected his gun, his ridged tongue thick in his mouth. The Visqueen tarp they laid over rafters to keep out the rain stirred and rustled with his movement. He stepped over his uncle and made his way to the blind in the dark and waited for the world to lighten.

This time it was bigger, bear-shaped, hulking, and the boy had killed enough things not to let his surge of excitement race his heart into unsteadiness. He sighted and shot.

Down the ladder at the base of the tree he paused and rested his face on the metal again, cold against his cheek. Then he turned and walked to the fallen creature.

He'd opened it up and taken the liver, the patchwork thing, when Burl found him. Red from shoulders to hands and naked, standing over the thing with fur and feather. And this time, many many teeth. Hard to tell where boy stopped and beast began.

"Goddamn, Franklin," Burl said. The boy turned around, black shiny skin creeping up the neck and hands now just an imitation of human. Teeth jutting, cat-yellowed.

"You said things come through for a reason," the boy said, but his mouth was barely suited for words anymore. He extended a clawed finger, pointing where the piney woods grew clustered thick and dark, where bramble and snarls of briarthorne and brush huddled. "Where it came through," he said, a thick jumble. He turned and pushed forward, across the needled forest floor, into the brush and bramble.

Burl raised his gun, sighting the thing in the shape of a boy. Then he lowered the rifle and watched the boy disappear into the woods, as he had with the boy's father.

MURDER BALLADS

(Being an account of the children of *Southern Gods*—Fisk Williams, Lenora
Williams, and Franny Rheinhart)

1960
A Hardfaced Man

IT WAS hate in the end that drove him away from Gethsemane and
Franny and the Big House and out into the world carrying his guitar.
Love was not enough to keep him. Or maybe, it was Franny's love that
meant he had to go.

Only eighty miles away, but across the Mississippi, from the beaten
delta of Arkansas to Memphis. The world of niteries and the stroll of
Beale. The ruin of that street—the pawn shops and drug stores, the
panhandlers and abandoned buildings—none of that could dampen
Fisk's wide-eyed eagerness, new strings on his guitar. He might be cast
out, but there were pleasures outside of Eden. After days of wandering,
sleeping nights in the bed of the farm truck that Miss Sarah Rheinhart
had reluctantly deeded him in a strange, tearful manumission, he
listened to B.B. King on the radio, and Rufus Thomas, and sometimes
even George Klein with all that white bread rock-n-roll that sounded like
food that a chef just learned to spice—the grind, the sway, the drag, the
burn of rhythm and blues peppering the sounds but not enough to Fisk's
tastes. Running through all his saved money from working for the
Rheinharts back in Arkansas, he found himself in a large backroom of
Capitol Loans Pawn full of boxes and bags and hats, radios and toasters
and lamps, record players and televisions, lawnmowers and outboard

motors—all the detritus that washed up on a pawn shop's shores, stacked and tagged neatly, smelling of pomade and engine oil. It was a theater of desperation beneath a single, swinging and naked electric bulb. It was here on a Tuesday night where the local players gathered in the largest space between stacks in the warehouse and picked some, drank some. It was a womanless space by design, a gathering of men to sort out their pecking order. They called it cuttin' heads.

After breathlessly waiting and tuning and sitting uncomfortably in his folding metal chair the likes of which he had only seen at the local Gethsemane church during those infrequent times he had attended, once the men started to play Fisk learned he knew fewer tricks, funs, and licks than he thought. The senior man among the gathering, a gray-haired black man named Vester White, said, "Boy, you go back to the woodshed for a few years and come back when you know how to roll it." He held his guitar loosely, a smile playing around his mouth. "Ain't no stompin' gone come from that noise."

"My daddy was Calvin Williams, played these parts back after the war," Fisk said.

"My daddy was Calvin Coolidge," the old player said. "At least that's what my momma said. Now put up that thang and let us old dogs get to cuttin.'"

Fisk relinquished his chair to another man and moved back, out of the light. He took a seat on a wooden crate and watched from the shadows at the rear of the circle—the area and seating for the "newsies" and "wet boys" and "Arkansas johnnies" (players that had not as yet shown their mettle amongst the known men)—as the older men worked through "Scratch My Back" and "Crazy 'Bout You Woman," the ebullient "I'm Ready" and the morose "Sad Hours." They vamped some songs, making up words on the spot, rolling with it, spinning it, teasing it out.

Fisk watched and listened, avidly, like a retriever straining toward its goal. In the dimness of the back benches, another man sat down beside him and offered him a smoke and a pull off a pint of gin. Fisk took both, coughing with each. The man was well-oiled and even though his gray wool pants were a little ragged and out of style, they had been expensive once. His dark, burnished skin shone in the dim room's lights but from what Fisk could make out his teeth were crooked and his eyes were jaundiced yellow.

"I knew your daddy," the man said. "A good player, though he stopped coming 'round a good time back."

"You knew him?"

"Sure I did. Sure," the man said. He offered his hand. "Name's Ace, but everybody calls me Hardface."

Neither of those names sounded legit. "Fisk," he said anyway. He took the man's proffered hand and shook.

Hardface whistled. "First time I met anybody named after a damned school." He laughed. "Imagine you ain't enjoying this class too much."

They both turned back to the men playing. Lee Riley had pulled his mouth harp and Junior Black beat time on an apple box. The old dog—the grizzled white-haired guitarist named Vester White who had admonished Fisk to put away his guitar—alternated between hollering and working the fretboard.

When the song came to an end, the men chuckled and joked with each other. A bottle appeared and was passed around; the spritz of beer cans being opened sounded. The close room filled with smoke from cigarettes and cigars.

Hardface leaned close to Fisk, and for a moment Fisk thought he was taking in his scent. *Smelling him.* But then the man said close to Fisk's ear, "This place a graveyard. I know a place with *real* players. And they'll always welcome a new axe, you catch me?"

"Where?" Fisk asked.

"West Memphis," Hardface said. "There's a barn in a field inside the levee and damn, son, the head cuttin' going on there is something to hear."

"Let's go," Fisk said, snapping closed the latches of his guitar case and standing.

"You got some wheels?" Hardface asked.

"Sure I do," Fisk said.

"Let's high step, then."

The other men, Lee Riley and Festus Ward, looked up from their banter seeing Fisk making to leave. "Hey, hey there, boy. Where you making off to? Maybe you'd like to give it another go."

"Naw," Fisk said, embarrassed at the fields and cotton coming through his voice. He stood. "No. We're gonna go on over to West Memphis and play."

"We?" Lee Riley said. "Who's we?"

"Me and Hardface," he said, turning to his companion. Hardface had vanished.

The men's expressions darkened. A couple stood and made their way to the door. Junior Black tilted back his beer and, finding it empty, muttered, "Motherfuckin' Hardface. Gimme that bottle."

Lee Riley approached Fisk. "Hardface, you say?"

"That's right." Fisk looked around among the pawn shop's shelves and boxes. "He was just here."

"Let me tell you something, boy," Riley said when he was close enough for Fisk to smell the stale cigar reek pouring off his jacket. "You don't go nowhere with Hardface." His expression was blank but the intensity in his voice bled through. "Hardface ain't a man..." He paused, thoughtful. "Hardface ain't a *thing* you go to West Memphis with, you catch me?"

"He said there be players cuttin' heads."

"There's players right here, son," Riley said, shaking his head and smiling a little. "Come on up and take a pull off this bottle and show us that song again and maybe we can give you some pointers. And forget about that Hardface."

The older man took him by the elbow and led him back into the light of the single bulb swinging above the men as they once again began stomping their feet and slapping their guitars.

1960

Black Dog

Fisk was out of money in a week, never having had to buy food for himself, or put gas in a truck, or pay for a lodging in which to sleep or wash himself. At the Rheinharts', when he was old enough to move out of the shadow of Alice, his mother, and away from the Big House, they'd assigned him a shotgun shack close to the bayou with running water and his own kitchen, though he still took three meals a day from his mother's kitchen, and pumped gas into his truck from the farm tanks. In all things, Fisk had been groomed for adulthood and the mantle of farm responsibility: Miss Rheinhart had made sure both he and Lenora could read and write and speak well, educated right alongside Franny, despite their race. They were family, in all the ways that a favored black family might find themselves in relation to landowners. It was an uneasy, messy, one-sided love with blurred lines.

He hadn't considered what kind of resources life took on his own. He slept in the bed of the farm truck most nights, hand on his guitar case. There wasn't any work in Memphis for a wide-eyed farmboy from Arkansas now that the sanitation workers' strike was on and every other man was trying to make extra money.

He couldn't face going back to the farm in Gethsemane so when he heard men talking about work back across the Mississippi, he took himself to Horeshone Turpentine Camp thirty miles southeast of Pine Bluff, spending the long days stripping and chipping at the pines.

It was two months before Hardface appeared.

―――

This time, Hardface was a union buster, a slick-haired white man who came slipping up to camp sheened in sweat and soaking his shirtsleeves in the summer heat. Fisk was minding the fire on the turpentine still when he came in, appearing wraith-like in the harsh, acrid smoke, wearing another cheap suit, jacket draped over his arm, and a smile like oil on water. He caught Fisk's eye and winked—that same jaundiced eye as back at the headcutting—and, easy-as-you-please, asked Fisk where he might find the foreman. Fisk, alarmed and surprised, knew better than to tell him, despite his misgivings. It was a way in. A snake working his way into the henhouse, eventually he'd turn his attention to the egg— Fisk. But it was Fisk's good fortune that the foreman was a union man himself and sent Hardface packing.

Months later, when the weather had turned cold and the ground at Horeshone was rust-colored and silent with pine needles and cones and the trees bled into buckets, Fisk found himself in the back forest, miles away from the turpentine still and workhouse and mess when the sun passed into the treeline. He'd been cutting trees with the hooked awl as men had been doing since the eighteen hundreds or even before, when Europe's navies relied on tar, and pitch, and turpentine from the Americas to keep their ships afloat.

Hardface took the form of a black dog, Fisk saw. He did not tarry in the gloaming woods, he simply strode quickly through the failing light, back to his truck, but he still had a mile or so to go among the pines. He was ready for the Horeshone mess hall, and maybe a beer out behind the barracks where the slough met the land. His breath came in big heaves— he smoked too much now, like all the men in this womanless place.

The trees had lit up from underneath with the setting sun lowering in the west, filtering through the pines, and then it all dipped to half-light gray, a ghostwood. That's what Franny had called trees during this time of day. *When the sun goes down, they call that the golden hour, Fisk. But then, for a little while after it,* she had said once in the pecan orchard, *it becomes a moment of ghosts. See the trees? A ghostwood, isn't it?* She had slipped her hand in his and then kissed his cheek, and that was a surprise to him because there were rules against white women kissing black men but they still had their childhood hanging about them in tattered streamers. He thought about the scar that ran the length of her torso, bisecting it. And how maybe she could see a little farther into the dark than he could. But the kiss was sweet and her hand fit his perfectly.

The dog paced him through the woods, a moving shadow, passing behind the trees so that Fisk thought he might be dreaming.

But then it spoke.

1951
A Boy, A Bull, A Book

He was just a fatherless boy ready to become a man. When the one they called Bull came to them adrift upon the waters of the bayou like some character out of the bible, Fisk found himself endlessly fascinated by him. He was as huge as a mountain, and powerful. In Bull, the boy saw something of what he hoped he might become. There were few men— just the Norths, a white family of sharecroppers and fieldhands who worked the land at Miss Sarah's instruction—at the Rheinhart farm and none in the Big House, save for Fisk his ownself.

He would creep into the bedroom where the man lay insensate and look upon him, thinking about his size, the unlined oblivion of his face, the scars crisscrossing his body. His dogtags and tattoos. *USMC. Semper Fi.* But his scars most of all. Puckered wounds on his legs, his chest. Slashes. Knifemarks. Scar tissue on his knuckles. This was before they knew even his name and Fisk didn't realize that, eventually, he would have much worse scars. As would Franny.

It had been the day after Bull had awoken from unconsciousness that Fisk found himself alone in the library. He knew his momma didn't like him in there, and that Miss Sarah had been spending extraordinary amounts of time in the library's confines with the doors shut. He and Franny and Lenora had put their eye to the crack where the pocket doors met and peered in to see what Franny's mother had been up to, but she had only been reading what appeared to be a small, thin, but very old book. A curiosity sparked in Fisk then. His mother, when describing his father Calvin whom he had never met, had called it *the burn* that Fisk always figured was some sort of wanderlust and he thought the way his mother said it maybe it was just *lust* but in him something like that rose up to meet his curiosity and became one. He waited until he was alone and slipped in.

The book was covered in handwritten pages in Miss Sarah's fine hand, but as she had begun to take an interest in his education, it was easy enough to read. Strange stanzas, grotesque couplets. Scratched out words and rephrased sentences.

He pushed the sheets aside and revealed the book itself.

There were words he could not understand, though the letters were clear enough. On the page, ink strokes and intaglios of rough drawings swam in his vision. Wolves with human faces, men and women with the faces of wolves, a bleak field with a skeletal figure pointing to a house, a man cutting out his own eye, his hand, his sex. A priaptic man fornicating with a corpse, its head and limbs chopped away. A gnarled palm with thirty coins. A splayed corpse with a crowned man crawling from the chest cavity. More and more. And like the first time he had seen a guitar played by a field hand, he had simply *understood*.

Any movement of power would cost him dear.

1961
The Black Dog Speaks

"Hello again, young buck," Hardface said through the black dog's mouth.

"Hello yourself," Fisk said, still hustling, arms pumping with the tree awl swinging in his tight grip. Trees bleeding into buckets passed; his day's work, scoring pines. Ahead, a half-a-mile, maybe more, his truck and a 20 gauge with two in the breach.

The dog loped alongside him, gangrel and mean, mouth open and a slathered red tongue lolling out, weaving in and out of the darkening trees.

"I ain't got no problems with you, boy," the black dog said. The shape of the creature's mouth wasn't suited for words, and the slaver and tongue gave the sound of his voice a meaty, slobbered timbre. "I just want the girl. I need you to let me in."

Fisk knew exactly whom the dog wanted. *Franny.* In coming back from beyond and Bull giving up everything to bring her back, she'd become something more. A gate. A tunnel maybe, with a highway running right through her. They were so young then. Fisk couldn't keep what happened to all of them in his head at once. But something devilish, for sure, had occurred. And now Hardface dogged him, literally. Of course the two things were connected. He might not have been able to draw that line except for the glance he'd had of the *book*.

Wolves with the faces of men. Men with the faces of wolves.

He could kick himself for not seeing Hardface for what he truly was in the head cuttin' session. His pride had blinded him.

"Don't call me that," Fisk said. "Ain't no boy, dog." He stopped and turned to the black thing loping in the darkness. He raised the awl. It was hooked for leverage when scoring at the pines surface to let the sap flow, down and down into the buckets and then harvested and distilled to turpentine. But the awl had been dulled by his labors throughout the day. Nevertheless, it was what he had.

"Ain't no dog, boy," Hardface said. "This is just a Sunday suit and I'm just a messenger. A whisker, a pricked-up ear. And I've been sent to find you. For you to present me an invitation. A foot in the door." The black dog had stopped now, when Fisk had. He moved as shadows moved, shifting beneath trees. "And bring you an offer."

"Wouldn't give you Franny for nothing," Fisk said.

"That's good, because I've been told to offer up *something* which is, if you didn't know, more than nothing."

Fisk thought then of Franny and Miss Sarah—Madame Reasoner, his tutor—correcting his grammar, when he slipped into fieldhand speak, as he had just then, conversing with the damned dog. *Franny, I'm still just a black country boy,* he had said, once.

"I wouldn't give you Franny for anything," Fisk said. "And even I don't know where she's…" He almost said *at* but the dog's rebuke of his use of nothing made him wary. *Ignorance is weakness, a dark room it's hard to find your way out of,* Miss Sarah had said once, and that had followed him all the way here. He didn't want to show Hardface his weakness. "I don't know where she is."

The black dog laughed, a strangled sound, halfway between a bark and a gargle. For a moment Fisk could picture the tortured throat and mouth of the creature, contorting to make these human sounds, as if the bones of the jaw and flesh had cracked and reshaped themselves. Were being ripped asunder by their own muscles and connective tissue. It was a sad realization to Fisk that this was a real dog, and Hardface—whatever Hardface was—had infested the dog with something far worse than fleas. Himself.

"You like that guitar, don't you?" the dog said. "We can make it so you can play it like…"

"Ringing a bell?" Fisk said, shaking his head. "I can already play like that." The men at the pawn shop had said, *Go on back to the woodshed,* and Fisk had. Running songs and scales and fingerings every night, even when he was bone tired and stinking of pitch. He did it anyway. That glimpse of the book showed him many things, and most of them were foul and forbidden, but underneath it all was the idea—*nothing good can come without some suffering. You got to sacrifice for what you desire.*

"That right?" the black dog asked. "Well, how 'bout this. When we're done with her, you can have the girl. Her momma. Everything. Down to their skin and bones." The dog licked its chops. Even in the failing light, Fisk could see the silvered saliva pouring from the thing's red maw.

"Don't want nothing from you," Fisk said. *And Franny already is mine,* he thought. *No, that's not right. I am Franny's and we belong to each other in this world that don't want us to be together. If I was with her, now and always, I'd always be a lever they could use to open her up. I guess I still am.* He thought about the dog and the dog's master. "Why do you want her so bad?"

The black dog shifted, growing impatient. "Yours is not to wonder why, young buck. Yours is but to do—"

"Or die," Fisk said.

"That's right," Hardface said, and shifted. It was almost fully dark now. "And since you ain't real talkative right now—"

"I might could offer you an invite if you told me something in return."

"And that's the whys and wherefores? That's what you want to know?"

"Yes," Fisk said.

"Like I said, I'm just the whisker, son, but there's a whole other bigger dog I'm connected to, bucking to get in."

"Get in?"

Hardface, the black dog, was just a shadow now. It looked around at the trees and the earth and the vault of sky above, the stars beginning to prick the curtain of night.

"To get *in*. To this fine house you got here all to yourselves." It came forward and before Fisk could respond or move, the black dog was right in front of him. Fisk's grip tightened on the wooden haft of the awl. He had sharpened it in the morning and hoped, after his day's work, the cutting blade was still sharp enough to do what he had to do. He had seen the book and this much was clear. Knives need to be sharp to make sacrifices.

"Now it's your turn," Hardface said and cocked its head, waiting. Fisk gripped the blade of the awl in his other hand and placed it at the knuckle of his smallest finger on his right hand. The pain, when it came, was outrageous and dull simultaneously, as the cutting-edge bit into skin, severed tendon, tore through cartilage. "Not going to give a yes, are you?" the black dog said. "No matter. I can rummage around in your meat easy enough and take what I want." The thing swelled and bloomed in the darkness. The raiment of the dog fell away in a welter of flesh and fur and crimson painted black in the gloom and Hardface grew into a towering bloody mist, rising up on the night air, malevolent. Bone glinted. It had kept only the teeth and claws and sharp bits of fragmented bone.

Fisk's fingertip separated from his body and he dropped it to the ground as the blood began to flow and his body thrummed with power, either from fear or from the wound, he could not tell.

"Don't think so," Fisk said and raised his wounded hand in a chopping gesture. Blood lanced out in a cutting arc from his hand and Hardface screamed wordlessly and shrank away. Fisk stepped forward.

"You could run faster if you hadn't killed the dog," Fisk said, and lashed out.

Hardface fled before him, mewling. Shrinking, skittering away.

It wasn't until later that Fisk realized how much of his music he'd just cut away.

⌁

1968
Rosalee's Juke Joint, Howard, Arkansas

Seven years had passed and the bright, smoking lights of the Chitlin' Circuit were lost to him.

"Integration's done a number on us," the promoter and barman said, a thick, fat-fingered black man named Morris "Hogleg" Randall. They were in a little town called Howard's End in Quapaw County, within spitting distance of the Mississippi levee, in a juke joint in the back of a long, narrow general store, its name forgotten as the paint that fixed it had been eaten away by the sun and no one cared anyway, since it was the only store. The bar faced a stage tucked in among tins of potted meat and sardines and stacks of toilet paper and boxes of Borax, of Ivory Soap. A Coca-Cola glasstop cooler chugged away behind Randall, full of soda and cheap beer. Pigs feet, pickles, and eggs swam in large brine-filled jars on the counter and, judging by the smell of grease in the air, there was a grill that fried bologna and Spam and egg sandwiches after dark somewhere in the back.

Randall looked Fisk up and down, from his worn wingtip broughams, battered guitar case, amplifier and applebox to his disheveled suit, one size too big—the dead man it came off was wider in the shoulders and with longer sticks, so his trouser cuffs pooled around the scarred leather of his shoes and hung on Fisk's lean frame, drooping at the shoulders—to his wide face that shone open and pained under the upturned brim of his porkpie, cigarette in the crook of his mouth.

"You saying you don't have a crowd on a Saturday night?" Fisk said. No crowd meant no change, no extra spending money, no gas to get on to the next town. But more than that, it meant no release of *the burn*.

Randall wiped the bar with a dirty rag. Behind him, the cooler rattled, sending vibrations through the shoe-worn floorboards of the general store bar.

"Used to be, a player comes in, we was the only game in town. But now, with the Diamond Club over in Darcy and all them longhaired ofays coming in from Memphis, we don't get all the folks we used to. Locals, farm boys and their women coming in for some cold beer." He pointed to the Select-O-Matic jukebox glowing in the corner. "Most nights, they satisfied with a few dollars pumped into that thing."

Fisk held up his right hand, showing his missing finger. Randall's eyes widened.

"'Course, we got a spot for you, wanderer. Fisk, is it? Been hearing about you. Last weekend you was at—"

"Helena. And the week before that, El Dorado."

"You could make a bundle if you went on over to Greenville," Randall said but hastily added, "but not tonight. We got a spot for you here. Dansho's frying a mess of catfish and puppies out back, so you're in luck, wanderer."

Fisk smiled and they worked out the details of the gig: dinner and as much beer as Fisk could drink, which was not much, honestly. Inconstant life on the road wreaked hell on his digestion, and he'd been on the road for years now, possessed of only dreams of Franny and home to keep him sane. And, Randall promised, *a ten dollar guarantee.* Which was five more than he had got in Helena. "Provided I can get on the horn and let the local folks know the nine-fingered man has rolled into town for a stomp. That should bring 'em in, for sure. And, 'course, whatever tips you can gennie up."

When he still had all of his fingers, Fisk had dreamed of being a player in Louis Jordan's Tympany Five, or the Rabbit Foot Minstrels, or even backup in Alexander's Harmony Kings—the big rhythm and blues bands from a decade or more past—and playing the Dreamland Ballroom, or Club Paradise before the throngs on the niteries of Beale. No matter he'd be just a member of a band, one among the many. He was fine with that, if it meant the greater work of making music to shake the heavens.

His momma called it *the burn,* that desire to play, and not just in the woodshed. If he couldn't be with Franny, he was not content to labor solely in the fields. He'd known a field player by the name of Buster Smith in Wabbaseka who had a number of stomps in his pocket, and Fisk had spent a week with him, learning what he knew, and watching his hands. "Might have but nine fingers, but you shore can play," Buster had said. "The real trick of it is the muscles. The smaller the muscle you move, the more you get paid for it." The man had raised his hands and waggled his fingers at Fisk. "Legs, back, ass, arms. They only pay you a few cents on the pound. But them fingers. Or a tongue if you've the knack of speaking like a preacher or singing."

"There's another muscle," Fisk had said, smiling.

"Ain't never gotten paid for that one. Just the opposite," Buster had said, and laughed.

Fisk took the unnamed stage and tuned up his guitar and drank a beer and smoked. Randall brought out a small church public address system with a mic and set it up in front of Fisk and he checked the levels with his guitar and amp and ran through "I'm Ready," which was only appropriate, and then vamped a little, making little runs while holding down the one to Randall's delight. Fisk placed his tambourine on the floor so he could tap it with his foot to really get the asses out of the seats and then went outside to look around a bit and calm himself before the stomp was to begin. He ate some catfish and chatted with the man Randall had called Dansho and walked down the irrigation ditch in the dying heat of the day as a thick cottonmouth grown fat on bullfrogs and field mice and maybe even rats from the juke joint paced him in the water trying to make up its mind whether to slide out of the ditch and protect its territory or just let the loping land thing be and Fisk thought, *Ain't that just the story of my goddamned life,* and, *Hardface, that you?* and considered the strange journey away from the woman he loved to this juke joint by this tiny farm town blessed by nothing but a train track running east to Mississippi and west to Little Rock.

The burn started to prick up in Fisk as the sun dipped beyond the treeline. To play before other living souls, to set them in judgement upon your skill, your heart, was really the only thing that sustained him, so far from home and near-banished from all he loved.

Music was a magic he could work, if any magic was real and he knew it was, he knew it in the finger he'd cut away, he knew it in his heart. It cost so much and would take everything if you let it. All your fingers. All your love.

———

1960
Franny

He thought of it as a courtship but she never did. He would bring her flowers, and buy her sweets from the rolling stores that stopped in Gethsemane. Ribbons and combs and mirrors. But after enough times, times when she held his presents in her hands and looked at him softly, smiling, and then put them aside, he came to know she didn't care for them. He never knew her to eat much. Something inside propelled her more than any food could.

Yet he never felt as though she didn't care for him.

They would walk. Out among the pecan trees. Down into the mosquito-swarmed muddy edges of Bayou Bartholomew. She preferred the wild sprawl of water over the ordered rows of orchard. It wasn't until he offered to take her out in the johnboat did she understand what he was trying to do and kissed him, in full view of the Big House.

"Franny," he said, pulling her away as gently as he could. "Don't. Farm manager sees us, Mister Jimson or Bill North's boys, and they'll come for me at night and nothing your momma says to them will matter."

"I don't give one good goddamn about them," Franny said and tried to kiss him again and frowned when he danced away.

"You give a damn about me, don't you? Let's go fishing," Fisk had said. "Got a mess of worms."

"'A mess of,'" she said.

Fisk grinned. "I can't help it, sometimes. Still a country boy." He straightened, giving his best Madame Reasoner impression. "'Mister Fisk! Collective noun for worms—with alacrity!'"

Franny said, "A mess. A jarful?"

"A squirm."

"A gooey tangle."

"That's a phrase, not a word," Fisk said.

"Fooey," Franny said, and took his hand. That made Fisk nervous. They had grown up together, hand in hand, but he was eighteen and she was seventeen now and he worked the farm most days with the men when he wasn't closeted with Madame Reasoner, Franny and Lenora. Lenora first looked upon Fisk and Franny with concern, then outrage, then envy.

"What do you think you're doing?" she asked him once, after seeing the two of them down by the bayou, closer than they should've been.

"What'dya mean?" he responded, knowing exactly what she meant.

"We were raised up in the same house, Fisk! She's near to being your damned sister."

Fisk pulled back his sleeve, exposing his forearm. "She don't look like me at all, 'Nora," he said. "A bit fairer complexioned."

Lenora let a look pass her features as if she'd just sucked an unsugared lemon. "Don't play me like that," she said. "You know it's not right."

"It doesn't have anything to do with you, sis," Fisk said.

"First the farm—you're Miss Sarah's golden boy and what am I? And now Franny. It's like everything I love, you want to take."

"How am I taking anything from you?" Fisk asked, honestly puzzled. At his sister's inability to answer, he said, "I thought so."

It was understood he would be Miss Sarah's man, her trusted first lieutenant on all matters once he knew enough. After all, she was paying for his education, and look how fine he turned out. *Look how well the boy speaks, even for a darkie,* he had heard young Stephen North say once when he thought Fisk was out of earshot. *But you want to take orders from him? Do you?*

It warred within him, the growing awareness of how the world viewed black men like him and the pocket of reality here, on the Rheinhart farm. The outer world didn't know what they'd been through. Not him, not Franny.

Fisk had seen the book, and in that glimpse had vast expanses of terror and pleasure and power revealed to him.

But Franny had seen worse. Franny had gone beyond.

They went down to the dock and took the johnboat out onto the smooth green waters of Bartholomew, the boat barely making a wake with their passage. Fisk knew how to skulk, as all the farmers called it—paddling with one hand from the prow—so they made their way in and out of shadow, Franny making sure her weight countered Fisk's. There was something in that, the balancing act of their weights in the boat, but Fisk couldn't puzzle out its greater meaning.

Franny eased, Fisk could see it in her face and the way she held her body. It was as if they were flying, here, on the face of the water. They moved in and out of the cypress, caught on the sluggish current.

"Come here," Franny said, eventually. "No one can see us now."

And he did.

That was the first time. There were many more Saturdays and Sundays together on the waters.

One, they stripped and looked upon each other's bodies in the sun, full of wonder and delight. His skin sheened and shining with sweat, hers almost alabaster.

One, they found a dry island and he took a slingblade to it and killed the snakes and made a dappled spot for them to sit, out away from the world of man. A blanket, a basket, bologna sandwiches for him. A jug of lemonade and Zapp's potato chips. Fat dill pickles. A thick can of sprayable Deet for the mosquitos. He ate happily in the sun, sweat trickling down his back, and Franny traced the muscles of his arm.

One, Franny stole a bottle of gin from the Big House bar and they drank, hissed at each other like cats, laughing, singing songs. Elvis and

Carl Perkins and Fats Domino. Later, they pissed together on the bank, Fisk with his cock in hand, weaving drunk, and Franny holding a tree, watchful for cottonmouths, but laughing. Fisk remembered being surprised in his drunkeness at the sound her urine made. So forceful. *Yes, she has a body, just like me. Each with its own needs.*

One, they lay together, him poised above her. Franny opening her legs to let him in. "I don't want to hurt you," he said, looking at the scar running from her navel to collarbone. It was as if she was an unfinished thing, the great seamstress who stuffed every doll on earth had sewn her up messily. She looked down at herself and to Fisk, on his knees, rampant. "There's nothing you could ever do to hurt me. Me. Who has been hurt beyond all hurts," she had said, and there was something of the beyond in her eyes that gave Fisk a great sadness. She saw it growing in him and reached out and led his body into hers.

One, they had rowed out far beyond where they had ever been before and Fisk worried they'd not make it home before dark. In the trees, in the shadows, despite the high summer sun, something moved. A man maybe. A bear. Franny crossed her arms over her breasts and her face grew dark. In that moment Fisk realized how white her hair was—parchment white. The white of snow. "They're looking for me. No, that's not right. They know where I am. They're trying to get in." And when Fisk asked who she meant, Franny only touched her stomach in response. They were quiet for a long time and she said, "Except on the water. They can't find me on the water. It happened on the water. You knew that, right?" He said, "What they did to you?" And she said, "What they did to all of us. Yes. On the water." And he said, "Then we'll stay on the water."

One, he said, "I got a song for you." And the look on her face he'd never forget. It was cooler then, and the cypress fronds had matted the banks in umber and rust. He wished he'd brought his guitar with him then, but it was his most prized possession and he didn't want it to get wet. "When did you write it?" she asked, and he responded, "I've always been writing it." Franny centered herself then almost as though readying her body for a blow and said, "Sing it for me," and he nodded and began, *Put on your little coat, my heart's up in my throat.* Franny's eyes widened and her shoulders slumped. *Put on them darling shoes, I don't know what to do, with the love I have for you. Fill up the sky with planes, I'll never be the same. Fill up the sky with blue, I don't know what to do. With the love I have for you.* He stopped then, embarrassed. Franny frowned and tsked. "'Put on them darling shoes,' Mister Fisk? Very poor grammar." But then she began to cry and said, "Come here, you absolute fool."

One, at night, in their bathing suits from the day's swimming, a cooler full of bream and bass and crappie on ice. Lying in the gunwale of the johnboat, looking at the stars, Franny in the crook of his arm. "They won't let us be together," Fisk said. "You know that, right?" She shushed him. "You can see Sputnik if you watch hard enough," Franny said. Fisk: "You told me they're trying to get in. Who're *they*?" Franny said, "I don't know but you do believe me, don't you?" And Fisk said, "I looked in the book," and she tensed. "They'll never stop," she said. "Never."

Not knowing that night would be their last.

1968
Rosalee's Juke Joint, Howard, Arkansas

The *burn* caught hold of the crowd when they saw Fisk was missing his finger. Rumor and reputation were the fastest things on earth, no device of man could match them. Fisk took the stage and swung through the old favorites: "Big Legged Woman" and one of his songs he called "Conspiracies" and then "I'm Ready" and "Hoochie Coochie Man" and "Smokestack Lightning." He'd never met Howlin' Wolf nor Muddy Waters, but he'd felt them, their spirit, their stomp, and he knew that whatever magic he could work came some from those wellsprings.

Every man and woman is a river, he sang, his hands moving in surges on the neck of his guitar, his foot stomping the tamborine. He watched the crowd, their history written in every face. Malaria, hookworm, pellagra, the comet's tail of every cruel year. Buster Smith had once sung,

Someone told me Wall Street fell, we was so poor we couldn't tell. Livin' on whipporwill peas and poke salat.

Fisk sang, *Every heart a damned bass drum.* This crowd looked pious enough, some of the women surely wearing the same hats they'd go to church in tomorrow, so he edited himself. No *goddamns*. No sacrilege. If he was clever enough, he'd figure out some way to sing, *There are no gods only devils, only men,* in a palatable way but it was beyond him. He knew that true sentiment would get him knifed when he went to piss or get another beer. The world will not tolerate, man will not tolerate, any water that erodes the banks of belief.

It's a weird trick of the human mind, Fisk thought, that I can be performing and thinking upon the nature of god and man, all at once.

By the time Fisk rolled through "I'm Feelin' Alright" and "Little Anna May," the women were up and dancing and the men had nothing left to do but join them. It was getting hot in the juke, sweat pricking up on skin. The sun had gone down entirely but the tension of the *burn* was rising, catching all those souls gathered here in its net. A flash of thigh, a glimpse of the upper slope of tit, open mouths and eager hands. He stomped through a bumptious "Spoonful" and "I Can't Quit You" and then just vamped for a long time in a shuffle, holding down the root chords and walking the bass but making up words as he went, forgotten as soon as he sang them. A young man approached the stage, pushing aside the men and women hooting and hollering and shaking their asses and raised a pair of drumsticks with a question in his expression. A young man, six or seven years Fisk's junior. He had a narrow nose and thin lips and a rusty complexion with green eyes and a spray of freckles across his cheeks with a white man bucking in his mother's or his grandmother's stall back down the line as the old saying went. But Fisk liked the look of him and nodded and told all those gathered we was going for a smoke and beer and a bit of fresh air. Quarters slipped into the Select-O-Matic and the dancing continued, but without as much vim or vigor. There's no substitute for the connections formed between performer and audience when the *burn* is running hot.

The room was packed and Fisk didn't bother surveying the faces— there was no woman that could stir him save one and she was far away and he didn't care at all for the men. He slipped out the backdoor where Dansho had fried the fish and the young black man with the drumsticks followed him out.

"What you got?" Fisk said.

"Just a kick and high-hat and snare," the young man said. "Gotta get 'em back to church before dawn."

"Kick, high-hat, snare? That's about all you need. Go on and hit me something and show me you ain't wasting my time."

The young man held the sticks in a modified drummer's grip, left hand with the thick part of the drumstick locked under thumb but in the right hand, the direction reversed, and patted out a quick rhythm on the meat of his thigh. Fisk smiled.

"All right," Fisk said. "What's your name?"

"Vernon Banks," he said.

"I imagine I'll have a dollar for you after the show, Mister Banks, if you don't lose too much time. Go on, get your shit."

The young man's face brightened. Vernon trotted off toward the parking lot. Fisk watched him go and stood in the dark smoking and observing the insects swarm the sodium light hanging over the parking lot now full of Chevrolets and Fords and Packards and Chryslers and Oldsmobiles. When Vernon returned, kick drum held tightly in a circle of gangly but strong looking arms—a small Slingerland toy kit—he set it down and half-jogged back to the parking lot and returned shortly with a high-hat and snare and the kick drum's detached foot pedal. They chatted some and Fisk gave him some instructions on how he wanted the rest of the night to sort itself out.

The excitement in Vernon was rising, he too had been caught up in the *burn*. The young man said, "You're drawing them in from all over, Mister Fisk. Saw a white man pull up in a big black Olds and get out neat as you please looking like he's from a record company, black suit, sweet tie."

The *burn* brought some extras and Fisk was entirely aware of them. One was a heightened sense of surroundings. Another was a hyper-sensitivity to the out of place. And at Rosalee's Juke on the edge of an irrigation ditch and cotton field, a white man in a fine suit was about the same thing as a cottonmouth drowsing on a church pew. He felt himself not just tense, but fray a little at the edges, static coming through the signal.

"Go on and set up your kit," Fisk said, frowning. The young man hastily loaded in his drums while Fisk stood in the dark chewing his lip. He raised his right hand and considered it for a long while. He took out his pocketknife and set the blade against the nub of his pinkie but did not cut.

Wonder if there's enough of that river still running in me? Fisk thought and then folded the knife and slipped it back into his pocket.

He entered the juke and wondered how many fingers he'd have by the end of the night.

<hr />

1968
Rosalee's Juke Joint, Howard, Arkansas

The crowd had only gotten more raucous in Fisk's absence. At his entry, a series of hoots sounded out and the Select-O-Matic went silent. He gained the stage in one easy step and someone put a Budweiser can beading with condensation from the heat at his feet near his tambourine and he made a great show of popping the tin and drinking it. Women clapped and men laughed. If there was one thing Fisk knew, crowds liked to believe that their performer was just as tight as they were. That the same river flowed through them all.

He searched the faces in the crowd and couldn't find the white man.

Fisk rolled into "Stagger Lee," always a good one to get the asses out of seats, and had the rafters dropping dust with the shaking from the dancers as he sang, *Go Stagger Go*, over and over while Vernon held down the back beat. The young man could play, that was for sure. It was a real shame he couldn't spend more time with him, teach him what he knew about the *burn* and life on the road. After tonight, young mister Banks would not be content to sit home.

Next, "Seventh Son" rolled into "Messin' with the Kid" which caromed right into "Blow Wind Blow" and "Blues with a Feeling." The men and women of the juke were steaming in the dark, yelling, hollering, tilting back beers and taking pulls from hipflasks. It had been a while since Fisk had had such an enthusiastic crowd. The worry regarding the white man dissipated and the *burn* took over full force and he blazed through the rest of the night without much thought other than being a passage for the music to come into the world. That was enough.

At the end of the evening he gave Vernon his dollar and thanked the young man and endured the awkward conversation that followed when he asked Fisk if he could come with him and Fisk had to say no. "I'm fixing to go on home for a bit, check on things," Fisk replied and didn't even realize, until he said it, that it was true.

He was loading his guitar and amp in the farm truck when the white man in the suit stepped forward out of the dark and said, "Mister Williams, I presume."

Fisk froze, stuck his hand inside his pocket, withdrew the knife and unfolded it and cut deep into the scarred tissue at the nub of his missing finger. His body hitched and thrummed with the pain. He'd cut deeper than he had intended.

For a while, there was no sound except for the soft *pat pat pat* of blood dripping on the gravel and then the man said, "I hardly think that was necessary, Mister Williams."

"I'm not much concerned with what you think," he said, faltering at the end, for he did not know to whom he spoke. "Is that you, Hardface?"

The man, immaculately dressed in a three-piece suit with a bit of sartorial geometry of a handkerchief poking from the breast pocket, chuckled and moved closer to Fisk. In response, Fisk raised his bleeding hand.

"Hardface? No, the person you're referring to has been…reassigned." A thoughtful look passed over the man's features. He was well-formed, to say the least, with high cheekbones and a nose like a chisel, and a strong jaw, blued at the edges. He seemed to Fisk like a man who could grow a beard by noon, if he didn't shave. As an afterthought, a pair of glasses possibly one size too small for his face sat perched on the bridge of his nose. "I see you are an initiate," the man said. Fisk's bloody hand made him stop and take a step back. "Allow me to introduce myself. My name is Wilson Cleave. I am a preparer of the way. An emissary."

"That's too bad. I thought you were an A&R man," Fisk said, and walked to the door of his truck. It was awkward, but he managed to get his keys from the opposite pocket from his unbloodied hand. "Unless you're going to tell me Chess Records got a contract for me, we don't have anything to talk about."

"Oh, I think we do, Mister Williams. You know what we require."

An invitation. The devil's got to be asked to come inside. It was something Fisk would never give.

Cleave could see it on Fisk's face. "The thing you call Hardface was—how would you say—clumsy. Brutish. He might have threatened to rummage through your integument of flesh to get what we want, but that is, of course, impossible. We know where the girl is. Mostly. We just require entry. It's that simple."

"Why didn't you come as a dog? Or a cat this time?"

Cleave allowed a smile to ghost across his face. "A dog or cat? No, for me, I need something with a more tailored cut, if you follow my meaning. Man-sized. Nine fingers."

And that is the invitation they want. To get inside me. And getting there, access to Franny.

Fisk unlocked the truck door and slipped behind the wheel and started the engine, never mind the blood getting on his interior and seats and wheel. Cleave's implacable face watched him and even though Fisk did not roll down the window, he knew every word the thing wearing the man that wore the tailored suit said: *An unwise decision. There is another way.*

Fisk's heart didn't slow until he was halfway to Gethsemane.

⁓

1960
Franny

One, she followed him back to the world of the farm from the dock and there she kissed him, not knowing that in the shadows of a far cypress, a black man by the name of Lukas Cross sat collecting his trot line—fat bluegill catfish in a neat string—and watched as they made their adieus and protestations of love in each other's embrace. Within three days, the rumor of their relationship had spread out into the world and circled back to Miss Sarah, who first tried to laugh it away and then brought them before her and asked, "Is there something going on between you two that I should know about?" and Fisk had bowed his head, fearful for them both, but Franny had answered, "We are in love," and Miss Sarah began to cry then because that truth had been staring her in the face since Fisk and Franny had both gotten their first growth. "No, no. With all you've suffered, you take on this burden, too," Sarah had said to Franny, her daughter. And Franny had frowned and said, "This is just a small thing compared to that," and stopped before she added that her mother was only thinking of herself. Miss Sarah, though, never forbade their love. But the farm manager and his boys caught Fisk that night outside of his shotgun shack, within earshot of the Big House, and beat him until he couldn't stand and then two days later, once he could stand again, he gathered up his guitar and asked Miss Sarah if he could take the truck he'd used in his duties as her second and she had tearfully agreed but she did not stop him. Franny, for her part, would not kiss him when he came to say goodbye. She had said only, "The world is a monster, my love, and it makes monsters of us. We have to give up bits of ourselves to survive." And Fisk, never feeling more alone, said, "They won't be satisfied with just beating me. You won't be safe." Franny, looking at him sadly: "I'd rather be unsafe with you than safe all alone." But he had left anyway.

1968
A Thought, a Worry, a Change of Course

Cleave's last words ate at Fisk like a steady riverflow eroding a mudbank. *An unwise decision. There is another way.*

What he could've meant by that, Fisk could not guess, but he knew he did not like it.

He arrived in Gethsemane at first light, and parked the truck in the farm motor pool by the grain dryers and silos. Checking himself in the truck's mirror, he did what he could to straighten himself up, changing shirts underneath the lightening sky turning blue, striated with pink veins. He threaded his tie and slapped his face a few times.

"We can do that for you," a voice came, near a combine poking its nose from the metal quonset hut that served as the farm's machine shop. It was a soft voice, with hard syllables, giving it a clandestine air. Fisk looked and saw Stephen North smoking in the shadow of the combine. From what Fisk understood, Stephen was next in line to become farm manager, now he was gone.

Fisk turned to face him, inexpressibly tired. He could not muster the strength for deference. "You got your pals with you?"

Stephen raised his eyebrows and spat. "Giving us lip now? I thought we beat that out of you, boy."

The anger, when it sparked, burned hot and white. But he'd learned enough since he left the farm to not let it show on his face. He thought about cutting his nub, to see how that crimson river would flow and what it would do to this man. But he was afraid that this garden variety monster would not run before the bloodtide, as Hardface had. The blood that had stopped Cleave in his tracks.

Fuck it, Fisk thought, and held up his right hand. It was not a wave, or a greeting. It was a gesture for North to stop. And he did. Fisk could not tell if it was due to his missing finger, or the dark expression on Fisk's face, or the fact that North was alone.

"If you've got a welcome party gathered 'round when I get back, *boy*," Fisk said. "Some of you are likely to get ventilated. Catch me?" When North did not respond, he said again, "Catch me?"

"Oh, we'll catch you," North said.

"Better pray you don't," Fisk said, and turned and straightened his tie in the truck's mirror. Then he walked to the Rheinhart Big House, went around back, and entered the kitchen.

———

He had grown up here, in this house, the son of a servant, Alice Williams. It had been eight years since he had left. Two spent at the turpentine camp, one working the barge floating cotton down the Arkansas between Pine Bluff to the Mississippi to Darcy and south to Greenville. Five on the road, going town to town playing in juke joints and tonks, barn stomps and side road bars. A life lived outside, or on the road, in smoke-filled halls, where men fought and scrapped in parking lots underneath sodium-vapor lights. Fisk knew he had a haggard, gangrel look, the mirror told him so, every morning. His clothes hung loose on his frame and were threadbare and worn. He wasn't a boy anymore, and looked older than his years.

His mother was rolling out biscuits and humming spirituals in her low, musical voice, accompanied only by an old, grizzled mutt that raised his shaggy head as Fisk opened the screen door, springs creaking and popping, and then set his whiskered chin back on the floor. Apparently, Fisk passed whatever test the dog had seen fit to give him.

When she caught sight of her son, he thought she might screech, or make some sort of exclamation. She did not. She simply dusted her hands on her apron and took him in her arms and pressed him close to her heart and held him that way for a long time.

When she was through, she held him at arm's length and looked him up and down and said, "The world ain't been kind to you, has she?"

Fisk shook his head. It was a simple truth. He said, "We get along all right, Momma. Most of the time."

Wordlessly, Alice turned back to her dough, cut the biscuits and placed them on a greased tray in the oven and moved on to frying bacon. In between tasks, she poured herself and Fisk cups of coffee and he sat at the table and crossed his legs, leaning back against the wall, letting his exhaustion pass over and through him, invisible forces and tides tugging at his flesh. He wanted to see Franny, desperately, but he was scared as well for the meeting. Scared of what she might say. It had been years with only a few phone calls in between. Franny had always been braver than him, and careless, and wild. He was a coward, he had gone away into the cruel world beyond the borders of the Rheinhart plantation. It would've been harder here, he knew. He'd taken what he thought was the only way out but now he saw it was the easy way.

He lit a cigarette and got a quick outraged expression from his mother who opened her mouth to say something, and then she caught sight of his right hand when he drew the cigarette to his mouth and she paused in her task and said, "So, you're the nine-fingered player everybody been talking about. The 'Wanderer.' Never thought it would play out this way, but you sure took after your father. Calvin. He only played small towns and tonks and shaker shacks, never the big halls. They say you're a ghost and don't even have a name."

Fisk laughed. "That's not really by choice."

"Why not?"

Fisk gestured at the walls and looked toward the ceiling and the upper floors of the Big House where Miss Sarah Rheinhart kept her suite of rooms. "This place. That big man. Bull. Everything that happened to Franny." He shifted in his seat, suddenly uncomfortable. "All that followed us down through the damned years. You ever heard of a...a man named Hardface?"

"Hardface?" Alice's own face grew dark. "No, never heard of him. There's a fella named Kenneth that everyone calls Flatface over in Coy, but I've never heard of anyone named Hardface."

"That's good," Fisk said. He drew smoke deep inside and let it sit there in his chest for a long time. The events of that summer so long past were still somewhat of a mystery to him. The priest. The book with the pictures, those terrible, luscious pictures. The bull that was a man. Something happened then, something beyond his ability, or his mother's ability, to understand. And now, with its comet's tail of wreckage trawling after them, putting the pieces together beggared his ability to understand. So he simply said, "You believe in devils, don't you?"

"The Devil?"

"No. Just devils."

Alice's hand went to the cross at her throat and then smoothed her apron. "I reckon I do."

"And you know something beyond our ken happened with that man Bull, don't you?"

She nodded, slowly. "Sarah told me about the book and what happened on the boat."

"The book." Even now, the book's illustrations wormed and writhed in Fisk's mind's eye. "Is it still here?"

"That's a question for Sarah," she said. "But after what happened, she locked up the library for a long time and didn't go back in it. Franny needed her then." She stopped. "But now Franny's—"

"Franny's what?" Fisk asked.

"I'll let Sarah do the telling," his mother said, and Fisk felt something hitch inside him.

"Those things—" Fisk began, with more intensity than he meant to convey. "Those that did what they did to Bull and Franny...they haven't gone away. They're sniffing around like dogs." Alice did not respond and Fisk said, "But you knew that, didn't you?"

"Every other week or so, a man or woman will come around, asking to come inside the house. Always something off about them. And Chester"—his mother indicated the old hound quietly slumbering with his haunches half in the pantry and his forepaws facing Alice—a fat dog, with rolls of flesh filled out with love and scraps tossed from Alice's kind hands. "They come around and even Chester would rouse himself and start a'baying and they wouldn't stay around long." She paused, thinking. "Then Sarah did something—she keeps up quite the correspondence—and now they don't even come on the property." Alice shook her head. "But you'll see cars parked at the end of the drive with men, women, behind the wheel." A shiver ran through her, despite the rising temperature of the day compounded by the oven. "Once, I had gone to the general store, and saw a car at the end of the drive. It was a young white girl, hair cut short. Maybe eight or nine behind the wheel of a big old Packard maybe thirty years old. She gets out of the car, neat as you please, and starts yammering at me. And as I passed her, I could've sworn the insides of her mouth were pure black, as if she'd drank a gallon of paint."

"What did Sarah do?"

"You'll have to ask her. She ain't feeling too good these days so you'll need to go upstairs and pay your respects." She smiled. "But not before breakfast."

The agitation in Fisk grew as they took their breakfast together. His mind turned and turned again, always back to Franny—where she might be. Why the deferral to Miss Sarah. He knew he would not get an answer from his mother; once she made a proclamation, she never backed away from it. Quickly, their conversation was reduced to Fisk asking after folk he used to know and learning whether they still lived, or worked on the farm. And then fell to discussing the breeding and habits of Chester.

Finally, when he'd buttered and ate the last biscuit and swallowed the last bit of bacon and chased those with the dregs of his coffee, his mother said, "I figure it's time you went and paid your respects."

When he was a boy, Miss Sarah—not really a "miss" as she had been married and made a mother, but such is the nomenclature of farmlife when a single woman, an attractive and marriageable widow, declines to remarry. It might have been different if she had come home back then in '51 with a husband in tow but he had drunk himself to death, never giving her a chance to assume the mantle of "Missus Sarah." And maybe that wasn't something that rankled her, after all.

Fisk made his way up the grand stairs to the upper rooms and suites, past inlaid fleur de lis and wooden scrollwork brought up the Mississippi by New Orleans craftsmen who built this plantation house over a century before. Down a hall where the various noble and ignoble oil-painted faces of Rheinharts from the ages looked down their equestrian noses at him, walking quietly forward. The house was just as he remembered—cavernous, dark, full of shadow. As a boy, he had rarely made his way this far upstairs—he kept to the servants' quarters off the kitchen, where his mother slept, where Lenora slept. Where Franny slept, as like as not, burrowing into Lenora's bed at night.

He knocked at Miss Sarah's old room and after a long silent minute, pushed open the door and found it empty and un-lived in.

She will have taken her mother's chambers, he thought to himself, and he felt his heartbeat increase. There were few people who frightened him. Cleave, of course. And Hardface. Whatever sort of creature those two men were.

Elizabeth Werner Rheinhart had frightened him more than both of them. She had been a vile and evil woman, even before whatever cursed bargain she had made with the creatures like Cleave. Fisk had to admit, he was glad she was dead.

He knocked on the door to what was once Elizabeth Rheinhart's suite. From inside a familiar voice said, "Come in, come in."

Fisk turned the handle and pushed the door open. The room was bright and dark all at once—a slanted pillar of light lanced down through the drawn heavy curtains to light up a Persian rug and settee brilliantly, while the rest of the room was cloaked in heavy shadow. He walked farther into the room and made out the shape of a woman sitting at the vanity beyond the spill of light. Miss Sarah. Her back was to him.

As he stepped into the brightly lit area, as if he was finally taking the stage at one of the big club's in Memphis—the Paradise maybe, or the Diamond Lounge—Sarah's gaze shifted to the mirror and she turned to face him.

"Oh, Fisk. Fisk," she said, and rose. She was still pretty, he could see, though her hair had become gray with years, an imitation of Franny's white, giving her a great dignity. It wreathed her face like a halo. *No, Fisk thought. Like a crown. She's queen here, ain't she? And I'm just her damned subject.*

Sarah approached, reaching out her hands to take his. This he allowed. Her gaze took him in just as his evaluated her—a fine craquelure of lines etched into the corners of her mouth, a sallowness to her once alabaster skin, rheumy-looking eyes, and a roseate spattering across her cheeks as if she'd been wind- and ice-whipped in the cold. But it was warm here, and a General Electric fan hummed and oscillated back and forth on a table near her bed. There was a cane there, too, with a silver handle.

"Oh, how we've missed you," Sarah said. She took his hands and drew him closer to her. He could smell the perfume she used, and a hint of mint and mentholatum and a whiff of decay. The sour smell of someone who has spent too much time in bed.

"And I, you," he said and immediately regretted it. Honestly, he had not thought of her much at all—his thoughts were always reserved for Franny—and the fact that he'd slipped so easily into the formal intonations and grammar that she had drilled into him, his sister, and Franny as children—his "white" voice—made him feel a burning shame in his chest.

She kissed his rough hands and then stopped and looked at the scabbed wound on his nub. "What is this? What is this?" she said. "Oh, Fisk, how did this happen?"

Fisk didn't say anything. What was there to tell?

Everything. I could tell her everything. And she'll have to tell me everything too. If this was poker, I'd be pushing in all my goddamned chips on the first hand.

"I figure you know something about this," he said, drawing his hand away, not ungently. "When I was a boy, I snuck into the library and took a long look at the book."

Here face went through a series of expressions—surprise, anger, shock, and fear. "You shouldn't have done that."

Fisk shrugged. "If I hadn't, we might not be talking right now."

"It is called the *Opusculis Noctis*," she said, her voice precise.

"Is that right? I've only ever thought of it as *the book*. That damned thing."

"Yes," Sarah said. "That damned thing." She faltered at that moment and Fisk clutched her elbow and helped her back to the cushioned seat at the vanity. She withdrew a cigarette from a mother-of-pearl case, snapped the case shut with a *snick* and lit the cigarette with a silver and gold lighter the size of a baseball. Having lived so hard, for so long on the road, Fisk tried to keep from evaluating what he might get for such a thing at a pawn shop, or the back room of a general store, and failed. Twenty dollars? More than he made in a night playing, that was for sure.

"So, maybe you know what happened to my hand, then." He gestured to the window and the outer world. "Them things, trying to get at Franny."

"*Those things,*" Sarah said.

"Whatever they are. I was approached by a—" He had to think a moment. "A big boss man. Went by the name of Cleave. Wanting me to let him in. To get at Franny." Fisk wanted at Franny, too, he realized. But for other reasons. "Where is she? Came a long way to see her."

"She's somewhere safe. Tell me about this man," Sarah said.

He tensed. For an instant, he imagined himself grasping her shoulders and shaking it out of her. But he'd be strung up on the nearest tree if he did that. In this world, the only way to lose control was surrounded by other black folks; otherwise, he'd never survive it. *Keep the tamp down, son*, he thought to himself. "I guess both you and I know he weren't wholly a man," Fisk said.

"Wasn't. And, yes. We've had mongrels prowling our grounds here as well."

"This one wanted to cut a deal."

Her face became lined with concern. "That's disconcerting."

"When I turned him down, he said I made a bad decision and that there's another way." He raised his hand. "But I cut away a part of myself and let the blood run and that stopped him well enough."

"He said there's another way? Hmm, that's unlikely."

"What do you mean? Momma said that you 'did something,'" Fisk said. "What did you do?"

"I made sure this place remains safe," she said, and touched her cheeks, where the crimson rash colored her skin. "I let the red river flow," she said, and smiled weakly.

By cutting away his finger, he'd given up some of his music and opened a gateway to power. What had she done?

"Lupus," she said. "I am become my mother."

<center>~~~</center>

They were quiet a long while. Sarah smoked her cigarette and softly asked him to ring downstairs for something to drink, and he did. His mother came up with some coffee mixed with a little something extra, maybe, some rum or bourbon, Fisk thought, if he hadn't lost all sense of smell. *So it's like that now? She surely has become her mother. Except for the fearfulness. And Miss Sarah's bargaining went the other way, didn't it?*

Alice set the tray down by Sarah and then sat down beside her and held her hand. They had been very close since they were girls. Now that Fisk had gone out into the world and lived there at its mercy, he saw the two of them and their relationship for what it was—a bond of complacency. His mother traded away some of her independence for security, and Sarah had done the same, in some ways, by allowing Alice to do all those things she could not. Mother her children. They were like two lovers locked in a strangling embrace, each trying to suffocate the other with care.

"Time was, I would've done anything for you, for Franny, for this farm. This life," Fisk said. "But maybe by leaving, I can't do that anymore. But I never really left, never truly left in my heart. You have to know this."

"Of course," Sarah said. "I never wanted you to go away in the first place."

"That's a conversation better left for another time," Fisk said. He went to the window and looked out. Once there were peafowl that walked these grounds, but no more. "I thought I needed to, but now I've come to think maybe I was wrong. That I was meant to be here. For something."

"The man said there was another way. Like blood moving through a body, those things don't travel down small or obscure paths, do they?" Sarah asked. After drinking from her laced coffee, her face seemed flushed, the rash standing brightly against her skin, giving her, yes, a lupine aspect. "What do you think he meant?"

"Ain't got a clue," Fisk said. "But it makes me want to see Franny all the more. So let's stop dicking around. Where is she?"

Sarah put down her cup and said, simply, "She's out on her boat."

~~~

Explanations

With Fisk gone, Franny had a growing unease, as Sarah told it. The mongrels came around more, the feral creatures of whatever animating force that drove Hardface and Cleave. She spent less time on land, and more in a johnboat, out on the face of the bayou. Once she was gone for days and they considered dragging the bayou for her body, except Bayou Bartholomew spanned from Pine Bluff to near Louisiana and farther, slithering like a cottonmouth in and out of the sloughs and brakes fed from the great floods. Instead, they sent out farmhands in all the johnboats they could muster, but Franny was not to be found. Its seething waters teemed with the rot of thousands of men, women and children killed in '27 when the Mississippi and Arkansas overran their levees and drowned the earth in tideflow.

"She told me, 'I am lost out there,'" Sarah said. "And I couldn't understand what she meant. I thought she didn't know where she was, and that might be true. But I came to understand that the way she meant it was she wanted to be lost, from this world."

"What're we talking here? Just paddling out and camping in a tent or something?"

"No," Sarah said. "This was before." She touched her cheek. "Before I made my choice. I insisted I come with her on an outing and we went out together in the johnboat. Franny paddled as easy as you please and told me you taught her how—skulking, she called it—and we moved between the cypress and willows and old-growth cottonwoods and oaks out to where there were just tussocks in the bayou's sluggish waters. She said you couldn't get to where you really wanted to go using an outboard motor. You had to paddle there, by strength of your own will, she said. I thought she meant her arms but came to know she meant something else entirely. Of course, I didn't quite understand but she seemed so certain. Mothers will allow almost anything from a child as long as it seems reasoned—we are easy creatures in this way.

"A mist rose up around us, making the sun distant and watery, and we drifted. We ate some of the sandwiches I packed and drank the coffee and fished but it was as if all of time had collapsed and we had become untethered, truly untethered since we could not see the shore. At some point Franny lay down in the bottom of the johnboat—Bill North had tricked it out where the bilge water remained beneath some wooden running boards—and went to sleep and I found myself feeling tired and closing my eyes and when I opened them, slumped against the tilted outboard, it was a murky dark, and then I closed them again and the sun was in a different position in the sky and the light…the quality of the light…seemed alien. Not unwholesome or tainted. But different. Bluer. Whiter. We seemed very far away." Sarah drank more of her coffee. "Things bellowed and cooed in the mist," she said, a puzzled look flashing across her features. "And that delighted Franny."

Fisk could feel a nervousness begin to affect him. His hands began to shake so he stuffed them in his pockets. "And then what?"

"We came back to dock and found Bill North and his boys in a tizzy, since we'd been gone for days," Sarah said.

"So, you're telling me she just goes out in a johnboat to who knows where for what? Days? Weeks?"

"Yes. 'Who knows where.'" Sarah said. "But like you said, I think both you and I know it's somewhere no one could point out on a surveyor's map." She looked pointedly at Fisk's missing digit on his right hand. "And she doesn't go out on a johnboat. We bought her a pole barge."

"You encouraged this?"

Alice said, "Fisk! Ain't your place!"

Fisk looked at his mother. "Whose place is it then, to look after Franny?"

He could feel Sarah's gaze and it was not unkind. "You must understand. We fought it. *I fought it.* But I also know what happened to her, so long ago. They cut her from—" She stopped. "They took everything from her and she was dead and only because of Bull, and his sacrifice, is she alive now. But the one thing they couldn't take from her? The fight. She never surrendered to them, and she came out of the ordeal with more than she or they could have imagined. We're just seeing how much."

Fisk could only nod. He knew she was right. Franny was always so much stronger than him. "A pole barge?"

"Yes, small, with no draft at all, and a little hut on top with bed and a stove, and a little six horse Johnson motor on the rear for moving faster if she needs it." Sarah looked at Fisk with a question and a hope in her expression. He realized he was scowling and he tried to soften his features.

It made a perverse sort of sense. What happened to Franny before occurred on the river—*on the water*—and it was on the water she felt herself lost to the world. She was owning her past, rather than being ruled by it.

It made Fisk ashamed for running away eight years before.

"I'm going to find her."

Alice looked to Sarah, who only nodded. It was inevitable.

<hr/>

Into the Mist

He went out the back screen door—the servants' entrance, that irony was not lost on him—to avoid whatever Stephen North might've planned and took the path down to the dock where the land became sodden and slumped into the bayou. The bayou itself was low, puddling at the knees of the bald cypresses.

He took off his broughams, rolled up his trousers to his knees and stepped into the algae-topped water and pulled one of the johnboats away from the shore, his feet sinking into the cool mud. He hoisted himself back onto the dock and tied off the johnboat's lead line and rummaged through the farm's other boats and canoes for a bailer and paddle. Once he was done, he took off his jacket and hat and placed them on the stern seat and took the prow and untied the johnboat and pushed away from the dock and moved out into the water of the bayou, bailing the bilge water that had gathered in the bottom.

When he was far enough from the shore, he unfolded his pocketknife and re-opened the wound on his nub—this time cutting as deep as he could endure, cutting right on top of the closed scab that he'd made only a day before. Then he took up the paddle in his bleeding hand and let the blood from his finger trace the length of the wood and then dipped it into the water and began to skulk—the slow one-handed paddling that he'd spend much of his childhood perfecting. The line of crimson between his hand and the surface of the bayou was like a live wire suddenly making a connection.

He allowed a moment to center himself, and then he moved the boat into the slow current of Bayou Bartholomew.

Miles then, and miles more, out into the flow. The mist rose up and he was gone.

Time was, Fisk knew the bayou near the Rheinhart plantation better than most men alive, but now, in the mist, recollection was lost to him. He tried to make for the picnic island where Franny and he had dallied so many summer days, but he could not find it in the gauzy light. So he just thought about her, pictured her face in his mind until a shape came out of the gloom.

A barge. Franny sat on the roof.

"I knew you'd come, eventually," Franny said. There was something about her that had changed. Was her hair whiter? Was that even possible? She looked as though she had not aged a single day. *No, that's not right. She looks as though she'll never age,* Fisk thought. But he said, "Can I come aboard?"

"Of course," she said, slipping from the roof.

He tied off the johnboat on the barge's gunwale and made the unsteady step from his boat to her larger one. She was there to take his hand and steady him as he came aboard. She remained holding his hand—his bleeding one, missing his pinkie—and frowning at it.

"They got at you, didn't they?" she said.

Fisk shrugged, pulling his hand away. She disappeared inside the little hut on the barge and re-emerged moments later with a kerchief that she used to clean and wrap his nub. "Why'd you do this?" she asked.

There was no reason to dissemble to Franny. "Old devil named Hardface was trying to get at you. So I had to give up something to stop him." The oldest story.

She put both her hands on his face and drew his head down to hers and kissed him. "I was mad at you for so long I nearly lost myself to it, but I understand now why you left."

"I don't even know if I understand why I did. But I did. And now I'm back and I don't intend to be separated from you again in this life," Fisk said.

A sadness crossed her then, and it was not lost on Fisk. But when he opened his mouth to ask her about it she stopped him with a kiss and drew him inside the hut—banging his head upon the doorjamb with his entry, causing Franny to tumble into peals of laughter. Then they disrobed and spent a long time in each other's embrace before moving to the bed and giving each other the gift of themselves. The barge shifted underneath them with their movements and the johnboat knocked softly at the other vessel's hull, as though a visitor knocking upon a wooden door.

When they were through, Franny rose and went to her small larder and brought out a sleeve of saltines and cut an apple and knifed peanut butter on crackers and fed them to Fisk. They drank unsweetened tea and then she poured white corn whiskey from an unmarked bottle into small jam jars they used as glasses and they drank and laughed and he shared what cigarettes he had and they smoked and drank, feeling the ease of once more being in the company of someone who loves and is loved back. They slept curled against each other in a hot tangle on the barge's small bed. By interludes, he told her the long story of his life until then, sparing nothing.

In the morning she boiled coffee and they drank it and ate more saltines and peanut butter until she said, "Come on, let's wet a line."

She had cane poles and a bait caster and some spinning rods sticking out like an insect's antennae on the barge's roof, and in a small tackle box beetle spins and Rappalas and plastic worms. They fished and she instructed Fisk how to pole the barge through the mist and pointed out the best places to catch fish in the hazy shore. Water and wind moved differently out here, in the mist. He had taken the red river to get here and he could not be altogether certain where "here" was.

They hit a patch of crappie away from shore and took in six slabs and could've caught more but she asked, "How hungry are you, Fisk? Are you eight fish hungry?" and he allowed he was probably only six crappie hungry.

She sat at the back of the barge where the draft was lowest and her feet could dangle into the water and filleted the crappie, dropping the guts and the speckled skins of the fish between her legs into the dark water. Fisk sat near her but raised up in surprise when he saw a large triangular head slip out from under the vessel and snatch a tangle of crappie innards.

"Don't mind him," Franny said. "He's sweet."

"It's a damned cottonmouth," Fisk said. "He must be fifty pounds." Having had enough frightening encounters with water moccasins, he knew to leave them well enough alone. Cottonmouths are territorial, and mean by nature, he'd always thought. Nothing had ever disabused him of that notion.

"We have an arrangement," Franny said. "I give him guts and scales and skin and he doesn't get ornery with me."

"It's like he's extorting you!" Fisk said.

She laughed. "It's not extortion if you enjoy the company. I need a man around sometimes," she said, and winked. "But only sometimes. I've gotten used to the sound of my own thoughts."

Fisk didn't know what to say to that. So Franny continued on.

"You've been gone eight years. You never took up with another girl?" she asked.

He saw no reason to lie. "I thought about it, I truly did. But I could never get you out of my mind. It was as thought I was in some half-lit world, where I couldn't be with you, and couldn't be without you. No other woman would do."

That sadness again crossed her features. "I fear I'm an anchor that will weigh you down all of your days." She tossed another snarl of blue, white and yellow guts and the cottonmouth lanced out and snatched it, one of the snake's twists of belly hooked around her ankle, as if using Franny for leverage. Fisk recoiled.

"Never," he said. "Just the opposite."

She finished her work and placed the filets in a small ceramic bowl and took them inside the hut, and returned to the stern and lay down on her stomach and washed her hands in the exact spot where the cottonmouth's head had been with a bar of Ivory soap. The snake was nowhere to be seen.

When her hands, her fingernails, her forearms were clean of blood and scales, she took Fisk's wounded hand in her own and kissed it. "Tell me the rest, then."

He finished his story—the events of the most recent days. The otherworldly Cleave approaching him, his coming home.

"And what is it that he said, again, when you came here?"

"There is another way," Fisk said, watching her brow furrow.

"What did he say exactly?" she said, becoming intense.

"He said he needed me to let him in. Like I was a suit he would wear. And then I let my blood flow and—"

"I got all that," she said and rubbed her chin. "Hardface sought you out and followed you. And then you started moving all around, from juke joint to the next, town to town. Somehow he knew you were the closest to me."

He nodded, it made sense.

"But I love others, as well, Fisk. Not as I love you. But others."

And then it all made sense.

Lenora.

———✵✵✵———

Lenora

She had left because of love, Franny said. Love drives us all away, scatters us all to the wind. And love is what *they* need to get in.

Lenora had fallen for a Little Rock man by the name of Big Jim Crouch, who made his living installing air conditioners for the black community, that was his preference—those who could afford them—and performing installation and maintenance on the white folks's HVAC units. Indeed, that was how he came to the Rheinhart plantation. He arrived on a warm spring day in May, and by the time he had installed the two large cooling units on cement slabs and run what vents he could without causing any destruction to the ante-bellum edifice of the Rheinhart family manse, he and Lenora were engaged to be wed. Big Jim, by all accounts Fisk had heard, was quite prosperous and kept a storefront on 9th street, only a stone's throw from the Dreamland Ballroom, the finest niterie in the mid-south, or so the signage proclaimed. Fisk had sat in there once, three years before, with Mollie Merchant and the Flamethrowers when their guitarist, a junkie by the name of Benton Byers, disappeared one night and never turned back up. Fisk had been playing at the White Water for just one night—cities made him nervous, the wolfish faces, the possibilities of other men, other creatures like Hardface—but when Mollie had approached him, he could not refuse. It was an easy enough gig.

The next day, he stopped in to visit his sister, to catch up, and meet her son, a rambunctious six-year-old, either hollering at the top of his lungs or dashing about the house with a toy air play, or holstered pop-guns, or a sackful of marbles, or a bouncing rubber ball. He hit himself in the head twice with a yo-yo violently enough that the boy Lenora had named Sylvester but they just called Tank staggered and looked like he might sit down hard on his ass. The little tyke shook it off and went back to play. Lenora sighed and Fisk got the idea that, no, Lenora would never want her boy to be hurt, but she wouldn't mind a bit of rest and down time.

She seemed happy enough, though she missed Momma and Franny and even Miss Sarah. But the good lord had placed her where she needed to be, praise Jesus. She had always been more religious than Fisk. Unlike many men, *her* man Jim seemed to have a knack for making money, and where to put it so that it made more, and their house was, while by no means ostentatious from the outside, very well appointed and not lacking in any comfort. But Lenora had her plate full, and so much so, she did not even notice the state of Fisk's hand and he did not bother to point it out. After a good long conversation, he left, promising to write, or call, and to not be a stranger. He had not seen her since. Lenora had always been a center point, a pivot around which he and Franny wheeled in their wild gyrations. She had never spoken to him about his relationship with Franny save once—*you were always never going to be together,* she had said—and it had driven a wedge between them, that he would surmount his sister in the girl's affections. That Miss Sarah had, for the time when he was groomed to become her manager, chosen him and in some ways left Lenora out rankled her. She would always be in his and her mother's shadow. What was left for her?

"Fast Fisk, always eating the first biscuit," she used to chide. Or call him "Mister Greedy Guts" when he would commandeer Franny's attention. The day he left the farm, she stopped him and said with an expression he couldn't read, "You and Franny were always meant to never be together."

"I have to go," Fisk said. "It might already be too late."

"Yes," Franny said. "And I must stay here. The water will keep me safe."

A great urgency pressed on his chest, and he felt as thought he'd been sniffing cocaine, something he'd done once and only once one night when he'd had too much whiskey during a stomp.

But her words made him pause. "But how do you know? That you'll be safe?"

"I—" She looked scared then. "I don't. But it feels right. And more right with you here. I don't want you to leave."

He drew her to him and kissed her. She tasted of all things—smoke and mist and cigarettes and sugar and fish and cinnamon and baked bread and bayou water. The totality of their environment. "I've got to. If Cleave gets to Lenora—or her boys—I don't know what to do. I'll have to ride the river. Maybe more."

Franny trembled and caught his hands in hers. "Don't. Remember my song?"

"How could I forget?"

"You'll know how, when the time comes," she said, and kissed him again. "Now go. Go."

<center>~~~</center>

Cleave and Company

Fisk opened the wound on his nub with his pocketknife once more and took the red river back, paddling briskly to the dock. Something in his movements seemed to leech the vapor from the already humid air and indicated he had crossed over some invisible threshold. Venturing out had been a journey of more than miles and water.

He found no one at the dock to greet him, though when he approached the area by the Quonset hut he found the windows of his truck broken, his tires slashed, and his guitar pulled from the cab and stomped on until fractured far beyond repair. A great anger had driven those actions, he knew, but it did not concern him much for the time being. He trotted over to the Big House, passed through the servants' entrance without knocking, and said to his mother, "I need to talk with Miss Sarah." Alice, seeing the expression on his face, disappeared upstairs and returned quickly to escort him up. Sarah awaited him at her vanity when he entered her suite.

"Franny and I think those interested parties we discussed yesterday—"

"A week ago," Sarah corrected.

"It was just yesterday I paddled out," he said.

"What are we doing here? I have become my mother and you know the power of blood so why is this hard to understand? You've been out for a week."

"All right," Fisk said, thinking about his time with Franny. Was it a week? They had made love and it had been sweet. Once? No. The memory of him pushing into her, crashing against her body, was as a wavefront collapsing all at once in his recollection. They had slept and ate and slept again and made love many times in between. Maybe. He shook his head as if clearing out the cobwebs. "All the more reason to hustle. They said there is another way. Franny thinks they mean Lenora."

"Oh my," Sarah said.

"That's right. I'm a goddamned rolling stone. But Lenora's got moss all over her and beaucoup leverage. All they gotta do is press her in the right spot. The boy. Jim. Whatever they need."

A look of horror passed over Sarah and was reflected in Alice's face. Whether it was because they were talking about forces and movements of power they did not precisely understand, or the vulnerability of the youngest of the children who had come of age in their tutelage and guidance, Fisk could not tell.

"I need a car. Some of your men trashed my truck, destroyed my guitar, and I have to get to Little Rock."

"It was the North boy and his cronies, I'm sure," Sarah said. "I will deal with him and his father. You can take my car." She turned and dug around in her vanity. From a drawer she pulled out a dark, heavy object with a wide bore. "You will remember the man whose gun that is." She stopped. "Was. Bull. I think you should have it."

The pistol was like a stone in Fisk's hand. Many bluesmen and player packed heat, for sure, but Fisk never did. He was good enough with his fists to deal with any minor disagreements without too much injury, and in his experience the addition of any firearm to an argument usually ended with someone on the ground, leaking. And, since the first days of his motion away from the Rheinhart farm and Franny, he was concerned with a different sort of adversary. The firearm was distasteful to him but he could understand how it could be of good use. He tucked it into his jacket's pocket.

"The keys are downstairs. Alice, give him however much money he'll need. Go! Go fast."

Fisk was down the stairs before the sound of her voice faded away, with his mother right behind him. She snatched a set of keys from a roll top desk in a corner of the front atrium, then dashed down the hall toward the kitchen. She returned with a wad of cash that she handed to Fisk and that he stuffed in his pocket. Then he was out the front door and moving across the plantation grounds to the detached garage in a flash. Inside he found a black Lincoln Continental, rather new, that matched the key in his hand, and it started with a rumble. He threw it into gear and lurched out onto the gravel drive and shot down the length of the pecan orchard, the Continental's rear wheels slewing back and forth, searching for traction on the loose rock. He was going sixty miles an hour when he hit the highway, bounced onto the tarmac, and gunned the vehicle west, as fast as it could go.

<hr>

After an hour, his panic diminished and he slowed his speed. It would not do to be pulled over by police for speeding and end up spending a night (or worse) in jail until the police could determine that he was authorized to be driving Mrs. Sarah Rheinhart's vehicle.

He filled up the gas tank in Stuttgart, bought cigarettes and an RC Cola and peanuts, dumped the peanuts in the bottle and drank as he drove, crunching the salty dregs.

An hour away from Little Rock, he wracked his memory for the layout of Lenora's home. Where was the boy's room? Where was the master bedroom? The backdoor? He constructed a facsimile of the dwelling in his mind as he drove and worked out a rough plan.

In Little Rock, he made his way west, to 27th Street near the new university where Lenora lived, passed her address once and, seeing no movement nor car in her drive, parked the Lincoln on the adjacent block, 26th Street. The houses on this street were small enough, and their spacing wide enough, Fisk felt sure he could see Lenora's reddish-brown roof peeking over a fence down a driveway. Knowing he was taking a risk, he walked down the drive past a Chrysler coupe, moved into the house's backyard and vaulted the wooden fence with an athleticism he hadn't even known he still possessed. The oblivion of the road had worn on his health.

He found himself in a bizarre little alley—not intended for automobile traffic, but an easement for access to powerlines and sewage, grown wild and rank with shrubs and tall grass and holly bushes and honeysuckle. He was unexpectedly surrounded by redolent nature, bees suckling at open flowers and buzzing around his head, long grass and thick weeds that had conquered the peagravel of the alley snagging his trousers. Robins sat on a powerline that bisected the heavens. Piles of yard refuse and mulch steamed in the heat. A dog barked in the middle distance, possibly sensing him.

He pushed his way through the lush growth, stopping at the far fence. Chain link. Fisk was positive that the house he looked on from the rear was Lenora and Jim's. There was an overturned tricycle. A red striped inflatable ball. A tire hanging from an oak tree's limb. The window of the door leading into what Fisk thought was Lenora's kitchen revealed nothing.

Fisk worked the toe of this brougham into the mesh of the chest-high chainlink and pushed himself over, getting a jab in his inner thigh from the metal twists at the fence's rim, and winced as his trousers tore. He stumbled slightly as his feet hit the earth.

The backdoor knob turned under his hand, and he opened the door as slowly as he could and entered the kitchen. It was the fetid odor of rotting meat he smelled first.

"Come join us, Mister Williams," a familiar voice called. "Come, we were just about to have an afternoon drink."

Fisk found the Morley in his tight and sweaty grip, its hammer cocked. He cursed himself for not thinking to cut his hand. For an instant, he pictured placing the pistol's bore on the center of his palm and pulling the trigger, but he wasn't sure he could act *and* endure the pain that would overwhelm him then. Or that the red tide loosed from that shot would be enough to drive Cleave before him and out into the street. In the end, he realized, he didn't know enough about the situation to make a decision and he walked from the kitchen into the den, where three dark shapes sat huddled around a dead television set. The stench had grown; it was almost an invisible pressure on his head, his sinuses, making it hard for Fisk to think. Once, when he was young, he went out in the bottoms near Bartholomew, walking through the lowlands in his hipboots with a little .22 rifle to take what squirrels and small game he could. He found himself in a sun-dappled field that should've smelled sweet and clean but it had a stench much like this one. As he penetrated the glade further, he found a heaping mound of swimming flesh that looked to be the remains of a horse, bloated and beyond grotesque. He gave a little yelp and the dead mound began to shift and writhe. Before Fisk could understand what was happening, three possums erupted from what was once the anus of the horse, slick and gleaming and red, and Fisk was took dumbstruck to shoot them or react in any way other than to stagger far enough away to fall to his knees and vomit up his last meal in a hot, bilious torrent.

This stench was very similar to that one.

One of the shadows shifted, elongating, and a light came on. Cleave sat in a wingback chair nearest a sideboard, composed and neat in his suit, hand on the lamp's switch. Lenora leaned into the sofa with her son, Tank, pressed into her side, one hand on the boy's belly, and one on his throat in a twisted claw. The expression on the boy's face was almost too much for Fisk to bear; she had stuffed what appeared to be a sock in his mouth and duct taped it in. His face was red, distressed, and he breathed heavily through his nostrils, caked in snot. His eyes streamed with tears. Fisk's sister, on the other hand, had an almost familiar exultant smirk.

"Hello, young buck," Lenora said, twisting the words viciously in her mouth.

"*Hardface,*" Fisk said. He raised the gun and pointed it at Lenora.

In response, she smiled wide, showing a mouth that was black as tar, a gullet to whatever hell these things came from.

"Aw, pard, you gonna shoot your ole buddy, Hardface?" The thing wearing Lenora let out a chuckle. "And muss this lovely dress?" It released Tank's stomach and with its free hand cupped Lenora's breast, leering.

"That's enough," Cleave said. "Be silent now." Hardface shut its black ichored mouth.

Fisk shifted his weight and pointed the gun at the man in the wingback chair. An expression of disappointment colored Cleave's handsome face. "I wouldn't think you need this explained to you, Mister Williams, but should you shoot this—" He paused, searching. His eyes took on a faraway look and focused on something beyond where they were currently locked in such a strange tableau. He made a sound that Fisk could not understand but later, years later, would re-emerge in his consciousness like a fat bluegill rising to the surface of the bayou, making a widening circle in the algae. Cleave shook his head, looking for all the world like a school-teacher disappointed with one of his student's dimness.

"If you shoot this *vessel*," he said. "Then the entity you refer to as Hardface with tear out the boy's throat. Shoot Hardface? You'll kill your sister and Hardface will migrate to the boy. A tight fit, indeed, and the boy will never be the same, for sure, but on the bright side he'd never survive the ordeal anyway."

Cleave withdrew a pack of unfiltered Pall Mall cigarettes and shook out one and offered it to Fisk.

"Here, Mister Williams. Put down your gun, have a nice, refreshing cigarette. It's quite cloying in here, is it not? We've been waiting for you for a long while. Days and days while you dallied in the *passage*. Dallied while we had naught to do but watch the way of all flesh. Long enough for your brother-in-law's integument to near slough away—" Cleave titled his head toward the door to the foyer and front stairs. Fisk turned to look. Framed in the doorway was a man-shaped lump, suppurating and bloated. Jim, Lenora's husband. "He has deliquesced. Is that the word? He has *positively* ripened." Cleave's face grew firm. "Put down your gun. And, as they said in a movie I had the pleasure of watching recently, keep your hands where I can observe them. I must insist."

Thoughts wheeled in Fisk's beleaguered mind, and his heart hammered away in his chest. He put the gun's bore in his fist. Cleave's eyes widened marginally. He snapped his fingers and Tank, even through his muzzle, began to mewl and whimper.

Cleave stood. "*I must insist*," he said again, holding out his hand.

With a look at Tank—his wide innocent eyes brimming with fear and desperation—Fisk handed over the pistol. Cleave whisked it away, tucking it into his jacket pocket. The claw at the boy's throat unclenched, slightly.

"Very good! Very satisfactory," Cleave said. "You possess some degree of reason. A remarkable feat for someone of your social status."

"Anybody ever told you, you talk too much?" Fisk said. It was hard for Fisk to fathom how this vile *thing* vomited out of some hot Hell could lord itself over him, but there it was. Even devils think they're better than a black man in this America. "How 'bout that smoke?"

Cleave shook his head, sadly. "We have been waiting long enough," he said. "I'm afraid the cigarette will have to wait for the car ride."

Hardface wearing Lenora unlimbered himself from the couch, as if Fisk's sister's body was ungainly—too short in legs, too thick in the chest, balance off—but never loosened its grip on the boy.

Fisk said, "Don't know how long you've been sitting here, but has the kid eaten? Gone to the pisser? He's just a boy."

Cleave looked about. "I believe the child soiled himself initially. It's hard to keep up with the necessities of these bodies. It has since dried, though you might not have smelled it with all of this…stench." He looked meaningfully at Hardface, who shrugged.

"I can tend the boy," Hardface said, and chuckled. "I am his mother, after all."

"I'll take care of him," Fisk said. "You can stand right behind me and make sure I don't do nothing. Bring the gun, whatever makes you comfortable." If Fisk could help it, he would do all he could to lessen the injury to the child, injury in either body or soul. Whatever he could do.

Hardface turned to Cleave, who gave an almost imperceptible nod.

The thing turned, the boy dangling from its hands, feet swinging, and offered him to Fisk. Fisk took him in his arms as Hardface took the gun from Cleave. Fisk carried the boy farther into the house, covering his eyes as he stepped over the body of his putrefying father, and soon found a bathroom. Though Hardface wore Lenora's body, no true vestige of her personality shone through, and while Fisk had no trouble discerning the difference there, he worried about Tank.

He knelt near him and in his ear, quietly, he said. "Don't know if you remember me, but I'm Uncle Fisk, catch me? I'm gonna take this out of your mouth and it's gonna hurt like the dickens but I need you to do something for me. Two things," Fisk said. "First, you gotta keep absolutely quiet when the gag comes off, however much it hurts, because if you cry, they're gonna want to put it back. You understand, Tank? Gimme a little nod if you understand."

Fisk could feel the boy was on the verge of a breakdown—trembling, streaming with snot and tears—but he turned his large, liquid brown gaze on his uncle and nodded.

"All right, then," Fisk said, cutting a quick look at Hardface. Hardface seemed fascinated by what was unfolding before him, but made no move to stop Fisk. It was as if Fisk and Tank were simply bizarre animals still capable of surprising him, still moderately amusing.

Even lower, Fisk said, "And you got to remember, always, that ain't your momma. You catch me? That ain't her. Something bad is wearing her, but it's not her."

With that, Fisk pulled the duct tape with a brisk movement and tore the gag from the boy's face. Tank took in a great draught of air as if to scream, or bawl, but then looked Fisk directly in the eyes and exhaled. After a long moment, he collapsed into Fisk's chest and began to silently sob. Fisk held him close.

"Well, this is mighty touching, but I don't think we should keep Mister Cleave waiting," Hardface said. He placed the pistol on the boy's head. Fisk clutched him harder to his chest.

"All right, Tank, let's get you on the pot."

The child was nearly catatonic. Fisk helped him drop his pants and pointed the absent and traumatized boy in the right direction. Fisk turned to face the door where Hardface stood and used his body as shield to allow the boy as much privacy as the situation would allow.

When the boy was done, Fisk said, "That's my Tank. All right, we gotta go with these folks, but I'm gonna be with you, right? As long as you stay quiet, you'll not get the gag again. Ain't that right, Hardface?"

"Come on, young buck," Hardface said, waving the gun in Fisk's face. "I'm getting real tired of these pup games."

They returned to the living area where Cleave remained standing.

"I'll make the boy something to eat," Fisk said, and walked into the kitchen.

As he opened the refrigerator, he felt something at the small of his back. From the living room, Cleave said, "Mister Williams, it would serve you in good stead if you did not take any initiative that has not been given permission first."

Fisk stood straight. "If you're gonna have Hardface shoot me, go ahead. If not, I'm gonna make the kid a damned sandwich."

He withdrew mayo and mustard, bologna and cheese, and rummaged in cabinets until he found a a loaf of Wonder Bread and quickly made a stack of sandwiches. In a cabinet, he found a coffee thermos and filled it with water and screwed the lid on tight. He wrapped the sandwiches in waxed paper and folded them as his mother had shown him, so long ago. Hardface watched this process with an amused expression playing about his features. The minutiae of the living, how droll.

When he was done, he could feel that he had absolutely exhausted the patience of the entities that possessed Cleave and Lenora. Fisk could only surmise that Cleave, like Lenora, had been a regular joe once, with a job and a family and maybe a nice little house with a picket fence and the whole white folks happily ever after bag. Despite all that, Fisk figured he'd kill him anyway, if he had the chance and it wouldn't endanger the boy. Hardface had the gun but not the pocketknife, and Fisk could still let the red power loose and follow it as far as it would take him. But he'd have to sacrifice. Nothing came without it. What would happen if he took off his own thumb? Or his tongue? He'd never be able to play, or sing, again. Goddamn, that would be a price to pay to survive, but he realized now he was willing to do it. It would render to him great power, this he knew with assurance.

They hustled Fisk and Tank outside and into a black Oldsmobile sedan, and had Fisk drive with Tank riding shotgun. There was ample room for Hardface to sit on the bench seat and press the pistol into the boy's side. If fired, the weapon would drive a bullet through the boy and into Fisk all in one deadly motion.

Cleave took the backseat.

"You know where we're going, since you just came from there. You might be considering alerting the police of your predicament by driving wildly or wrecking the car. I will say only this: I am a white man, riding in the backseat, and if Hardface does not manage to kill both of you in such a misguided event—which he most certainly will—the authorities will not look kindly upon you by dint of the color of your skin. I would prefer no one get killed, but I will allow it should you try to be a hero. We have entre to the sanctum sanctorum with the mother, anyway. She's still in there somewhere, isn't she, Hardface?"

Hardface grinned. "Sure. You want me to let her out for a hot second?"

"I think that might be a good reminder to Mister Williams where we stand," Cleave said. "I'll take the gun for the nonce." Hardface handed it over.

Once Hardface had turned over the pistol, its expression crumpled and suddenly Lenora was there with them in the car. She slumped forward, quivering involuntarily, her hands held loosely in her lap.

She screamed.

It was an agonized sound, piercing the close confines of the cab and tearing through the car.

Whether it was out of fear, stress, rage, violation, or all of the above, Fisk could not tell but he imagined there was a little bit of all of those things mixed together in that desperate vocalization. It was a sound that would live with him for the rest of his days.

Lenora began, "Tank, oh, Tank, baby, I should never have let them—"

Whatever else she might have said was cut off. She spasmed and Hardface was once again with them, gloating and unctuous. Tank pressed into Fisk's side, shaking.

"Now we have that all sorted," Cleave said from the backseat in an upbeat voice. "It's time for you to chauffeur, Mister Williams."

———

Homecoming

Thing were coming to an end, Fisk could tell. There was an invisible rising tension in the cab and beyond. Something about Hardface and Cleave began to radiate. The only experience Fisk had to compare it to was when a stomp was going exceedingly well and the *burn* started jumping from musician to musician, and musician to audience, and soon the whole damned shack with all the people, all the flesh, all the life within earshot were vibrating on the same harmonic wavelength. But with Cleave and Hardface, it was like an electric storm. It was the swimming black motes at the edges of your vision after a coughing fit. Black sap rising in the trees. A curled moccasin on the macadam, ready to strike.

Fisk had felt power before. Power he had cut parts of himself away to access. He was no fool. Whatever rode in this car with him cut a wake through invisible waters and those waves would crash upon the shores soon, bringing darkness and despair.

His mind jumped from Franny, to Lenora, to the boy, indiscriminately. He could see no way out of taking them to where they wanted to go. And that was into the mist. Out onto the bayou. The path they wanted to take went through his love. They—or *something*—had been there before until Bull had stopped them. And now it was only Fisk left.

What had Franny said?

They arrived in Gethsemane just as the shadows grew long and the sky bloomed full of color—pinks and purples striated with orange—in the western sky. As they passed onto the Rheinhart land, Hardface said something in a tongue that Fisk could not recognize, let alone understand, but it was said with some urgency and a hint of desperation, and he watched as both of his captors hitched with pain as they crossed over some invisible boundary. They had gotten in.

"Now to the water," Cleave said. "With my three fine bargaining chips."

The surface of Bayou Bartholomew was absolutely still, a flat dark green suface, when they came to the waterfront. Cleave held the gun on the boy Tank as Fisk prepared and bailed the standing water from a johnboat and found a paddle. He pulled it into the bayou, sending out sluggish ripples in widening circles outward to lap thickly at the shore and the ballroots of cypresses. Mosquitos swarmed him, biting his neck and cheeks as he labored with the boat, hip deep in the opaque water. Their wings whined faintly in the air.

He pulled the johnboat alongside the dock and Cleave stepped into the craft, the boy followed, and Hardface came last. Fisk had chosen, due to their number, one of the larger boats, sixteen feet long and heavier than the others. He double checked that the boat plug was stoppered at the stern, though he considered what might happen had he left it out. Would Cleave or Hardface know how to swim? He didn't see how they could. Lenora had never liked dark water, and she might be able to dog paddle, but swimming? No. And what about Tank? Could the boy keep himself afloat? Better not to risk it.

Fisk pulled himself up and over the gunwale, his trousers sodden, dripping and speckled with blue-green algae, barely visible in the dying light. He took a moment's pleasure in the alarmed expression coloring Hardface with the shifting of the johnboat's balance with Fisk's entry. Cleave remained inscrutable and remote.

Cleave.

Now that they were on the water, something about the man—the entity that wore the man—was changing. His demeanor was that of a man with his attention focused on two things, or more, and at least one of them was not in his current presence. Fisk sensed, more than saw, thin streamers of connections—dark, writhing, tenuous—snaking out and away from where the johnboat sat in the sluggish, thick waters.

"Paddle," Cleave said to Fisk. "We require some locomotion for this to work and our tasks to come to an end."

Our tasks to come to an end? Fisk did not like the sound of that at all. Tension rose in him, settled in his shoulders and back. He gripped the paddle, hard, thinking of how he might strike Hardface without injuring or disturbing Tank. Hardface and the boy had taken the middle seats facing the stern and Fisk, and Cleave had perched on the fore one, sitting sideways, so that he could look ahead. He could reach out and bash Hardface, easily enough.

Instead, he followed Cleave's instruction, dipping the paddle into the water on either side of the johnboat, putting his strength into the pulls. Hardface watched him, a smile playing about its black mouth. His sister's mouth, now grotesque with what evil infested her. Hardface kept one arm looped around Tank's neck, clawed hand at the boy's throat. The boat moved across the face of the bayou, slowly. Vapors had begun to gather with the nightfall and the mist was rising, and Fisk shifted his leg to feel the reassuring weight of the folding knife still in his trouser pocket.

For its part, Hardface was changing too. The vile stuff that blackened its mouth gathered at the corners of Lenora's lips and dripped down onto her chest, spilling onto Tank's shoulder. Hardface's expression turned from mocking to rapturous as they moved into the mist.

Fisk paddled on, his discomfort and internal agitation growing with each stroke of the paddle. He thought on Franny. He wondered if she could sense them coming. On the barge, she seemed to have a preternatural connection with the bayou—the fish, the sweet moccasin, the barge appearing like some wraith—and he hoped she could sense their approach. They were fully in the mist now and nothing other than the boat itself and the hard, indifferent stars directly above stood visible to the naked eye. There were intimations of things in the gloom—a hulking shape discoloring the mist but indistinct, just a clotted and heavier piece of darkness passing slowly by. Cleave sat staring into the mist, and Fisk felt a vague sense of forces gathering around the man.

If Franny could sense anything, it would be him.

Bayou Bartholomew spanned hundreds of miles, but Fisk was certain, like Dorothy in the Wizard of Oz, they weren't in Arkansas anymore. Franny could be anywhere, and the mist, the farther in it they progressed, seemed vast and limitless. But Fisk had the feeling that in the mist there were only two true places one could be: either hidden or revealed.

His mind kept returning to Franny. Their time together. Even though it spanned most of their lives, now, in this moment, it seemed so desperately short. There were so many things he wished he could say to her. Things he never got to do with her. A car ride in the fall through the dappled light of the highway. A movie, holding hands. A trip to Memphis, or Nashville, or St. Louis, where the disparity in the color of their skin might not mean enough to find him beaten, or attacked. A child? That he might have a son or daughter was something he'd never allowed himself to think. And now...

And now an irrevocable certainty crept on him that any love he had for her was also a danger. To her, and to him. And to the world.

His life of music, following the *burn* just like his father had, all seemed like a waste in this moment. A futile and selfish indulgence. All time and effort he could've spent with the woman he loved. He had never sung a song truer than that.

Except maybe one.

"Now we are come to the vault of many shifting doors, steeped in the ancient air," Cleave said. In response, Hardface emitted a sound that was a gleeful gurgle, emanating deep from Lenora's throat, full of black phlegm and ill intention. Its clawed hand tightened on Tank's neck, either with purpose or involuntarily from his rising excitement, Fisk could not tell. The boy began to weep, at first breathing heavily, and then slowly sobbing.

Cleave, irritated, snapped, "The child!" Hardface snarled and gave the boy a vicious shake and tossed him to the hull of the johnboat.

Fisk stopped paddling and, grabbing Tank by his shoulders, drew the boy to him, pressing his face into his chest. To blot out this world and situation for the boy, if only for a second.

"I got you," Fisk said. "Gonna be all right, my little man. I got you."

"Uncle Fisk," Tank said. The timbre of the child's voice made Fisk feel unfamiliar and uncomfortable things in his expanding chest. This was the first time, Fisk realized, that the boy had ever really spoken to him. "I'm scared." Tank raised his face to look at Fisk's in the low starlight. The pain and distress was evident, and Fisk knew it would be something the boy would carry with him the rest of his life. A severed finger that no one would ever see.

"As well you should be," Cleave said. "Now be silent or you'll be thrown overboard. Your usefulness to me is rapidly coming to an end."

The boy shivered and thrummed with new panic in Fisk's embrace. He knew nothing to do to ease the lad's growing tension, except possibly to sing him a song to calm his nerves that would aggravate Cleave even more. And he knew no lullabies, anyway, or any other song that might suit.

A song. The song, Fisk thought, eyes widening. God, not that. I will lose everything with nothing left.

———

Any extended time on the water brings with it a certain attenuation of the senses. A boat on the bayou possesses an undeniable and ineluctable presence. Perhaps it is the displaced water, perhaps it is the constant and connected flux of the vessel's suspension causing the boat to shift, moan, pop, creak. Whatever the case, despite the mist, Fisk abruptly knew they approached another boat.

Cleave stood, their johnboat shifting underneath him. The distracted demeanor was gone now. The thing that called himself Cleave was firmly rooted in the present moment, and the only vaguely sensed connections streaming away from the man were now fully on view: squirming coils of insubstanial though deadly looking twines of...what? Muscular tissue? The limbs of some prehistoric creature erupting from out of time and Cleave's body? Semi-opaque arms for all the world looking like rain-wet branches of a crepe myrtle? These appendages shifted and writhed with each thought that skittered across Fisk's consciousness and flowed away from Cleave like a cloak caught in the wind. No, a shroud, snaking into the mist and connecting to...larger things only sensed at the edges of perception. Moving titanically. Very far away and very close, all at once. Urgent, and waiting.

In the mist, a square shape began to take form in the gloom, surmounted by the silhouette of a slim, defiant figure, feet spread wide for balance.

Franny.

Her head pivoted and she located them in the mist. She held her arms loosely at her sides and held something in one tight fist. A baseball bat? A machete? A crowbar? Fisk could not tell.

A vibration filtered into Fisk's awareness, a thrumming, like the electrical buzz of a transformer about to blow from too many amps and musical equipment drawing power. The johnboat yawed slightly beneath them, making Tank cry out in fear.

Cleave rose into the air. For a moment, Fisk questioned why he had ever thought this was a suited A&R man. Cleave had distended, changed, and the raiment he had worn had been more than a suit. Or flesh.

He appeared now as a roiling, quicksilver mass of darkness. And rose up into the mist to meet Franny.

Fisk felt an icy stillness settle on his heart. The time for disguises were over. He drew Tank tight against him.

"Ah, yesss," Cleave said. "The closed door shall be opened. So close. So deliciously near."

Hardface giggled. Fisk regarded the nearer devil. Lenora. His poor sister. To have her features so twisted, so tortured.

"Fisk!" Franny called, her voice sounding out clear as if she had spoken into a microphone at a shaker shack. "You know what to do, don't you?"

"I don't want to," he said softly. But Hardface's head pivoted around as if on gimbals and bared black teeth at him.

"I'm not your concern anymore," Franny said. "Though I still love you. That won't change. Ever."

"Silence!" the thing that had been Cleave hissed. It moved across the face of the water between their johnboat and Franny's barge. "I am the opener of the way, child. It will be less painful if you do not struggle."

"Fisk," Franny said. "Do it. Give me up."

Lenora's features shifted, cracked. Fisk recalled when Hardface had worn the black dog and erupted out of its body into blackness, keeping only its teeth and claws and the sharp bits of bone. He could not save his sister, he knew.

When he opened his mouth to give voice to the song, Fisk knew the necessities of the process, the incantation, the bargain he was making did not require him to ride the red river. It simply required his irrevocable commitment and intention. The mysterious forces of the universe that he was now maybe more than an initiate of would do the rest.

His voice echoed over the waters and reverberated through the mists.

"Put on your little coat," he sang for the last time in this life. "My heart's up in my throat. Put on them darling shoes, and I don't know what to do—"

As he sang, Tank gripped his chest tighter. Each word that came from Fisk burnt like an ember upon his tongue and evaporated into the air. The words struck the ears of all who could hear like hammerfalls on metal, a bright percussive noise, sending out sparks.

"With the love I have for you," Fisk sang, his voice loosening and growing stronger. "I don't know what to say, but I'll love you anyway."

The thing that was Cleave thrashed in the grip of the song. Instead of a barge roof, Franny seemed to stand on a ledge. Her face was wreathed in shadow and indecipherable to Fisk, but he imagined she wept. And then he knew tears streamed down his own cheeks. The air wavered, as if steam or heat from the macadam occulted his vision. And Franny began to move away. The longer he sang, the more she diminished, as if traveling fast straight away from them, on some unknown plane that existed only in opposing directions. A diminuendo, a ritard. The ledge became a cliff. The cliff became a mountain top.

Fisk's love, his connection, dwindled with each word, matching Franny's diminishment, until eventually, both were gone from this world.

Fisk felt nothing save emptiness.

Hardface erupted then, swelling into the air as whatever Cleave had finally become screeched and thrashed. The tearing of flesh and the popping of bones shocked Fisk. In a bloody mist, the thing rose, the boat shifting at the lack of weight. Salty hot droplets spattered Fisk's face and exposed skin. The boy flinched in his grasp.

Cowering, they were showered with gouts of gore and blood, bits of flesh, as the entity destroyed Lenora. Then it gathered only the evil and deadly bits of that great rending to hazard the humans left among them.

A hollow strength filled Fisk. He had sacrificed everything to save Franny, and in the aftermath, he was a husk. But the boy was at risk, now. He reached into his pocket, withdrew the knife, and with a quick easy gesture, popped it open with one hand as he gripped the boy with the other. Bringing the knife up, he brought his hands together, encircling the child—like a circle round the sun, he thought crazily—and with a deft twisting motion, Fisk cut away the smallest finger of his own left hand. It fell, hitting the gunwale, splashing into the water.

"We're gonna take a ride, you and me, motherfucker," Fisk said and lashed out with his hand, the arc of blood cutting like the blade of a sword. What was left of Lenora—poor Lenora!—cringed and shrank before his lashing blood, like a school of fish evading a larger predator.

Fisk rose, the power shaking through him, like the powerful bass of a kick drum, or the *burn* in full stomp. He had made a sacrifice, and the power was there for him to wield.

Again he struck with his red hand, the blood splashing forward in a hot, vital torrent. It ripped at Hardface, now thrashing and mewling in the bilgewater, sloughing away parts of itself. The thing's cries bit and tore at the air and with a last, great heave, the morass of Lenora's animated flesh lost cohesion and whatever energy that held it afloat began to become diffuse, moving over the gunwale and disappearing into the waters of the bayou.

Setting the boy down, Fisk found his balance and set his feet wide.

He looked for Cleave, a bloody hand at the ready, but the swirling mass of the creature had done what it could to follow where he had released Franny to, and failed. They had come out of the mist now. That in-between world was gone.

Cleave hung in the air like a man lynched, his glamour of humanity re-established now they were returned to the real world. But shabby, frayed at the edges, indistinct. To Fisk, Cleave looked a washed-out specter. A haint, as the old men would say over guitars and beer.

Franny had moved away from them, away from everything, and passed into the beyond. She was unobtainable now, and forevermore.

Fisk recognized he should care, should weep, but no emotion churned in his currents, no feelings marked the surface of his calm. All that remained was the shatter of sacrifice and the echoes of the power that ripped through him with the red river.

"Come on then, boy," Fisk said. So many white men had called him boy in all of his years as a full-grown man. It was a fine thing to turn those words back against them. Cleave hitched and twisted with each syllable as if being struck by physical blows. "Come on! I've got a little something for you." He raised his wounded left hand, now missing a finger and matching his right, and made a clenched fist with what was left. The blood flowed down his forearm in thick pumps, the burning throb like holding a naked electrical wire.

"I think not, Mister Williams," Cleave said and made a noise that sounded very much like a sigh. The man grew distant, still hanging in the air. The dark snaking tendrils—of what, Fisk couldn't say—that had been so evident in the mist were not perceivable now. Still, the man hung there, as if suspended high in invisible waters. The distance between them grew and grew until Cleave was beyond any hope of reach. "There are other shores than these, mortal. And other opportunities."

The moon had risen over the far treeline, casting a long and inconstant reflection on the surface of the bayou. Cleave merged with the shadows of the cypress at the shore. "Count your blessings—and your fingers—Mister Williams, those that are left to you, and pray to whatever gods you hold dear we do not meet again in this world. For I have a score to settle with you," Cleave said, faintly, and then he was gone.

Alone on the face of the water, under the brilliant night sky, they were alone. Off in the distance an owl hooted and the low chug of a bullfrog sounded against the hushed cacophony of the bayou.

Fisk sat back down on the johnboat's seat and drew the boy Tank to him and embraced him for a long while, reveling in the feel of another human heart beating so close and so strongly to his. He held him out at arm's length and realized he had left smears of blood all over the child's shoulders and back.

No matter. He would clean up right nice. Just like Fisk's injured hand.

"What did I tell you, little man?" Fisk said, observing the child's face. He had fine cheekbones and a questioning and intelligent expression, no doubt riddled with hurt and trauma, concentrated in the eyes. As Fisk looked at him, he could see Lenora plainly in his features, the shape of his lips, the soft curve of his cheek.

"I got you, Tank," Fisk said. "I got you and I ain't letting go."

Still holding the boy, Fisk picked up the paddle in his unbloodied hand and began paddling back to shore.

ABOUT THE AUTHOR

John Hornor Jacobs is an award-winning author of genre-bending adult and YA fiction. His first novel, *Southern Gods*, was nominated for a Bram Stoker Award® for Excellence in a First Novel and won the Darrel Award. The Onion AV said of the book, "A sumptuous Southern

Gothic thriller steeped in the distinct American mythologies of Cthulhu and the blues . . . *Southern Gods* beautifully probes the eerie, horror-infested underbelly of the South."

His second novel, *This Dark Earth*, Brian Keene described as "...quite simply, the best zombie novel I've read in years" and was published by Simon & Schuster's Gallery imprint. Jacobs's acclaimed series of novels for young adults beginning with *The Twelve-Fingered Boy*, continuing with *The Shibboleth*, and ending with *The Conformity* has been hailed by Cory Doctorow on BoingBoing as "amazing" and "mesmerizing."

Jacobs's first fantasy novel, *The Incorruptibles,* was nominated for the Morningstar and Gemmell Awards in the UK. Pat Rothfuss has said of this book, "One part ancient Rome, two parts wild west, one part Faust. A pinch of Tolkien, of Lovecraft, of Dante. This is strange alchemy, a recipe I've never seen before. I wish more books were as fresh and brave as this."

His recent collection of two short novels, *A Lush and Seething Hell,* was nominated for the Shirley Jackson Award and garnered rave reviews.

His fiction has appeared in *Playboy Magazine, Cemetery Dance, Apex Magazine*, and his essays have been featured on *CBS Weekly* and *Huffington Post*.

Follow him at @johnhornor on Twitter or visit johnhornor.com to learn more.